The Hunters and the Hunted!

All at once, from around a bend in the street, a horseman appeared. As he came into sight, the hounds, which surrounded his beast's feet, an undulation of savagery, began to bay. There were other riders behind him, but the leader was gigantic, dwarfing all. He wore a monstrous winged helmet framing a bearded face from which the eye glowed with the same green-blue light which flooded the village . . .

"Mother of God," said Sedenko. "I'll fight any man fairly, but not this."

I held my ground. "Drive us they might," I said, "and it would be good sport for them, no doubt . . . Those are hunters and I would say their prey is Man!"

THE WAR HOUND AND THE WORLD'S PAIN

MICHAEL MOORCOCK

A TIMESCAPE BOOK
PUBLISHED BY POCKET BOOKS NEW YORK

Another *Original* publication of TIMESCAPE BOOKS

A Timescape Book published by
POCKET BOOKS, a Simon & Schuster division of
GULF & WESTERN CORPORATION
1230 Avenue of the Americas, New York, N.Y. 10020

ISBN: 0-671-83412-6

First Timescape Books paperback printing November, 1982

10 9 8 7 6 5 4 3 2 1

For Doctor A. C. Papadakis,
Valerie, Amanda, Charles Platt
and all those others who, with Jill, helped create the
circumstances that led to the writing of this book

THE WAR HOUND
AND
THE WORLD'S PAIN

Being the true testimony of the Graf Ulrich von Bek, lately Commander of Infantry, written down in the Year of Our Lord 1680 by Brother Olivier of the Monastery at Renschel during the months of May and June as the said nobleman lay upon his sickbed.

(This manuscript had, until now, remained sealed within the wall of the monastery's crypt. It came to light during work being carried out to restore the structure, which had sustained considerable damage during the Second World War. It came into the hands of the present editor via family sources and appears here for the first time in a modern translation. Almost all the initial translating work was that of Prinz Lobkowitz; this English text is largely the work of Michael Moorcock.)

Chapter I

It was in that year when the fashion in cruelty demanded not only the crucifixion of peasant children, but a similar fate for their pets, that I first met Lucifer and was transported into Hell; for the Prince of Darkness wished to strike a bargain with me.

Until May of 1631 I had commanded a troop of irregular infantry, mainly Poles, Swedes and Scots. We had taken part in the destruction and looting of the city of Magdeburg, having somehow found ourselves in the army of the Catholic forces under Count Johann Tzerclaes Tilly. Wind-borne gunpowder had turned the city into one huge keg and she had gone up all of a piece, driving us out with little booty to show for our hard work.

Disappointed and belligerent, wearied by the business of rapine and slaughter, quarrelling over what pathetic bits of goods they had managed to pull from the blazing houses, my men elected to split away from Tilly's forces. His had been a singularly ill-fed and badly equipped army, victim to the pride of bickering allies. It was a relief to leave it behind us.

We struck south into the foothills of the Hartz Mountains, intending to rest. However, it soon became evident to

11

me that some of my men had contracted the Plague, and I deemed it wise, therefore, to saddle my horse quietly one night and, taking what food there was, continue my journey alone.

Having deserted my men, I was not free from the presence of death or desolation. The world was in agony and shrieked its pain.

By noon I had passed seven gallows on which men and women had been hanged and four wheels on which three men and one boy had been broken. I passed the remains of a stake at which some poor wretch (witch or heretic) had been burned: whitened bone peering through charred wood and flesh.

No field was untouched by fire; the very forests stank of decay. Soot lay deep upon the road, borne by the black smoke which spread and spread from innumerable burning bodies, from sacked villages, from castles ruined by cannonade and siege; and at night my passage was often lit by fires from burning monasteries and abbeys. Day was black and grey, whether the sun shone or no; night was red as blood and white from a moon pale as a cadaver. All was dead or dying; all was despair.

Life was leaving Germany and perhaps the whole world; I saw nothing but corpses. Once I observed a ragged creature stirring on the road ahead of me, fluttering and flopping like a wounded crow, but the old woman had expired before I reached her.

Even the ravens of the battlegrounds had fallen dead upon the remains of their carrion, bits of rotting flesh still in their beaks, their bodies stiff, their eyes dull as they stared into the meaningless void, neither Heaven, Hell nor yet Limbo (where there is, after all, still a little hope).

I began to believe that my horse and myself were the only creatures allowed, by some whim of Our Lord, to remain as witnesses to the doom of His Creation.

If it were God's intention to destroy His world, as it seemed, then I had lent myself most willingly to His purpose.

I had trained myself to kill with ease, with skill, with a cunning efficiency and lack of ambiguity. My treacheries were always swift and decisive. I had learned the art of passionless torture in pursuit of wealth and information. I knew how to

terrify in order to gain my ends, whether they be the needs of
the flesh or in the cause of strategy.

I knew how to soothe a victim as gently as any butcher
soothes a lamb. I had become a splendid thief of grain and
cattle so that my soldiers should be fed and remain as loyal as
possible to me.

I was the epitome of a good mercenary captain; a
soldier-of-fortune envied and emulated; a survivor of every
form of danger, be it battle, Plague or pox, for I had long
since accepted things as they were and had ceased either to
question or to complain.

I was Captain Ulrich von Bek and I was thought to be
lucky.

The steel I wore, helmet, breastplate, greaves and
gloves, was of the very best, as was the sweat-soaked silk of
my shirt, the leather of my boots and breeches. My weapons
had been selected from the richest of those I had killed and
were all, pistols, sword, daggers and musket, by the finest
smiths. My horse was large and hardy and excellently furnished.

I had no wounds upon my face, no marks of disease,
and, if my bearing was a little stiff, it gave me, I was told, an
air of dignified authority, even when I conducted the most
hideous destruction.

Men found me a good commander and were glad to
serve with me. I had grown to some fame and had a
nickname, occasionally used: *Krieghund*.

They said I had been born for War. I found such opinions
amusing.

My birthplace was in Bek. I was the son of a pious
nobleman who was loved for his good works. My father had
protected and cared for his tenants and his estates. He had
respected God and his betters. He had been learned, after the
standards of this time, if not after the standards of the Greeks
and Romans, and had come to the Lutheran religion through
inner debate, through intellectual investigation, through dis-
course with others. Even amongst Catholics he was known for
his kindness and had once been seen to save a Jew from
stoning in the town square. He had a tolerance for almost
every creature.

When my mother died, quite young, having given birth
to the last of my sisters (I was the only son), he prayed for her

soul and waited patiently until he should join her in Heaven. In the meantime he followed God's Purpose, as he saw it, and looked after the poor and weak, discouraged them in certain aspirations which could only lead the ignorant souls into the ways of the Devil, and made certain that I acquired the best possible education from both clergymen and lay tutors.

I learned music and dancing, fencing and riding, as well as Latin and Greek. I was knowledgeable in the Scriptures and their commentaries. I was considered handsome, manly, God-fearing, and was loved by all in Bek.

Until 1625 I had been an earnest scholar and a devout Protestant, taking little interest (save to pray for our cause) in the various wars and battles of the North.

Gradually, however, as the canvas grew larger and the issues seemed to become more crucial, I determined to obey God and my conscience as best I could.

In the pursuit of my Faith, I had raised a company of infantry and gone off to serve in the army of King Christian of Denmark, who proposed, in turn, to aid the Protestant Bohemians.

Since King Christian's defeat, I had served a variety of masters and causes, not all of them, by any means, Protestant and a good many of them in no wise Christian by even the broadest description. I had also seen a deal of France, Sweden, Bohemia, Austria, Poland, Muscovy, Moravia, the Low Countries, Spain and, of course, most of the German provinces.

I had learned a deep distrust of idealism, had developed a contempt for any kind of unthinking Faith, and had discovered a number of strong arguments for the inherent malice, deviousness and hypocrisy of my fellow men, whether they be Popes, princes, prophets or peasants.

I had been brought up to the belief that a word given meant an appropriate action taken. I had swiftly lost my innocence, for I am not a stupid man at all.

By 1626 I had learned to lie as fluently and as easily as any of the major participants of that War, who compounded deceit upon deceit in order to achieve ends which had begun to seem meaningless even to them; for those who compromise others also compromise themselves and are thus robbed of the capacity to place value on anything or anyone. For my own part I placed value upon my own life and trusted only myself to maintain it.

Magdeburg, if nothing else, would have proven those views of mine:

By the time we had left the city we had destroyed most of its thirty thousand inhabitants. The five thousand survivors had nearly all been women and their fate was the obvious one.

Tilly, indecisive, appalled by what he had in his desperation engineered, allowed Catholic priests to make some attempt to marry the women to the men who had taken them, but the priests were jeered at for their pains.

The food we had hoped to gain had been burned in the city. All that had been rescued had been wine, so our men poured the contents of the barrels into their empty bellies.

The work which they had begun sober, they completed drunk. Magdeburg became a tormented ghost to haunt those few, unlike myself, who still possessed a conscience.

A rumor amongst our troops was that the fanatical Protestant, Falkenburg, had deliberately fired the city rather than have it captured by Catholics, but it made no odds to those who died or suffered. In years to come Catholic troops who begged for quarter from Protestants would be offered "Magdeburg mercy" and would be killed on the spot. Those who believed Falkenburg the instigator of the fire often celebrated him, calling Magdeburg "the Protestant Lucretia," self-murdered to protect her honour. All this was madness to me and best forgotten.

Soon Magdeburg and my men were days behind me. The smell of smoke and the Plague remained in my nostrils, however, until well after I had turned out of the mountains and entered the oak groves of the northern fringes of the great Thuringian Forest.

Here, there was a certain peace. It was spring and the leaves were green and their scent gradually drove the stench of slaughter away.

The images of death and confusion remained in my mind, nonetheless. The tranquillity of the forest seemed to me artificial. I suspected traps.

I could not relax for thinking that the trees hid robbers or that the very ground could disguise a secret pit. Few birds sang here; I saw no animals.

The atmosphere suggested that God's Doom had been visited on this place as freely as it had been visited elsewhere. Yet I was grateful for any kind of calm, and after two days without danger presenting itself I found that I could sleep quite easily for several hours and could eat with a degree of leisure, drinking from sweet brook water made strange to me because it did not taste of the corpses which clogged, for instance, the Elbe from bank to bank.

It was remarkable to me that the deeper into the forest I moved, the less life I discovered.

The stillness began to oppress me; I became grateful for the sound of my own movements, the tread of the horse's hooves on the turf, the occasional breeze which swept the leaves of the trees, animating them and making them seem less like frozen giants observing my passage with a passionless sense of the danger lying ahead of me.

It was warm and I had an impulse more than once to remove my helmet and breastplate, but I kept them firmly on, sleeping in my armour as was my habit, a naked sword ready by my hand.

I came to believe that this was not, after all, a Paradise, but the borderland between Earth and Hell.

I was never a superstitious man, and shared the rational view of the universe with our modern alchemists, anatomists, physicians and astrologers; I did not explain my fears in terms of ghosts, demons, Jews or witches; but I could discover no explanation for this absence of life.

No army was nearby, to drive game before it. No large beasts stalked here. There were not even huntsmen. I had discovered not a single sign of human habitation.

The forest seemed unspoiled and untouched since the beginning of Time. Nothing was poisoned. I had eaten berries and drunk water. The undergrowth was lush and healthy, as were the trees and shrubs. I had eaten mushrooms and truffles; my horse flourished on the good grass.

Through the treetops I saw clear blue sky, and sunlight warmed the glades. But no insects danced in the beams; no bees crawled upon the leaves of the wild flowers; not even an earthworm twisted about the roots, though the soil was dark and smelled fertile.

It came to me that perhaps this was a part of the globe as yet unpopulated by God, some forgotten corner which had been overlooked during the latter days of the Creation. Was I a wandering Adam come to find his Eve and start the race again? Had God, feeling hopeless at humanity's incapacity to maintain even a clear idea of His Purpose, decided to expunge His first attempts? But I could only conclude that some natural catastrophe had driven the animal kingdom away, be it through famine or disease, and that it had not yet returned.

You can imagine that this state of reason became more difficult to maintain when, breaking out of the forest proper one afternoon, I saw before me a green, flowery hill which was crowned by the most beautiful castle I had ever beheld: a thing of delicate stonework, of spires and ornamental battlements, all soft, pale browns, whites and yellows, and this castle seemed to me to be at the centre of the silence, casting its influence for miles around, protecting itself as a nun might protect herself, with cold purity and insouciant confidence. Yet it was mad to think such a thing, I knew.

How could a building demand calm, to the degree that not even a mosquito would dare disturb it?

It was my first impulse to avoid the castle, but my pride overcame me.

I refused to believe that there was anything genuinely mysterious.

A broad, stony path wound up the hillside between banks of flowers and sweet-smelling bushes which gradually became shaped into terraced gardens with balustrades, statuary and formally arranged flower beds.

This was a peaceful place, built for civilised tastes and reflecting nothing of the War. From time to time as I rode slowly up the path I called out a greeting, asking for shelter and stating my name, according to accepted tradition; but there was no reply. Windows filled with stained glass glittered like the eyes of benign lizards, but I saw no human eye, heard no voice.

Eventually I reached the open gates of the castle's outer wall and rode beneath a portcullis into a pleasant courtyard full of old trees, climbing plants and, at the centre, a well. Around this courtyard were the apartments and appointments of those who would normally reside here, but it was plain to me that not a soul occupied them.

I dismounted from my horse, drew a bucket from the well so that he might drink, tethered him lightly and walked up the steps to the main doors which I opened by means of a large iron handle.

Within, it was cool and sweet.

There was nothing sinister about the shadows as I

climbed more steps and entered a room furnished with old chests and tapestries. Beyond this were the usual living quarters of a wealthy nobleman of taste. I made a complete round of the rooms on all three stories.

There was nothing in disorder. The books and manuscripts in the library were in perfect condition. There were preserved meats, fruits and vegetables in the pantries, barrels of beer and jars of wine in the cellars.

It seemed that the castle had been left with a view to its inhabitants' early return. There was no decay at all. But what was remarkable to me was that there were, as in the forest, no signs of the small animals, such as rats and mice, which might normally be discovered.

A little cautiously I sampled the castle's larder and found it excellent. I would wait, however, for a while before I made a meal, to see how my stomach behaved.

I glanced through the windows, which on this side were glazed with clear, green glass, and saw that my horse was content. He had not been poisoned by the well water.

I climbed to the top of one of the towers and pushed open a little wooden door to let myself onto the battlements.

Here, too, flowers and vegetables and herbs grew in tubs and added to the sweetness of the air.

Below me, the treetops were like the soft waves of a green and frozen sea. Able to observe the land for many miles distant and see no sign of danger, I became relieved.

I went to stable my horse and then explored some of the chests to see if I could discover the name of the castle's owner. Normally one would have come upon family histories, crests and the like. There were none.

The linen bore no mottoes or insignia, the clothing (of which quantities existed to dress most ages and both sexes) was of good quality, but anonymous. I returned to the kitchens, lit a fire and began to heat water so that I might bathe and avail myself of some of the softer apparel in the chests.

I had decided that this was probably the summer retreat of some rich Catholic prince who now did not wish to risk the journey from his capital, or who had no time for rest.

I congratulated myself on my good fortune. I toyed with the idea of audaciously making the castle my own, of finding servants for it, perhaps a woman or two to keep me company and share one of the large and comfortable beds I had already sampled. Yet how, short of robbery, would I maintain the place?

There were evidently no farms, no mills, no villages nearby; therefore no rents, no supplies. The age of the castle was difficult to judge, and I saw no clear roads leading to it.

Perhaps its owner had first discovered the tranquil wood and had had the castle built secretly. A very rich aristocrat who required considerable privacy might find it possible to achieve. I could imagine that I might myself consider such a plan. But I was not rich. The castle was therefore an excellent base from which to make raids. It could be defended, even if it were discovered.

It seemed to me that it could also have been built by some ancient brigandly baron in the days when almost all the German provinces were maintained by petty warlords preying upon one another and upon the surrounding populace.

That evening I lit many candles and sat in the library wearing fresh linen and drinking good wine while I read a treatise on astronomy by a student of Kepler's and reflected on my increasing disagreement with Luther, who had judged reason to be the chief enemy of Faith, of the purity of his beliefs. He had considered reason a harlot, willing to turn to anyone's needs, but this merely displayed his own suspicion of logic. I have come to believe him the madman Catholics described him as. Most mad people see logic as a threat to the dream in which they would rather live, a threat to their attempts to make the dream reality (usually through force, through threat, through manipulation and through bloodshed). It is why men of reason are so often the first to be killed or exiled by tyrants.

He who would analyse the world, rather than impose upon it a set of attributes, is always most in danger from his fellows, though he prove the most passive and tolerant of men. It has often seemed to me that if one wishes to find consolation in this world one must also be prepared to accept at least one or two large lies. A confessor requires considerable Faith before he will help you.

I went early to bed, having fed my horse with oats from the granary, and slept peacefully, for I had taken the precaution of lowering the portcullis, knowing that I should wake if anyone should try to enter the castle in the night.

My sleep was dreamless, and yet when I awoke in the morning I had an impression of gold and white, of lands without horizon, without sun or moon. It was another warm, clear day. All I wished for to complete my peace of mind was a little birdsong, but I whistled to myself as I descended to the kitchens to breakfast on preserved herring and cheese, washing this down with some watered beer.

I had decided to spend as much time as I could in the castle, to recollect myself, to rest and then continue my journey until I found some likely master who would employ me in the trade I had made my own. I had long since learned to be content with my own company and so did not feel the loneliness which others might experience.

It was in the evening, as I exercised upon the battlements, that I detected the signs of conflict some miles distant, close to the horizon. There, the forest was burning; or perhaps it was a settlement which burned. The fire spread even as I watched, but no wind carried the smoke towards me.

As the sun set I saw a faint red glow, but was able to go to bed and sleep soundly again, for no rider could have reached the castle by the morning.

I rose shortly after sunrise and went immediately to the battlements.

The fire was dying, it seemed. I ate and read until noon.

Another visit to the battlements showed me that the fire had grown again, indicating that a good-sized army was on the move towards me. It would take me less than an hour to be ready to leave, and I had learned the trick of responding to nothing but actual and immediate danger. There was always the chance that the army would turn away well before it sighted the castle.

For three days I watched as the army came nearer and nearer until it was possible to see it through a break in the trees created by a wide river.

It had settled on both banks, and I knew enough of such armies to note that it was constituted of the usual proportions: at least five camp-followers to every soldier.

Women and children and male servants of various sorts went about the business of administering to the warriors. These were people who, for one reason or another, had lost their own homes and found greater security with the army than they would find elsewhere, preferring to identify with the aggressor rather than be his victims.

There were about a hundred horses, but the majority of

the men were infantry, clad in the costumes and uniforms of a score of countries and princes. It was impossible to say which cause, if any, it served, and would therefore be best avoided, particularly since it had an air of recent defeat about it.

The next day I saw outriders approach the castle and then almost immediately turn their horses back, without debate. Judging by their costume and their weapons, the riders were native Germans, and I formed the impression that they knew of the castle and were anxious to avoid it.

If some local superstition kept them away and thus preserved my peace, I would be more than content to let them indulge their fears. I planned to watch carefully, however, until I became certain that I would not be disturbed.

In the meanwhile I continued my explorations of the castle.

I had been made even more curious by the fearful response of those riders. Nonetheless, no effort of mine could reveal the castle's owner, nor even the name of the family which had built it. That they were wealthy was evident from the quantity of rich silk and woollen hangings everywhere, the pictures and the tapestries, the gold and the silver, the illuminated windows.

I sought out vaults where ancestors might be buried and discovered none.

I concluded that my original opinion was the most likely to be true: this was a rich prince's retreat. Possibly a private retreat, where he did not wish to be known by his given name. If the owner kept mysteries about him as to his identity, then it was also possible that his power was held to be great and possibly supernatural in these parts and that that was why the castle went untouched. I thought of the legend of Johannes Faust and other mythical maguses of the previous, uncertain, century.

In two days the army had gone on its slow way and I was alone again.

I was quickly growing bored, having read most of what interested me in the library and beginning to long for fresh meat and bread, as well as the company of some jolly peasant woman, such as those I had seen with the army. But I stayed there for the best part of another week, sleeping a good deal and restoring my strength of body, as well as my strength of judgement.

All I had to look forward to was a long journey, the business of recruiting another company and then seeking a fresh master for my services.

I considered the idea of returning to Bek, but I knew that I was no longer suited for the kind of life still lived there. I would be a disappointment to my father. I had sworn to myself long since that I should only return to Bek if I heard that he was dying or dead. I wished him to think of me as a noble Christian soldier serving the cause of the religion he loved.

On the night before I planned to leave I began to get some sense of a stirring in the castle, as if the place itself were coming to life.

To quell my own slight terrors I took a lamp and explored the castle once more, from end to end, from top to bottom, and found nothing strange. However, I became even more determined to leave on the following morning.

As usual, I rose at sunrise and took my horse from the stable. He was in considerably better condition than when we had arrived. I had raised the portcullis and was packing food into my saddlebags when I heard a sound from outside, a kind of creaking and shuffling.

Going to the gates, I was astonished by the sight below. A procession was advancing up the hill towards me. At first I thought this was the castle's owner returning. It had not struck me before that he might not be a temporal prince at all, but a high-ranking churchman.

The procession had something of the nature of a monastery on the move.

First came six well-armed horsemen, with pikes at the slope in stirrup holsters, their faces hidden in helmets of black iron; then behind them were some twoscore monks in dark habits and cowls, hauling upon ropes attached to the kind of carriage which would normally be drawn by horses. About another dozen monks walked at the back of the coach, and these were followed by six more horsemen, identical in appearance to those at the front.

The coach was of cloudy, unpainted wood which glittered a little in the light. It had curtained windows, but bore no crest, not even a cross.

The regalia of the riders looked popish to me, so I knew I would have to be wary in my responses, if I were to avoid conflict.

I wasted no time. I mounted and rode down the hill towards them. I wished that the sides of the hill were not so steep here, or I should not have had to take the road at all. I could not, as it happened, make my departure without passing them, but I felt happier being free of the castle, with a chance at least of escape should these warriors and monks prove belligerent.

As I came closer I began to smell them. They stank of corruption. They carried the odour of rotting flesh with them. I thought that the coach contained perhaps some dead cardinal.

Then I realised that all these creatures were the same. The flesh appeared to be falling from their faces and limbs. Their eyes were the eyes of corpses. When they saw me they came to a sudden stop.

The horsemen prepared their pikes.

I made no movement towards my own weapons, for fear of exciting them. Nonetheless, I readied myself to charge through them if it should prove necessary.

One of the riders spoke sluggishly and yet with horrifying authority, as if he were Death Himself and that pike in his hand the Reaper's scythe:

"You trespass, fellow.

"You trespass.

"Understand you not that this land is forbidden to you?"

The words came as a series of clipped phrases, with a long pause between each, as if the speaker had to recall the notion of language.

"I saw no signs," said I. "I heard no word. How could I when your land is absolutely free of population?"

In all my experience of horror I had witnessed nothing to compare with this talking corpse. I felt unnerving fear and was hard put to control it.

He spoke again:

"It is understood—

"By all. It seems.

"Save you."

"I am a stranger," I declared, "and sought the hospitality of this castle's lord. I did not expect the place to be empty. I apologise for my ignorance. I have done no damage."

I made ready to spur my horse.

Another of the riders turned his iron head on me.

Cold eyes, full of old blood, stared into mine.

My stomach regretted that I had broken its fast so recently.

He said:

"How were you able to come and go?

"Have you made the bargain?"

I attempted to reply in a reasonable tone. "I came and went as you see, upon my horse. I have no bond, if that is what you mean, with the master of this castle."

I addressed the coach, believing that the castle's owner must sit within:

"But again I say that I apologise for my unwitting trespass. I have done no harm, save eat a little food, water my horse and read a book or two."

"No bargain," muttered one of the monks, as if puzzled.

"No bargain he is aware of," said a third horseman.

And they laughed amongst themselves. The sound was a disgusting one.

"I have never met your lord," said I. "It is unlikely that I know him."

"Doubtless he knows you."

Their mockery, their malicious enjoyment of some secret they believed they shared, was disturbing my composure and making me impatient.

I said:

"If I may be allowed to approach and present myself, you will discover that I am of noble birth . . ."

I had no real intention of talking with the occupant of the coach, but should I be able to advance a little farther I would gain time and distance—and with some luck I might break free of them without need of my sword.

"You may not approach," said the first rider.

"You must return with us."

I spoke with mock good manners:

"I have already sampled your hospitality too long. I'll impose upon it no further."

I smiled to myself. My spirits began to lift, as they always do when action is required of me. I began to experience that cool good humour common to many professional soldiers when killing becomes necessary.

"You have no choice," said the rider.

He lowered his pike: a threat.

I relaxed in my saddle, ensuring that my seat was firm.

"I make my own choices, sir," I said.

My spurs touched my horse and he began to trot rapidly towards them.

They had not expected this.

They were used to inducing terror. They were not, I suspected, used to fighting.

I had broken through them in a matter of seconds. Barely grazed by a pike, I now attempted to ride the monks down.

I hacked at the cowled men. They did not threaten me but were so anxious not to release their grasp on the carriage's ropes that they could not move from my path. They seemed perfectly willing to die under my sword rather than give up their charge.

I was forced to turn and face the riders once more.

They had no battle skill, these people, and were uncertain in their movements, for all their arrogance. Again I received an impression of hesitation, as if each individual action had to be momentarily remembered. So clumsy were they that their pikes were tangled by a few passages of my sword.

I used the bulk of my horse to back farther into the press of monks. They offered the heavy resistance of corpses.

I turned the steed again.

I let him rear and strike down two monks with his hooves.

I jumped first one taut rope and then the other and was aiming for the grassy flanks of the steep hillside when the riders from the rear came galloping forward to cut me off.

I had a balustrade before me, some statues to my left, an almost sheer drop beyond these.

Again I was forced to pause. I tried to pull a pistol loose and fire in the hope it would startle their horses. I did not think I could delay their charge by wounding one.

My horse was moving too much beneath me, ready to gallop, yet not knowing where to go. I reined him tight, standing firm against that rocking nest of pikes which was now almost upon me.

A glance this way and that told me that my chances had improved. There was every possibility of escape. I no longer felt in terror of my attackers. At worst I could calculate on a few flesh wounds for myself and a sprained tendon or two for my horse.

The pikes drew closer as I reached for my pistols.

Then a clear, humorous voice sounded from the interior of the coach:

"There is no need for this. It wasn't planned. Stop at once, all of you. I demand that you stop!"

The riders drew in their own reins and began to raise their pikes to the slope.

I put my sword between my teeth, drew both pistols from the saddle-holsters, cocked the flints and fired.

One of the pistols discharged and flung a rider straight out of his seat. The other needed recocking, having failed to spark, but before I could see to it, I heard the voice again.

It was a woman. "Stop!"

I would let them debate her orders. In the meantime I had a little time in which to begin my descent. I sheathed my sword and looked down the hillside. I had planned to skirt this party and continue down the road if possible. It would mean driving directly through the pikes, but I believed I could do it fairly easily.

I prepared myself, while giving the impression that I was relaxing my guard.

The door of the coach opened.

A handsome woman of about thirty, with jet-black hair and wearing scarlet velvet, clambered swiftly onto the coachman's seat and raised her arms. She seemed distracted. I was impressed by her bearing and her beauty.

"Stop!" she cried to me. "We meant no harm to you."

I grinned at this. But since I now had something of an advantage and did not wish to risk either my life or my horse more than necessary, I paused. My loaded pistol was still in my gloved hand.

"Your men attacked me, madam."

"Not upon my orders." Her lips matched her costume. Her skin was as delicate and pale as the lace which trimmed her garments. She wore a matching broad-brimmed hat with a white ostrich feather trailing from it.

"You are welcome," she said. "I swear to you that it is so, sir. You came forward before I could present myself."

I was certain that all she was doing now was to change tactics. But I preferred these tactics. They were familiar enough.

I grinned at her. "You mean you had hoped that your servants would frighten me, eh, madam?"

She feigned puzzlement. She spoke with apparent sincerity, even urgency: "You must not think so. These creatures are not subtle. They are the only servants provided me." Her eyes were wonderful. I was astonished by them. She said: "I apologise to you, sir."

She lowered her arms, almost as if she appealed to me. She struck me as a woman of substance, yet there was an engaging touch of despair about her. Was she perhaps a prisoner of those men?

I was almost amused: a lady in distress, and myself a knight-errant to whom the notion of chivalry was anathema. Yet I hesitated.

"Madam, your servants disturb me by their very appearance."

"They were not chosen by me."

"Indeed, I should hope that's so." I retained my pistol at the cock. "They were chosen by Death long since, by the look of 'em."

She sighed and made a small gesture with her right hand.

"Sir, I would be much obliged if you would consent to be my guest."

"Your men have already invited me. You'll recall that I refused."

"Will you refuse me? I ask," she said, "in all humility."

She was a clever woman and it had been some years since I had enjoyed such company. It was her eyes, however, which continued to draw me. They were wise, they were knowing, they contained in them a hint of deep terror and they were sympathetic, I thought, to me in particular.

I was lost to her. I knew it. I believe she knew it. I began to laugh.

I bowed to her.

"It is true, madam," said I, "that I cannot refuse you. Boredom, curiosity and what is left of my good manners drive me to accept. But most of all, madam, it is yourself, for I'll swear I see a fellow spirit and one as intelligent as myself. A rare combination, you'd agree?"

"I take your meaning, sir. And I share your feeling, too." Those wonderful eyes shone with ironic pleasure. I thought that she, too, could be laughing, somewhere within her. With a delicate hand she brushed hair away from the left side of her face and tilted her head to look at me. A conscious gesture, I knew, and a flirtatious one. I grinned this time.

"Then you'll guest with me?" she said.

"On one condition," said I.

"Sir?"

"That you promise to explain some of the mysteries of your castle and its surrounds."

She raised her brows. "It is an ordinary castle. In ordinary grounds."

"You know that it is not."

She answered my grin with a smile. "Very well," she said. "I promise that you shall understand everything very soon."

"I note your promise," said I.

I sheathed my pistol and turned my horse towards the castle.

I had taken my first decisive step towards Hell.

Chapter II

I GAVE THE lady my arm and escorted her through her
courtyard, up the steps and into her castle, while her horrid
servants took horse and coach to the stables. Curiosity had
me trapped.

Lust, half-appreciated as yet, also had me trapped.

I thought to myself with a certain relish that I was, all in
all, thoroughly snared. And at that moment I did not care.

"I am Ulrich von Bek, son of the Graf von Bek," I told
her. "I am a Captain of Infantry in the present struggle."

Her perfume was as warm and lulling as summer roses.
"On whose side?" she asked.

I shrugged. "Whichever is the better organised and less
divided."

"You have no strong religious beliefs, then?"

"None."

I added: "Is that unusual for men of my kind in times like
these?"

"Not at all. Not at all." She seemed quietly amused.

She took off her own cloak. She was almost as tall as I
and wonderfully formed. For all that she gave the impression
of possessing a strong and perhaps even eccentric will, there

was yet a softness about her now which suggested to me that
she was presently defeated by her circumstances.

"I am Sabrina," she said, and gave no title or family
name.

"This is your castle, Lady Sabrina?"

"I often reside here." She was noncommittal.

It could be that she was reluctant to discuss her family.
Or perhaps she was the mistress of the powerful prince I had
originally guessed as owner. Perhaps she had been exiled here
for some appalling crime. Perhaps she had been sent here by
her husband or some other relative to avoid the vicissitudes
either of love or of war. From tact I could ask her no other
questions on the matter.

She laid a fair hand upon my arm. "You will eat with me,
Captain von Bek?"

"I do not relish eating in the presence of your servants,
madam."

"No need. I'll prepare the food myself later. They are
not permitted to enter these quarters. They have their own
barracks in the far tower."

I had seen the barracks. They did not seem large enough
for so many.

"How long have you been here?" She glanced about the
hall as we entered it.

"A week or two."

"You kept it in good order."

"It was not my intention to loot the place, Lady Sabrina,
but to use it as a temporary refuge. How long has your home
been empty?"

She waved a vague hand. "Oh, some little while. Why do
you ask?"

"Everything was so well-preserved. So free of vermin.
Of dust, even."

"Ah. We do not have much trouble of that kind."

"No damp. No rot."

"None visible," she said. She seemed to become impatient with my remarks.

"I remain grateful for the shelter," I said, to end this
theme.

"You are welcome." Her voice became a little distant.
She frowned. "The soldiers delayed us."

"How so?"

"On the road." She gestured. "Back there."

"You were attacked?"

"Pursued for a while. Chased." Her finger sought dust on a chest and found none. She seemed to be considering my recent remarks. "They fear us, of course. But there were so many of them." She smiled, displaying white, even teeth. She spoke as if I would understand and sympathise. As if I were a comrade.

All I could do was nod.

"I cannot blame them," she continued. "I cannot blame any of them." She sighed. Her dark eyes clouded, became in-turned, dreamy. "But you are here. And that is good."

I should have found her manner disturbing, but at the time I found it captivating. She spoke as if I had been expected, as if she were a poor hostess who, delayed abroad, returns to discover an unattended guest.

I offered some formal compliment to her beauty and grace. She smiled a little, accepting it as one who was very used to such remarks, who perhaps even regarded them as the opening feints in an emotional duel. I recognised her expression. It caused me to become just a little more remote, a little more guarded. She was a gameswoman, I thought, trained by one or more masters in the terrible, cold art of intellectual coquetry. I found the woman too interesting to wish to give her a match, so I changed the subject back to my original reason for accepting her invitation.

"You have promised to explain the castle's mysteries," I said. "And why there is no animal life in these parts."

"It is true," she said. "There is none."

"You have agreed with me, madam," I said gently, "but you have not explained anything to me."

Her tone became a shade brusque. "I promised you an explanation, did I not, sir?"

"Indeed, you did."

"And an explanation will be forthcoming."

I was not, in those days, a man to be brushed off with insubstantial reassurances. "I'm a soldier, madam. I had intended to be on my way south by now. You will recall that I returned here at your invitation—and because of your promise. Soldiers are an impatient breed."

She seemed just a fraction agitated by my remark, pushing at her long hair, touching her cheek. Her words were rapid and they stumbled. She said: "No soul—that is no free soul, however small—can exist here."

This was not good enough for me, although I was intrigued. "I do not follow you, madam," I said with deliberate firmness. "You are obscure. I am used to action and simple facts. From those simple facts I am able to determine what action I should take."

"I do not wish to confuse you, sir." She appealed to me, but I refused to respond to her.

I sighed. "What do you mean when you say that no soul can exist here?"

She hesitated. "Nothing which belongs," she said, "to God."

"Belongs? To God? The forest, surely . . . ?"

"The forest lies upon the"—she made a baffled gesture—"upon the borders."

"I still do not understand."

She controlled herself, returning my stare. "Neither should you," she said.

"I am not much impressed by metaphysics." I was becoming angry. Such abstract debate had caused our present woes. "Are you suggesting that some sort of plague once infested this land? Is that why both men and beasts avoid it?"

She made no reply.

I continued: "Your servants, after all, suffer from disease. Could they be suffering from an infection local to this area?"

"Their souls—" she began again.

I interrupted. "The same abstraction . . ."

"I do my best, sir," she said.

"Madam, you offer me no facts."

"I have offered you facts, as I understand them. It is hard . . ."

"You speak of a sickness, in truth. Do you not? You are afraid that if you name it, I shall become nervous, that you will drive me away."

"If you like," she said.

"I am afraid of very little, though I must admit to a certain caution where the Plague is concerned. On the other hand I have reason to believe that I am one of those lucky souls apparently immune to the Plague, so you must know that I shall not immediately run quaking from this place. Tell me. Is it a sickness of which you speak?"

"Aye," she said, as if tired, as if willing to agree to almost any definition I provided. "It could be as you say."

"But you are untouched." I moved a pace towards her. "And I."

She became silent. Was I to think, I wondered, that the signs of that horrible sickness which possessed her servants had not yet manifested themselves in us? I shuddered.

"How long have you lived at the castle?" I asked.

"I am here only from time to time."

This answer suggested to me that perhaps she was immune. If she were immune, then so, perhaps, was I. With that consideration I relaxed more.

She seated herself upon a couch. Sunlight poured through stained glass representing Diana at the hunt. It was only then that I realised not a single Christian scene existed here, no crucifix, no representations of Jesus or the saints. Tapestries, glass, statuary and decoration were all pagan in subject.

"How old is this castle?" I stood before the window, running my fingers over the lead.

"Very old, I think. Several centuries, at least."

"It has been well-maintained."

She knew that my questions were not innocent or casual. I was seeking further knowledge of the estate and the mysterious sickness which haunted it.

"True," she said.

I sensed a new kind of tension. I turned.

She went from that room into the next and came back with wine for us. As she handed me my cup I observed that she did not wear a marriage ring. "You have no lord, madam?"

"I have a lord," she said, and she stared back into my eyes as if I had challenged her. Then, seeing my question to be fairly innocent, she shrugged. "Yes, I have a lord, captain."

"But this is not your family property."

"Oh, well. Family?" She began to smile very strangely, then controlled her features. "The castle is my master's, and has been his for many years."

"Not always his, however?"

"No. He won it, I believe."

"Spoils of war?"

She shook her head. "A gambling debt."

"Your master is a gambler, eh? And plays for good-sized stakes. Does he participate in our War?"

"Oh, yes." Her manner changed again. She became brisk. "I'll not be cryptic with you, Captain von Bek." She smiled; a hint, once more, of helplessness. "On the other hand it does not suit me to pursue this conversation further at present."

"Please forgive my rudeness." I think that I sounded cold.

"You are direct, captain, but not rude." She spoke quietly. "For a man who has doubtless seen and done so much in the matter of war you seem to retain a fair share of grace."

I touched the cup to my lips—half a toast to her own good manners. "I am astonished that you should think so. Yet, in comparison with your servants, I suppose I must seem better than I am . . ."

She laughed. Her skin appeared to glow. I smelled roses. I felt as if the heat of the sun were upon me in that room. I knew that I desired Sabrina as I had desired no one or nothing else in all my life. Yet my caution maintained distance. For that moment I was content merely to experience those sensations (which I had not experienced in many years of soldiering) and not attempt fulfillment.

"How did you come by your servants?" I sipped my wine. It tasted better than any of the other vintages I had sampled here. It increased the impression that all my senses were coming alive again at once.

She pursed her lips before replying. Then: "They are pensioners, you might say, of my master."

"Your master? You mention him much. But you do not name him." I pointed this out most gently.

"It is true." She moved hair from her face.

"You do not wish to name him?"

"At this time? No."

"He sent you here?" I savoured the wine.

"Yes," she said.

"Because he fears for your safety?" I suggested.

"No." Sadness and desperate amusement showed for a second in the set of her lips.

"Then you have an errand here?" I asked. Again I moved closer.

"Yes." She took a couple of paces back from me. I

guessed that she was as affected by me as I was by her, but it could have been merely that my questions cut too close to the bone and that I was unnerving her.

I paused.

"Could I ask you what that errand can be?"

She became gay, but plainly her mood was not altogether natural. "To entertain you"—a flirt of the hand—"captain."

"But you were not aware that I stayed here."

She dropped her gaze.

"Were you?" I continued. "Unless some unseen servant of your master reported me to you."

She raised her eyes. She ignored my last remark and said: "I have been looking for a brave man. A brave man and an intelligent one."

"On your master's instructions? Is that the implication?"

She offered me a challenging look now. "If you like."

The instinct which had helped me keep my life and health through all my exploits warned me now that this unusual woman could be bait for a trap. For once, however, I ignored the warning. She was willing, she suggested, to give herself to me. In return, I guessed, I would be called upon to pay a high price. At that moment I did not care what the price was. I was, anyway, I reminded myself, a resourceful man and could always, with reasonable odds, escape later. One can act too much in the cause of self-preservation and experience nothing fresh as a result.

"He gives you liberty to do what?" I asked her.

"To do almost anything I like." She shrugged.

"He is not jealous?"

"Not conventionally so, Captain von Bek." She drained her cup. I followed her example. She took both cups and filled them again. She sat herself beside me, now, upon a couch under the window. My flesh, my skin, every vein and sinew, sang. I, who had practised self-control for years, was barely able to hold onto a coherent thought as I took her hand and kissed it, murmuring: "He is an unusual master, your lord."

"That is also true."

I withdrew my lips and fell back a little, looking carefully at her wonderful face. "He indulges you? Is it because he loves you very much?"

Her breathing matched mine. Her eyes were bright,

passionate gems. She said: "I am not sure that my master understands the nature of love. Not as you and I would understand it."

I laughed and let myself relax a little more. "You become cryptic again, Lady Sabrina, when you swore that you would not be."

"Forgive me." She rose for fresh cups.

I watched her form. I had never seen such beauty and such wit combined in any human individual before. "You will not tell me your history?"

"Not yet."

I interpreted this remark as a promise, yet I pressed her just a little further:

"You were born in these parts?"

"In Germany, yes."

"And not very long ago." This was partly to flatter her. It was unnecessary, that flattery, I knew, but I had learned pothouse habits as a soldier-of-fortune and could not in an instant lose them all.

Her answer was unexpected. She turned to me, with a wine-cup in each hand. "It depends on your definition of Time," she said. She gave me my filled cup. "Now you probe and I mystify. Shall we talk of less personal matters? Or do you wish to speak of yourself?"

"You seem to have determined who and what I am already, my lady."

"Not in fine, captain."

"I've few secrets. Most of my recent life has been spent in soldiering. Before that it was spent in receiving an education. Life is not very brisk in Bek."

"But you have seen and done much, as a soldier?"

"The usual things." I frowned. I did not desire too much recollection. Magdeburg memories still lingered and were resisted with a certain amount of effort.

"You have killed frequently?"

"Of course." I displayed reluctance to expand upon this theme.

"And taken part in looting? In torture?"

"When necessary, aye." I grew close to anger again. I believed that she deliberately discomfited me.

"And rape?"

I peered directly at her. Had I misjudged her? Was she

perhaps one of those bored, lascivious ladies of the kind I had once met at Court? They had delighted in such talk. It had excited them. They were eager for sensation, having forgotten or never experienced the subtle forms of human sensuality and emotion. In my cynicism I had given them all that they desired. It had been like bestowing lead on gold-greedy merchants who, in their anxiety to possess as much as possible, could not any longer recognise one metal from another. If the Lady Sabrina was of this caste, I should give her what she desired.

But her eyes remained candid and questioning, so I answered briefly: "Aye. Soldiers, as I said, become impatient. Weary . . ."

She was not interested in my explanation. She continued: "And have you punished heretics?"

"I have seen them destroyed."

"But have taken no part in their destruction?"

"By luck and my own distaste, I have not."

"Could you punish a heretic?"

"Madam, I do not really know what a heretic is. The word is made much of, these days. It seems to describe anyone you wish dead."

"Or witches? Have you executed witches?"

"I am a soldier, not a priest."

"Many soldiers take on the responsibilities of priests, do they not? And many priests become soldiers."

"I am not of that ilk. I have seen poor lunatics and old women named for witches and dealt with accordingly, madam. But I have witnessed no magic performances, no incantations, no summonings of demons or ghouls." I smiled. "Some of those crones were so familiar with Mephistopheles that they could almost pronounce the name when it was repeated to them . . ."

"Then witchcraft does not frighten you?"

"It does not. Or, I should say, what I have seen of witchcraft does not frighten me."

"You are a sane man, sir."

I supposed that she complimented me.

"Sane by the standards of our world, madam. But not, I think, by my own."

She seemed pleased by this. "An excellent answer. You are self-demanding, then?"

"I demand little of myself, save that I survive. I take what I need from the world."

"You are a thief, then?"

"I am a thief, if you like. I hope that I am not a hypocrite."

"Self-deceiving, all the same."

"How so?"

"You hide the largest part of yourself away in order to be the soldier you describe. And then you deny that that part exists."

"I do not follow you. I am what I am."

"And that is?"

"What the world has made me."

"Not what God created? God created the world, did He not?" she said.

"I have heard some theorise otherwise."

"Heretics?"

"Ah, well, madam. Desperate souls like the rest of us."

"You have an unusually open mind."

"For a soldier?"

"For anyone living at this time."

"I am not quite sure that my mind is open. It is probably careless, however. I do not give a fig for metaphysical debate, as I believe I have already indicated."

"You have no conscience, then?"

"Too expensive to maintain nowadays, madam."

"So it is unkempt, but it exists?"

"Is that what you would say I hide from myself? Have you a mind to convert me to whatever Faith it is you hold, my lady?"

"My Faith is not too dissimilar to yours."

"So I thought."

"Soul? Conscience? These words mean little, I'm sure you'd agree, without specification."

"I do most readily agree."

We continued to debate this subject only for a short while and then the discussion broadened.

She proved to be an educated woman with a fine range of experience and anecdote. The longer we were together, however, the more I desired her.

The noon meal was forgotten as we continued to talk and to drink. She quoted the Greeks and the Romans, she quoted poetry in several tongues. She was far more fluent in the languages of modern Europe and the Orient than was I.

It became obvious to me that Sabrina must be highly valued by her master and that she was probably something more than his mistress. A woman could travel the world with a little more danger but a little less suspicion than a male envoy. I formed the impression that she was familiar with a good many powerful Courts. Yet I wondered how her servants must be received if they accompanied her to such places.

Evening came. She and I retired to the kitchen where, from the same ingredients, she prepared a far better meal than anything I had been able to make for myself. We drank more wine and then, without thought, took ourselves up to one of the main bedrooms and disrobed.

Sheets, quilts, bed-curtains, were all creamy white in the late sunshine. Naked, Sabrina was perfect. Her pale body was flawless, her breasts small and firm. I had seen no woman like her, save in statues and certain paintings.

I had not believed in perfection before that night, and although I retained a healthy suspicion of Sabrina's motives I was determined to offer no resistance to her charms.

We went quickly to bed. She became by turns tender, savage, passive and aggressive. I turned with her, whatever her mood, as she turned with mine. My senses, which had become almost as dead as those of Sabrina's servants, had come to life again.

I felt my imagination coming back to me, and with it a certain amount of hope, of the old optimism I had known as a youth in Bek.

Our union, it seemed to me, was preordained, for there was no doubt that she relished me as thoroughly as I relished her. I absorbed her scents, the touch of her skin.

Our passion seemed as endless as the tides; our lust conquered all weariness. If it had not been for that nagging memory that she was in some way pledged to another, I should have given myself up to her entirely. As it was, some small part of me held back. But it was a minuscule fraction. It need hardly have existed.

Eventually we fell asleep and woke in the morning, before light, to make love again. A week or two went by. I was more and more entranced by her.

Half-asleep as one grey dawn came, I murmured that I wanted her to come with me, to leave her ghastly servants behind, to find some other place which the War did not touch.

"Is there another place?" she asked me, with a tender smile.

"In the East, possibly. Or England. We could go to England. Or to the New World."

She became sad and she stroked my cheek. "That isn't possible," she said. "My master would not allow it."

I became fierce. "Your master would not find us."

"He would find me and take me from you, be assured of that."

"In the New World? Is he the Pope?"

She seemed startled and I wondered if, with my rhetorical question, I had struck upon the truth.

I continued: "I would fight him. I would raise an army against him if necessary."

"You would lose."

I asked her seriously: "Is he the Pope? Your master?"

"Oh, no," said she impulsively, "he is far greater than the Pope."

I frowned. "Perhaps in your eyes. But not the eyes of the world, surely?"

She stirred in the bed and avoided looking directly at me, saying softly: "In the eyes of the whole world, and Heaven, too."

In spite of myself, I was disturbed by her reply. It took another week before I found the courage to make a further statement. I would rather not have pursued the subject:

"You have promised to answer my questions," I said to her, again in the morning. "Would it not be fair to tell me the name of your all-powerful lord? After all, I could be endangering myself by remaining here."

"You are in no particular danger."

"You must let me decide that. You must offer me the choice."

"I know . . ." Her voice died away. "Tomorrow."

"His name," I insisted the next day. I saw terror reflected and compounded, hers and mine.

Then from where she lay in bed she looked directly into my eyes. She shook her head.

"Who is your lord?" I said.

She moved her lips carefully. She raised her head as she spoke. Her mouth seemed dry, her expression strangely blank.

"His name," she said, "is Lucifer."

My self-control almost disappeared. She had shocked me in several ways at the same time, for I could not decide how to interpret this remark. I refused to let superstition attack my reason. I sat up in bed and forced myself to laugh.

"And you are a witch, is that it?"

"I have been called that," she said.

"A shape-changer!" I felt half-mad now. "You are in reality an ancient hag who has englamoured me!"

"I am who you see me to be," she said. "But, yes, I was a witch."

"And your powers come from your compact with the Prince of Darkness?"

"They did not. I was called a witch by the people who determined to kill me. But that was before I met Lucifer . . ."

"You implied some time ago that you shared my opinions of witches!"

"Aye—of those poor women so branded."

"Yet why call yourself one?"

"You used the word. I agreed that I had been called that."

"You are not a witch?"

"When I was young I had certain gifts which I put to the service of my town. I am not stupid. My advice was sought and used. I was well-educated by my father. I could read and write. I knew other women like myself. We met together, as much to enjoy each other's intelligence as to discuss matters of alchemy, herbalism and the like." She shrugged. "It was a small town. The people were small merchants, peasants, you know . . . Women are, by and large, denied the company of scholars, even if they resort to the nunnery. Christians do not permit Eve wisdom, do they? They can only suggest that she was influenced by a fallen angel." She was sardonic. Then she sighed, leaning on one bare arm as she looked at me.

"Scholarly men were suspect in my town. Women could not admit to scholarship at all. Men are afraid of two things in this world, it seems—women and knowledge. Both threaten their power, eh?"

"If you like," I said. "Were there not other women in the town afraid of such things?"

"Of course. Even more afraid in some ways. It was women who betrayed us, in the end."

"It is in the way of events," I said. "Many speak of freedom, of free thought, but few would want the responsibility of actually possessing them."

"Is that why you insist that you are a soldier?"

"I suppose so. I have no great hankering after real freedom. Is that why you let me call you a witch?"

Her smile was sad. "Possibly."

"And is that why you now tell me that Satan is your Master?"

"Not exactly," she replied. "Though I follow your reasoning."

"How did you come to be branded a witch in your town?"

"Perhaps through Pride," she said. "We began to see ourselves as a powerful force for good in the world. We practised magic, of sorts, and experimented sometimes. But our magic was all White. I admit that we studied the other kind. We knew how it could be worked. Particularly by the weak, who sought spurious strength through evil."

"You came to believe that you were strong enough to resist human prejudice? You grew incautious?"

"You could say so, yes."

"But how did you come, as you put it, to serve Satan?" Now I believed that she spoke metaphorically, or that at least she was exaggerating. I still could not believe that she was insane. Her confession, after all, was couched in the most rational terms.

"Our coven was discovered, betrayed. We were imprisoned. We were tortured, of course, and tried, and found guilty. Many confessed to pacts with the Devil." Her expression became bleak. "I could not, in those days, believe that so many evil people would pose as good while we, who had done no harm and had served our neighbours, were submitted to the most disgusting and brutal of attentions."

"But you escaped . . ."

"I became disillusioned as I lay wounded and humiliated in that dungeon. Desperate. I determined that if I was to be branded an evil witch I might as well behave as one. I knew the invocations necessary to summon a servant of the Devil."

She moved carefully, looking full into my face before she spoke next:

"In my cell one night, because I wished to save myself from death and further barbarism; because I had lost belief in the power of my sisters, upon which I had faithfully relied, I began the necessary ritual. It was at my moment of greatest weakness. And it is at that moment, you must know, when Lucifer's servants come calling."

"You summoned a demon?"

"And sold my soul."

"And were saved."

"After the pact was made, I appeared to contract the Plague and was thrown, living, into a pit on the outskirts of town. From that pit I escaped and the Plague went from me. Two days after that, as I lay in a barn, my Master appeared to me in person. He said that He had special need of me. He brought me here, where I was instructed in His service."

"You truly believe that it was Lucifer who brought you here? That this is Lucifer's castle?" I reached out to touch her face.

"I know that Lucifer is my Master. I know that this is His domain on Earth." She could tell that I did not believe her.

"But He is not in residence today?" I said.

"He is here now," she told me flatly.

"I discovered no sign of Him." I was insistent.

"Could you recognise the sign of Lucifer?" she asked me. She spoke as if to a child.

"I would expect at least a hint of brimstone," I told her.

She gestured about her. "This whole castle, the forest outside, is His sign. Could you not guess? Why do even the smallest insects avoid it? Why do whole armies fear it?"

"Then why did I feel only a hint of trepidation when I came here? How can you live here?"

Her expression approached pity.

"Only the souls He owns can exist here," she said.

I shuddered and became cold. I was almost convinced by her. Happily, my reason once again began to function. My ordinary sense of self-preservation. I stepped from the bed and began pulling on my linen. "Then I'll be leaving," I said. "I have no wish to make a pact with Lucifer or anyone who calls himself Lucifer. And I would suggest, Sabrina, that you accompany me. Unless you wish to remain enslaved by your illusion."

She became wistful.

"If only it were an illusion, and you truly could save me."

"I can. On the back of my very ordinary horse. Leave with me now."

"I cannot leave and neither can you. For that matter, because the horse has served you, neither can your horse."

I scoffed at this. "No man is wholly free and the same, madam, may be said for the beast he rides, but we are both free enough to go from here at once!"

"You must stay and meet my Master," she said.

"I am not about to sell my soul."

"You must stay." She reached a hand to me. It trembled. "For my sake."

"Madam, such pleas to my honour are pointless. I have no honour left. I thought that I had made that perfectly clear."

"I beg you," she said.

It was my desire, rather than my honour, which held me there. I hesitated. "You say that your Master is in the castle now?"

"He waits for us."

"Alone? Where? I'll take my sword and deal with your 'Lucifer,' your enchanter, in my own habitual fashion. He has deceived you. Good, sharp steel will enlighten Him and prove to you that He is mortal. You'll be free soon enough, I promise you."

"Bring your sword if you wish," she said.

She rose and began to dress herself in flowing white silk. I stood near her, watching impatiently as she took pains with her clothing. I even felt a pang of jealousy, as a cuckolded husband knows when he sees his wife dressing for her lover.

It was odd, indeed, that such a beautiful and intelligent woman could believe herself in thrall to Satan Himself. Our times were such that human despair took many forms of madness.

I buckled my sword-belt about my shirted waist, pulled on my boots and stood before her, trying to determine the depth of her illusion. Her stare was direct and there was pain in it, as well as a strange sort of determination.

"If you are crazed," I said, "it is the subtlest form of insanity I've ever witnessed."

"The human imagination confers lunacy on everyone,"

she said, "dependent upon their condition. I am as sane as you, sir."

"Then you are, after all, only half-mad," I told her. I offered her my arm as I opened the bedroom door for her. The passage beyond was cold. "Where does this Lucifer of yours hold Court?"

"In Hell," she said.

We walked slowly along the passage and began to descend the broad stone steps towards the main hall.

"And His castle is in Hell?" I asked, looking about me in a somewhat theatrical fashion. I could see the trees through the windows. Everything was exactly as it had been during my stay there.

"It could be," she said.

I shook my head. It took much to threaten my rational view of the world, for my mind had been tempered in the fires of the War, by its terrors and its cruelties, and had survived the contemplation of considerable evil and delusion. "Then all the world is Hell? Do you propose that philosophy?"

"Ah," she said, almost gaily, "is that what we are left with, sir, when we have discarded every other hope?"

"It is a sign of Hope, is it, to believe our own world Hell?"

"Hell is better than nothing," she answered, "to many, at least."

"I refuse to believe such nonsense," I told her. "I have become grim and absolute, madam, in most of my opinions. We appear to be returning to the realm of speculation. I wish to see a concrete Devil and, if we are in Hell, concrete proof of that statement."

"You are overeconomical, sir, in the use of your intelligence."

"I think not. I am a soldier, as I've told you more than once. It is a soldier's trait. Simple facts are his trade."

"We have already discussed your reasons for choosing to become a soldier, sir."

I was amused, once more, by the sharpness of her wit.

We were walking down the steps, alternately through sunlight and shadow. The shift of light gave her features a variety of casts, which had become familiar to me.

Such strength of mind or of body was not usually associated either with witchcraft or with Satan-worship. In my experience, as Sabrina had already hinted to me, those who sought the aid of demons were wretched, powerless creatures who had given up hope of all salvation, whether it be on Earth or in Heaven.

We were crossing the main floor now, towards the huge doors of the library.

"He is in there," she said.

I stopped, loosening my sword. I sniffed.

"Still no brimstone," I said. "Has He horns, your Master? A long tail? Cloven hooves? Does fire come from His nostrils? Or is His enchantment of a subtler sort?"

"I would say that it was subtler," she told me softly. She seemed torn between proving herself and wishing to flee with me. Her expression was challenging and yet fearful as she looked up at me. She seemed even more beautiful. I touched her hair, stroking it. I kissed her upon her warm lips.

Then I strode forward and pushed the large doors open.

Sabrina put her hand on my arm and preceded me into the room. She curtseyed.

"Master, I have brought you Captain von Bek."

I followed immediately behind her, my sword ready, my mind prepared for any challenge, yet my resolve left me immediately.

Seated at the central table and apparently reading a book was the most wonderful being I had ever seen.

I became light-headed. My body refused any commands. I found myself bowing.

He was naked and His skin glowed as if with soft, quivering flames. His curling hair was silver and His eyes were molten copper. His body was huge and perfectly formed, and when His lips smiled upon me I felt that I had never loved before; I loved Him. He bore an aura about His person which I had never associated with the Devil: perhaps it was a kind of dignified humility combined with a sense of almost limitless power.

He spoke in a sweet, mature voice, putting down the book.

"Welcome, Captain von Bek. I am Lucifer."

I was speaking. I believed Him at that moment and I said as much.

Lucifer acknowledged this, standing to His full height and going to the shelves, where He replaced the book.

He moved with grace and offered the impression of exquisite sadness in His every gesture. It was possible to see

how this being had been God's favourite and that He was
surely the Fallen One, destroyed by Pride and now humbled
but unable to achieve His place in Heaven.

I believe that I told Him I was at His service. I could not
check the words, although I recovered myself sufficiently to
deny, mentally, the implications of what I said. I was
desperately attempting to secure my reason.

He seemed to know this and was sympathetic. His
sympathy, of course, was also disarming and had to be
ignored.

He answered my words as if I had offered them voluntar-
ily:

"I wish to strike a bargain with you, Captain von Bek."

Lucifer smiled, as if in self-mockery:

"You are intelligent and brave and do not deny the truth
of what you have become."

"The truth—" I began, with some difficulty, "is not—is
not . . ."

He appeared not to hear. "That is why I told my servant
Sabrina to bring you to me. I need the help of an adult human
being. One without prejudice. One with considerable experience. One who is used to translating thought into determined
action. One who is not given to habits of fearfulness and
hesitation. Such people are scarce, always, in the world."

Now my tongue was not thickened. I was allowed to
speak. I said: "It seems so to me, also, Prince Lucifer. But
you do not describe me. I am but a poor specimen of
mankind."

"Let us say you are the best available to the likes of me."

A little of my wit returned. "I believe you think you
flatter me, Your Majesty."

"Not so. I see virtue everywhere. I see virtue in you,
Captain von Bek."

I smiled. "You are supposed to recognise evil and
wickedness and appeal to those qualities."

Lucifer shook His head. "That is what humankind
detects in me: the desire to find examples for their own base
instincts. Many believe that if they discover an example it
somehow exonerates them from responsibility. I am invested
with many terrible traits, captain. But I, too, possess many
virtues. It is the secret of my power and, to a degree, your
own. Did you know that?"

"I did not, Your Majesty."

"But you understand me?"

"I believe that I do."

"I am asking you to serve me."

"You must have far more powerful men and women than I at your command."

Lucifer reseated Himself behind the desk. He seemed to give His full attention to every word that I uttered now. And this in itself, of course, was flattering to me.

"Powerful," He replied, "certainly. Many of them. In the way in which power is measured upon the Earth. Most of the Holy Church is mine now; but that's a fact well-known to thinking people. A majority of princes belong to me. Scholars serve me. Poets serve me. The commanders of armies and navies serve me. You would think that I am satisfied, eh? There have rarely been so many in my service. But I have few such as you, von Bek."

"That I cannot believe, Your Majesty. Bloody-handed soldiers abound in these times."

"And always have. But few with your quality. Few who act with the full knowledge of what they are and what they do."

"Is it a virtue to know that you are a butcher, a thief? That you are ruthless and without altruism of any kind?"

"I believe so. But then I am Lucifer." Again the self-mockery.

Sabrina curtseyed again. "My Lord, shall I leave?"

"Aye," said Lucifer. "I think so, my dear. I will return the captain to you in due course, I promise."

The witch withdrew. I wondered if I had been abandoned forever by Sabrina, now that she had served her purpose. I tried to stare back at the creature who called Himself Lucifer, but to look into those melancholy, terrible eyes was too much for me. I directed my attention to the window. Through it I could see the mass of trees that were the great forest. I attempted to focus on this sight, in order to preserve my reason and remember that in all likelihood I had been drugged by the accomplice of a man who was nothing more than a charlatan sorcerer of a very high order.

"Now," said the Prince of Darkness, "will you not accompany me to Hell, captain?"

"What?" said I. "Am I damned already? And dead?"

Lucifer smiled. "I give you my word that I shall bring you back to this room. If you are uninterested in my bargain, I will allow you to leave the castle unharmed, to go about whatever business you choose."

"Then why must I come with you to Hell? I have been taught to believe that Satan's word is in no way to be trusted. That He will use any means to win over an honest soul."

Lucifer laughed. "And perhaps you are right, captain. Is yours an honest soul?"

"It is not a clean one."

"But it is, by and large, honest. Yes?"

"You seem to place value on such honesty."

"Great value, captain. I admit to you freely that I have need of you. You do not prize yourself as highly as I prize you. Perhaps that is also one of your virtues. I am prepared to offer you good terms."

"But you will not tell me your terms."

"Not until you have visited Hell. Will you not satisfy your curiosity? Few are able to sample Hell before their time."

"And the few I have read of, Your Majesty, are usually tricked to return there soon enough."

"I give you my word, as an angel, that I am not about to trick you, Captain von Bek. I will be candid with you: I cannot afford to trick you. If I gained what I need from you by deception, then what I gained would be useless to me."

Lucifer offered me His hand.

"Will you descend, with me, to my domain?"

Still I hesitated, not entirely convinced that this was not a complicated and sophisticated enchantment wholly of human origin.

"Can you not bargain with me here?" I said.

"I could. But when the bargain was struck—if it was struck—and when we had parted, would you remain truly certain that you had negotiated with Lucifer?"

"I suppose that I would not. Even now I think that I could be in some kind of drugged glamour."

"You would not be the first to decide that an encounter with me had been nothing but a dream. As a rule it would be immaterial to me whether you decided you had experienced an illusion or were utterly sure that you had enjoyed a meeting with the Prince of Darkness. But I am anxious to prove myself to you, captain."

"Why should Lucifer care?"

A trembling of old Pride. Almost a glare of anger. Then

it was gone. "Be assured, captain," replied Lucifer in deep, urgent tones, "that on this occasion I do care."

"You must be clearer with me, Your Majesty." It was all that I could do to utter even this simple phrase.

He exerted patience. "I cannot prove myself to you here. As you doubtless know, I am largely forced to use humankind for my purposes on Earth, being forbidden direct influence over God's creations, unless they seek me out. I am anxious to do nothing further in defiance of God. I yearn for freedom, von Bek." His copper eyes showed a more intense version of the pain I had observed in Sabrina's. "I once thought I could achieve it. And yet I know now that I cannot have it. Therefore, I wish to be restored."

"To Heaven, Your Majesty?" I was astonished.

"To Heaven, Captain von Bek."

Lucifer applying for a return to Grace! And suggesting that somehow I could be His agent in effecting this! If this were indeed a spell, a trance, it was a most intriguing one.

I was able to say: "Would that not produce the abolition of Hell, the end of Pain in the world?"

"You have been taught to believe that."

"Is it not true?"

"Who knows, Captain von Bek? I am only Lucifer. I am not God."

His fingers touched mine.

Unconsciously, I had stretched my hand towards Him.

His voice was a throb of pleading, of persuasion. "Come, I beg thee. Come."

It was as if we swayed together in a dance, like snake and victim.

I shook my head. My mind was too full of conflict. I felt that I was losing both physical and mental balance at once.

He touched my hand again. I gasped.

"Come, von Bek. Come to Hell."

His flesh was hot but did not burn me. It was sensuous, that touch, though immensely strong.

"Your Majesty . . ." I was pleading, in turn.

"Will you not have pity, von Bek? Have pity on the Fallen One. Pity Lucifer."

The urgency, the pain, the need, the desperation, all conspired to win me, but I fought for a few seconds more. "I have no pity," I said. "I have scoured pity from my soul. I have scoured mercy. I feel only for myself!"

"That is not so, von Bek."

"It is so! It is!"

"A truly merciless creature would not even know what it was. You resist mercy in yourself. You resist pity. You are a victim of your reason. It has replaced your humanity. And that is truly what death is, though you walk and breathe. Help me restore myself to Heaven, and I shall help you to come to life again . . ."

"Oh, Your Majesty," said I, "you are as clever as they say you are." For all that I was, at that moment, His, I still attempted to strike some temporary sort of bargain. "I'll come, on the understanding that I shall be back in this room before the hour's over. And that I shall see Sabrina again . . ."

"Granted."

The flagstones of the library melted away before us. They turned to mercury and then to blue water. We began to float downwards, as if through a cold sky, towards a distant landscape, wide and white and without horizon.

Chapter III

MY SKIN NOW seemed to have turned almost as white as that featureless plain. I observed on my hands details of line, contours of vein and bone, which I had never before noticed.

My nails glittered like glass and appeared extraordinarily fragile.

I possessed virtually no weight at all. I thought that I might have been a crystal ghost.

"This is Hell?" said I to Lucifer.

The Prince of Darkness, too, was pale. Only His eyes, black as weathered iron, were alive.

"This is Hell," He said. "One part, I should say, of my domain. A domain which is, of course, infinite."

"And has infinite aspects?" I suggested.

"Of course not. You speak of Heaven. Hell is the Realm of Restraint and Bleak Singularity." His smile was almost hesitant, His glance sidelong, as if He was concerned that I should not miss His irony.

Lucifer seemed to exhibit a certain shyness with me. I could believe that He hoped for my good opinion. I was puzzled as to why this should be. He still gave off an aura of tremendous power and genius. I was still, against every effort of will, drawn to Him. I was certainly no match for Him in any conceivable terms. Yet it was my impression that He was nervous of me. What might I possess that He could not demand? Why should He be so desperate to own my soul?

But I saw no sense in trying to outguess Satan. Surely He could read every thought, anticipate every argument, forestall every action I chose to take.

It then occurred to me that perhaps He was refusing to do this. Perhaps His apparent delicacy was the result of His own reluctance to use the power that was His. The Prince of Darkness, who could manipulate kings and generals, Popes and cardinals, to whom such manipulation was second nature, was seeking somehow to be direct, was resisting in Himself the habits of an eternal lifetime.

This impression of mine could in itself have been created by means of careful deception.

There was plainly no point in attempting to understand Lucifer's motives or guess His character. Neither should I, I told myself, waste what few mental resources I still had in trying to anticipate either His actions or His needs.

I should merely trust that he would keep His word. I would let Him show me what He wished to show me of His Realm. And I would believe nothing to be wholly what it might seem to be.

"You are a pragmatist, captain," said Lucifer casually, "in your very bones. To your very soul, one might say."

My voice seemed fainter than was normal. There was a slight echo to it, I thought. "Do you see my soul, Your Majesty?"

He linked His arm in mine and we began to walk across the plain.

"I am familiar with it, captain."

I knew no fear at this statement, whereas on Earth I should have shuddered at least a little. Although aware of Lucifer's presence, my body was now neither corporeal nor ethereal, but somewhere between the two. Emotions which should have been strong in me were presently only hinted at; my brain seemed clearer, but that in itself could have been an illusion; my movements were slow and deliberate, yet they followed my thoughts well enough.

This state of being was not uncongenial, and I wondered if it might be the usual condition of angels and the more powerful orders of supernatural entities.

It did not strike me as strange, as I strolled through Hell, side by side with Lucifer, that I had begun to think in terms of spiritual creatures, of realms beyond my earthly world, when, for many years, I had refused to believe in anything but the most substantial and material of phenomena.

Flesh and blood—predominantly the preservation of my own—had been my only reality since my early days of soldiering. My mind and my senses had become blunted, almost certainly, but blunted sensibilities were the only kind one could safely have in the life I led. And the life I led was the only sane one in the world in which I had found myself.

Now, of a sudden, I was not only discovering a return of all my subtlest sensibilities, but exploring sensations—illusory or not—normally denied the bulk of humanity.

It was no wonder that my judgment was confused. Even though I allowed for this, I could not help but be affected. I fought to remember that I must make no pact with Lucifer, that I must agree to nothing, that no matter how tempting any offer He made I must play for time. For not only my life could be at stake, my fate for all Eternity could be the issue.

Lucifer seemed to be trying to console me. "I have given my word to you," He reminded me, "and I shall keep it."

An archway of silvery flames appeared immediately before us. Lucifer drew me towards it.

This time I did not hesitate, but entered the archway and found myself in a city.

The city was of black obsidian stone. Every surface, every wall, every canopy and every flag were black and gleamed. The folk of the city wore clothes of rich, dark colours—of scarlet and deep blue, of bloody orange and moss green—and their skins were the colour of old, polished oak.

"This city exists in Hell?" I asked.

"It is one of the chief cities of Hell," replied Lucifer.

As we passed, the people knelt immediately to the ground and made obeisance to their Lord.

"They recognise you," I said.

"Oh, indeed."

The city seemed rich and the people seemed healthy.

"Hell is a punishment, surely?" I said. "Yet these people are not evidently suffering."

"They are suffering," said Lucifer. "It is their specific fate. You saw how swiftly they knelt to me."

"Aye."

"They are all my slaves. They are none of them free."

"Doubtless they were not free on Earth."

"True. But they know that they would be free in Heaven. Their chief misery is simply that they know they are in Hell for all Eternity. It is that knowledge, in itself, which is their punishment."

"What is freedom in Heaven?" I asked.

"In Hell you become what you fear yourself to be. In Heaven you may become what you hope yourself to be," said Lucifer.

I had expected a more profound reply, or at least a more complicated one.

"A mild enough punishment, compared to what Luther threatened," I observed.

"Apparently. And far less interesting than Luther's torments, as he would tell you himself. There is nothing very interesting in Hell."

I found that I was amused. "Would that be an epigram to sum Hell up?" I asked.

"I doubt if such an epigram exists. Perhaps Luther would believe that it was. Do you wish to ask him?"

"He is here?"

"In this very city. It is called the City of Humbled Princes. It might have been built for him."

I had no wish to encounter Martin Luther, either in Hell, in Heaven or on Earth. I must admit to a certain satisfaction at the knowledge that he had not gained his expected reward but doubtless shared territory in Hell with those churchmen he had most roundly condemned.

"I believe I understand what you mean," I said.

"Oh, I think we both understand Pride, Captain von Bek," said Lucifer almost cheerfully. "Shall I call Luther? He is very docile now."

I shook my head.

Lucifer drew me on through the black streets. I looked at the faces of the citizens, and I knew that I would do almost anything to avoid becoming one of them. This damnation was surely a subtle one. It was their eyes which chiefly impressed me: hard and hopeless. Then it was their whispering voices: cold and without dignity. And then it was the city itself: without any saving humanity.

"This visit to Hell will be brief," Lucifer reassured me. "But I believe it will convince you."

We entered a huge, square building and passed into deeper blackness.

"Are there no flames here?" I asked Him. "No demons? No screaming sinners?"

"Few sinners receive that sort of satisfaction here," said Lucifer.

We stood on the shores of a wide and shallow lake. The water was flat and livid. The light was grey and milky and there seemed no direct source for it. The sky was the same colour as the water.

Standing at intervals in the lake, for as far as I could see, naked men and women, waist-deep, were washing themselves.

The noise of the water was muffled and indistinct. The movements of the men and women were mechanical, as if they had been making the same gestures for eons. All were of similar height. All had the same dull flesh, the same lack of expression upon their faces. Their lips were silent. They gathered the water in their hands and poured it over their heads and bodies, moving like clockwork figures. But again it was their eyes which displayed their agony. They moved, it appeared to me, against their will, and yet could do nothing to stop themselves.

"Is this guilt?" I asked Lucifer. "Do they know themselves to be guilty of something?"

He smiled. He seemed particularly satisfied with this particular torment. "I think it is an imitation of guilt, captain. This is called the Lake of the False Penitents."

"God is not tolerant," I said. "Or so it would seem."

"God is God," said Lucifer. He shrugged. "It is for me to interpret His Will and to devise a variety of punishments for those who are refused Heaven."

"So you continue to serve Him?"

"It could be." Lucifer again seemed uncertain. "Yet of late I have begun to wonder if I have not misinterpreted Him. It is left to me, after all, to discover appropriate cruelties. But what if I am not supposed to punish them? What if I am supposed to show mercy?" I noted something very nearly pathetic in His voice.

"Are you given no instructions?" I asked somewhat weakly. "Tens of millions of souls might have suffered for nothing because of your failure!" I was incredulous.

"I am denied any communion with God, captain." His tone sharpened. "Is that not obvious to you?"

"So you never know whether you please or displease Him? He sends you no sign?"

"For most of my time in Hell I never looked for one, captain. I am, as I have pointed out, forced to use human agents."

"And you receive no word through such agents?"

"How can I trust them? I am excommunicate, Captain von Bek. The souls sent to me are at my mercy. I do with them as I wish, largely to relieve my own dreadful boredom." He became gloomy. "And to take revenge on those who had the opportunity to seek God's grace and rejected it or were too stupid or greedy to recognise what they had lost." He gestured.

I saw a sweep of broad, pleasant fields, with green trees in them. An idyllic rural scene. Even the light was warmer and brighter here, although again there was no sense of that light emanating from any particular direction.

It could have been spring. Seated or standing in the fields, like small herds of cattle, dressed in shreds of fabric, were groups of people. Their skins were rough, scabrous, unclean. Their motion through the fields was sluggish, bovine. Yet these poor souls were by no means contented.

I realised that, although the shape of the bodies varied, every face was absolutely identical.

Every face was lined by the same inturned madness and greed, the same pouched expression of utter selfishness. The creatures mumbled at one another, each monologue the same, as they wandered round and round the fields.

The whined complaints began very quickly to fill me with immense irritation. I could feel no charity for them.

"Every single one of those souls is a universe of self-involvement," said Lucifer.

"And yet they are identical," I said.

"Just so. They are alike in the smallest detail. Yet not one of those men or women there can allow himself to recognise the fact. The closer they get to the core of the self, the more they become like the others." He turned to look sardonically down at me. "Is this more what you expected of Hell, captain?"

"Yes. I think so."

"Every one of these when on Earth spoke of Free Will, of loyalty to one's own needs. Of the importance of controlling one's own destiny. Every one believed himself to be master of his fate. And they had only one yardstick, of course: material well-being. It is all that is possible when one discounts one's involvement with the rest of humanity."

I looked hard at those identical faces. "Is this a specific warning to me?" I asked Lucifer. "I should have thought you would be attempting to make Hell seem more attractive to me."

"And why is that?"

I did not reply. I was too afraid to answer.

"Would you enjoy the prospect of being in my charge, Captain von Bek?" Lucifer asked me.

"I would not," I told him, "for on Earth, at least, one can pretend to Free Will. Here, of course, all choice is denied you."

"And in Heaven one can actually possess Free Will," said Lucifer.

"In spite of Heaven's ruler?" I said. "It would seem to me that He demands a great deal of His creatures."

"I am no priestly interpreter," said Lucifer, "but it has been argued God demands only that men and women should demand much of themselves."

The fields were behind us now. "I, on the other hand," continued the Prince of Darkness, "expect nothing of humanity, save confirmation that it is worthless. I am disposed to despise it, to use it, to exploit its weakness. Or so it was in the beginning of my reign."

"You speak as one who saw all humanity as His rival. I should not have believed an angel—albeit a fallen one—to admit to such pettiness."

"That rage, I still recall it. That rage did not seem petty to me, Captain von Bek."

"You have changed, Your Majesty?"

"I told you that I had, captain."

"You are frustrated, then, that you have failed to convince God of this?"

"Just so. Because God cannot hear me."

"Are you certain of that, Your Majesty?"

"I am certain of nothing. But I understand it to be the truth."

I felt almost sorry for this great being, this most defiant of all creatures, having come to a point where He was willing to admit to His defeat, and there being no one to acknowledge or perhaps to believe His admission.

"I am weary of the Earth and still more weary of Hell, captain. I yearn for my position in Heaven."

"But if Your Majesty is truly repentant . . ."

"It must be proved. I must make amends."

Lucifer continued: "I placed high value on the power of the intellect to create a luxury of wonders upon the Earth. I sought to prove that my logic, my creativity, my mind, could all outshine anything which God made. Then I came to believe that Man was not worthy of me. Then I came to believe that perhaps I was not worthy, that what I had sought to make had no substance, no definition, no future. You have seen much of the world, captain."

"More than most are permitted to see," I agreed.

"Everything is in decay, is it not? Everything. The spirit decays as the flesh and the mind decay." Lucifer uttered a sigh. "I have failed."

His voice became hollow. I found that I was pitying Him, even more than I pitied the souls who were trapped in His domain.

"I wish to be taken back into the certainty, the tranquillity, I once knew," Lucifer continued.

We stood again upon the white plain.

"I sought to show that I could create a more beautiful world than anything God could create. I still do not know what I did wrong. I have been thinking on that for many a century, captain. And I know that only a human soul can discover the secret which eludes me. I must make amends. I must make amends . . ."

"Have you decided how you can do that?" I asked quietly.

"I must discover the Cure for the World's Pain, Captain von Bek." He turned his dark eyes upon me and I felt my whole being shiver at the intensity.

"A Cure? Human folly, surely, is the cause of that Pain. The answer seems simple enough to me."

"No!" Lucifer's voice was almost a groan. "It is complex. God has bestowed on the world one object, one means of healing humanity's ills. If that object is discovered and the world set to rights again, then God will listen to me. Once God listens, I might be able to convince Him that I am truly repentant."

"But what has this to do with me, Your Majesty? Surely you cannot think that I possess a Cure for human folly."

Lucifer made an almost angry gesture with His right hand.

We were suddenly once more in the library of the castle. We faced one of the great windows. Through it I could see the green, silent forest and noted that very little time had passed. My body was now as solid as it had always been. I felt some relief. My ordinary senses were restored.

Lucifer said: "I asked you to help me, von Bek, because you are intelligent, resourceful and not easily manipulated. I am asking you to embark upon a Quest on my behalf. I want you to find me the Cure to the world's ills. Do you know of what I speak?"

"I have heard only of the Holy Grail, Your Majesty," I told Him. "And I believe that to be a myth. If I were shown such a cup I would believe in its powers as much as I would believe in the powers of a piece of the True Cross, or Saint Peter's fingernail."

He ignored these last remarks. His eyes flamed and became remote. "Ah, yes. It is called that. The Holy Grail. How would you describe it, von Bek?"

"A legendary cup."

"If it existed. What would you say it was?"

"A physical manifestation of God's mercy on Earth," I said.

"Exactly. Is that not the object I have described to you?"

I became incredulous. "Lucifer is commissioning a godless soldier-of-fortune to seek and secure the Holy Grail?"

"I am asking you to seek the Cure for the World's Pain, yes. Call it the Grail."

"The legend says that only the purest of knights is permitted to see it, let alone touch it!"

"Your journey will purify you, I'm sure."

"Your Majesty, what are you offering me, should I agree to this Quest?"

He smiled ironically at me. "Is it not an honour in itself, von Bek?"

I shook my head. "You must have better servants for such a monumental Quest."

Was Lucifer mad? Was He playing a game with me?

"I have told you," He said, "that I have not."

I hesitated. I felt bound to voice my feelings:

"I am suspicious, Your Majesty."

"Why so?"

"I cannot read your motive."

"My motive is simple."

"It defeats me."

His miserable, tortured eyes looked full on me again and He spoke in an urgent whisper: *It is because you fail to understand how great is my need. How great is my need! Such souls as yours are scarce, von Bek.*

"Can I assume that you are trying to buy my soul at this moment, Your Majesty?"

"Buy it?" He seemed puzzled. "Buy your soul, von Bek? Did you not realise that I own your soul already? I am offering you the chance to reclaim it."

I knew at once that He spoke the truth. I had known, within me, for some while.

It was then that Lucifer smiled, and in that smile I saw simple confirmation of what we both knew. He did not lie.

A coldness came into me. That was why He had shown me Hell; not to lure me there, but to sample my eternal doom.

I drew away from my Master. "Then I am already forbidden Heaven. Is that what you are telling me, Your Majesty?"

"You are already forbidden Heaven."

"If that is so, I have no choice, surely?"

"If I rejected you, it would allow you a new chance to be restored in God's grace—just as I hope to be restored. We do indeed have much in common, von Bek."

I had never heard of such a bargain before. Yet by taking it I could only lose my life a little sooner than I had planned.

I said: "Then in reality I have little choice."

"Let us say that your character has already determined your choice."

"Yet you cannot promise me that God will accept me into Heaven."

"I can promise you only that I will release your soul from my custody. Such souls do not always enter Heaven. But they are said to live forever, some of them."

"I have heard legends," I said, "such as that of the

Wandering Jew. Am I to try to save myself from Hell merely so that I may wander the world for Eternity seeking redemption?"

It occurred to me of a sudden that I was not the first mortal soul to be offered this bargain by Lucifer.

"I cannot say," said the Prince of Darkness. "But if you are successful, it is likely, is it not, that God would look with mercy upon you?"

"You must know more of God's habits, Your Majesty, than I." A strange calm was creeping into me now. I felt a degree of amusement.

Lucifer saw what was happening to me and He grinned. "It is a challenge, is it not, von Bek?"

"Aye, Your Majesty." I was still debating what He had said. "But if I am already your servant, why did you go to such elaborate means to ensure this meeting? Why send Sabrina?"

"I have told you. I am forced to use human agents."

"Even though she and I are already your servants?"

"Sabrina elected to serve me. You have not yet agreed."

"So Sabrina cannot be saved?"

"All will be saved if you find the Grail."

"But could I not ask one thing of Your Majesty?"

Lucifer's beautiful head turned down towards me. "I think I follow you, von Bek."

"Would you release Sabrina from your power if I agreed to what you ask of me?"

Lucifer had anticipated this.

"Not if you agree. But if you are successful. Find the Cure for the World's Pain, and bring it to me, and I promise you I will release Sabrina under exactly the same terms as I release you."

"So if I am doomed to eternal life, I shall have a companion with me."

"Yes."

I considered this. "Very well, Your Majesty. Where shall I seek this Cure, this Grail?"

"All that I know is that it is hidden from me and from all those already dwelling in infernal regions. It is somewhere upon the Earth or in a supernatural realm not far removed from the Earth."

"A realm not of the Earth? How can I possibly go to such a place?"

Lucifer said: "This castle is such a place, von Bek. I can allow you the power to enter certain parts of the world forbidden to ordinary mortals. It is possible that the Cure lies in one of those realms, or that it lies in a most ordinary place. But you will be enabled to travel more or less where you wish or need to go."

"Do you mean to make a sorcerer of me, Your Majesty?"

"Perhaps. I am able to offer you certain privileges to aid you in your Quest. But I know that you take pride in your own intelligence and skills and it is those which shall be most valuable to both of us. And you have courage, von Bek, of several kinds. Although you are mortal, that is another quality we have in common. That is another reason I chose you."

"I am unsure if I am entirely complimented, Your Majesty. To be Satan's representative upon Earth, some Anti-Pope." I changed the subject. "And what if I should fail you?"

Lucifer turned away from me. "That would depend, let us say, on the nature of your failure. If you die, you travel instantly to Hell. But should you betray me, in any way at all, von Bek—well, there is no way in which I cannot claim you. You shall be mine soon enough. And I shall be able to debate my vengeance upon you for all Eternity."

"So if I am killed in pursuit of my Quest, I gain nothing, but am transported at once to Hell?"

"Just so. But you have seen that Hell can take many forms. And I am able, after a fashion, to resurrect the dead . . ."

"I have seen your resurrections, Your Majesty, and I would rather be wholly dead. But I suppose I must agree to your bargain, because I have so little to lose."

"Very little, captain."

How radically had my life been turned about in the past twenty-four hours! I had over the years managed successfully to rid myself of all thoughts of damnation or salvation, of God or the Devil, during my career as a soldier. I had served many masters, but felt loyal to none of them, had never let them control my fate. I had believed myself my own man, through and through, for good or ill.

Now, suddenly, I had been informed by Lucifer Himself that I was damned and that I was to be offered at the same time a chance of salvation. My feelings, needless to say, were mixed. From a pragmatic agnostic I had been changed not only into a believer, but into a believer called upon to take part in that most fundamental of all spiritual concerns, the struggle between Heaven and Hell. And I had become an apparently important piece in the game. It was hard for me to accept so much at once.

I understood what Sabrina had meant when she had told me, also, that only souls already owned by Lucifer could exist in the castle and its environs.

I had originally refused to accept that knowledge, but it was no longer possible for me to resist it. The evidence had been presented to me. I was damned. And I had already begun (more than I would have admitted then, I think) to hope for salvation. As a result, I had committed myself, against all former habit, to a cause.

I bowed to Lucifer. "Then I am ready to embark upon this Quest, Your Majesty, whenever you wish."

It was ironic, I thought, that Hope had been revived in me by the Fallen One and not, as should be traditional, by a vision of the Madonna or a meeting with some goodly priest.

"I would like you to begin almost immediately," said the Prince of Darkness.

I looked outside. It was not yet noon.

"Today?" I asked Him.

"Tomorrow. Sabrina will spend some time with you."

At this hint of manipulation of my private emotions I bridled. "Perhaps I have no further desire to spend time with her, Your Majesty."

Lucifer clapped his hands lightly and Sabrina entered the library and curtseyed.

"Captain von Bek has agreed to my bargain," Lucifer told her. "You must now do as I instructed you, Sabrina." His voice had become gentle, almost kindly.

She curtseyed again. "Yes, Your Majesty."

I looked upon her beauty and I marvelled all the more. My feelings for her had not changed. At once I became almost grateful to Lucifer for sending her to me.

Lucifer returned to the central table, taking another book with Him, for all the world like a rural nobleman preparing himself for a little solitude before lunch.

"And Captain von Bek has involved you in this bargain,

my dear. He has news for you which you might find palatable."

She frowned as she rose. She looked enquiringly from her Master to myself. There was nothing I was prepared to say to her at that moment.

He was plainly dismissing us both. Yet I hesitated.

"I had expected a somewhat more dramatic symbol of our bargain, Your Majesty."

Lucifer smiled again. His wonderful eyes were, temporarily at least, free of pain.

"I know few mortals who would feel that a visit to Hell was undramatic, captain."

I bowed again, accepting this.

"Should you be successful in your Quest," Lucifer added, "you will return to this castle with what I have asked you to find. Sabrina will await you."

I could not resist one last question: "And if Your Majesty is displeased with what I bring Him?" I said.

Lucifer put down His book. The eyes had become hard again as they looked into mine. I knew, then, that He must surely own my soul, He understood it so well.

"Then we shall all go back to Hell together," He said.

Sabrina touched my arm. I bowed to my Master for the third and last time. Lucifer returned to His reading.

As she led me from the room, Sabrina said: "I already know the nature of your Quest. There are maps I must give you. And other things."

She curtseyed. She closed the library doors on the Prince of Darkness. Then she took my hand and led me through the castle to a small chamber in one of the northwestern towers. I could not remember having explored this particular region of the castle.

Here, on a small desk, was a case of maps, two small leather-bound books, a ring of plain silver, a roll of parchment and a brass flask of the ordinary kind which soldiers often carried.

These objects had been arranged, I thought, in some sort of pattern. Perhaps Sabrina's habits of witchcraft, with their emphasis on shapes and symbols, influenced her without her being aware of it.

By way of experiment, I stretched a hand towards the flask. I moved it slightly. She made no objection.

That action of mine, however, gave me pause. I realised that I had already begun to think in terms which a day or two earlier would have been ridiculous. My world was no longer what it had seemed to be. It was not the world I had trained myself to see. It was a world, in some ways, which threatened action. Imposed upon my world was another, a world in which the smallest detail possessed an extra significance. I attempted to dismiss this unwelcome awareness, at least from my conscious mind. It would not do, I thought, to observe potential danger in the way a bird flew across the sky, or see importance in the manner in which two tree branches intersected. This was the madness of those who thought themselves seers or artists, and I should always remind myself that I was a soldier. My concerns were with the physical world, with the reading of another man's eyes to see if he meant to kill me or not, with the signs of groups of infantry on the move, with the detection of a peasant's secret storehouse.

I turned to Sabrina. It was almost a plea for help.

"I am afraid," I said.

She stroked my arm. "You regret your bargain with our Master?"

I was unable to reply directly. "I regret the circumstances which have put us both in His power," I said. "But if it is so, I have little choice but to do what He asks of me."

"He suggested that something you had agreed with Him would be of significance to me." She spoke carelessly, but I think she was eager to hear what had been agreed. "The bargain you struck?"

"I am attempting to regain your soul as well as my own," I said. "If I find this—this Grail, we are both free."

At first she looked at me with hope and then, almost immediately, with despair. "My soul is sold, Ulrich."

"He has promised to restore it to you. If I am successful in my Quest."

"I am moved," she said, "that you should think of me."

"I believe that I love you," I said.

She nodded. I understood from her expression that she also loved me. She said: "He has commissioned you, has He not, to seek the Cure for the World's Pain?"

"Just so."

"And the chances of your success are poor. Perhaps that Cure does not exist. Perhaps Lucifer is as desperate as we are." She paused, almost whispering: "Could Lucifer be mad?"

"Possibly," I said. "But mad or not, He owns our souls. And if there is even a little hope, I must follow it."

"I shall forget hope, for my own part." She came towards me. "I cannot afford to hope, Ulrich."

I took her in my arms. "I cannot afford not to hope," I told her. "I must take action. It is in my nature."

She accepted this.

I kissed her. My love for her was growing by the moment. I had become increasingly reluctant to leave. Yet Lucifer, sane or insane, had convinced me that our only chance to be truly together lay in my fulfilling the terms of our bargain.

I drew away from her. I contained my emotions. I looked down at the desk.

"Show me what these things are," I said to her.

She could hardly speak. Her hand trembled as she picked up the map-case and gave it to me.

"The maps are of the world, both known and unknown. There are certain areas marked on them which are not marked on ordinary maps. These are the lands which exist between Earth and Heaven, between Heaven and Hell.

"This"—she picked up a box from the desk—"is a compass, as you can see. It will lead you through the natural world as surely as any good compass can. And it will point towards the entrances and exits of those supernatural lands."

She put down the compass and pointed to the brass flask. "That contains a liquid which will restore you to energy and help heal any wounds you might sustain. The books are grimoires, so that you may summon aid if you need it. They are to be used judiciously."

"And the ring?" I asked.

She took it from the desk and placed it carefully on the second finger of my right hand.

"That is my gift to you," she said. Then she kissed the hand.

I was moved. "I have no gift for you, Sabrina."

"You must bring yourself safely back," she said. "For surely if you are dutiful in your Quest, even if you fail, our Master will allow us some time together in Hell."

She was afraid of hope. I understood her.

There were tears in her eyes. I realised that I, too, was weeping. I forced control on myself again and said unsteadily:

"The parchment? You have not told me what it is."

"The parchment is to be opened if you succeed." Her voice, too, was trembling. "It informs you how you may return to the castle. But you must not open it before you find the Cure for the World's Pain."

She leaned down and picked up a pouch from the floor. "There are provisions in this," she said, "as well as money for your journey. Your horse will carry more provisions and will await you in the courtyard when you are ready to leave."

She began to pack the maps and the other objects into the pouch. She buckled it carefully and gave it into my hands.

"What next?" I asked her.

Her smile was no longer bold, no longer challenging. It was almost shy. I smelled roses again. I touched her hair, the soft skin of her cheek.

"We have until the morning," she said.

Chapter IV

My MOOD, UPON awakening the next morning, was peculiar. All kinds of conflicting feelings stirred within me. My love for Sabrina was coloured by the knowledge that she had helped to trap me, though I knew, too, that I had not really been trapped. Lucifer had, after all, offered me the opportunity of redeeming my immortal soul. My impressions of my brief visit to Hell were if anything stronger, and I believed almost without question that I had indeed encountered the Prince of Darkness and had accompanied Him to His domain. I had always claimed to welcome the truth; yet now, in common with most of us, I was resentful of the truth because it called upon me to take an unwelcome course of action. I longed for the grim innocence I had so recently lost.

Sabrina was still sleeping. Outside, a mist of light rain obscured the forest. I brooded upon the conversations which had taken place between myself and Sabrina, between myself and Lucifer. I sought for some saving logic, some means of questioning the import of what I had heard, and could find none. This castle, alone, convinced me. The previous night Sabrina had said: "You see the surface translated by your mortal eye. Your mortal mind could not, in normality, accept the truth. There is nothing to do in Hell: no fulfillment, no future, no hope at all. No faith in anything. Those souls who dwell there also had faith only in their own survival. And now they have lost that, also."

I had not answered her, after this. I had become absorbed in feelings which were impossible to put into thoughts, let alone words. At one time I had been flooded with anger and had said: "Sabrina, if all this is a deception, an enchantment in which you have conspired, I will surely return to kill you."

But my anger had disappeared even as I spoke. I knew that she did not wish me ill. My threat had been made from a habit of attitude and action which was virtually meaningless now.

I knew for certain that she loved me. And I knew that I loved her. We were like-minded in so many ways; we were equals. I could not tolerate the notion that I might lose her.

I returned to draw back the curtains and sit on the edge of the bed, looking down on Sabrina's sleeping face. She started suddenly, crying out, reaching her hand to where I had lain. I touched her cheek. "I am here."

She turned and smiled at me. Then her eyes clouded. "You are leaving?"

"I suppose that I must. Soon."

"Yes," she said, "for it is morning." She began to sit up. She sighed. "When I made my bargain with Lucifer I thought that I was resisting circumstance, taking my fate into my own hands. But circumstance continues to affect us. Can it even affect who we are? Is there any proof beyond ourselves that we are unique?"

"We feel ourselves to be unique," I said. "But a cynic sees only familiarity and similarity and would say that we are all pretty much the same."

"Is it because a cynic does not possess the imagination to distinguish those subtle differences in which you and I believe?"

"I am a cynic," I said to her. "A cynic refuses to allow distinctions of motive or of temperament."

"Oh, but you are not!" She came into my arms. "Or you would not be here."

I held her closely. "I am what I have to be at this moment," I said. "For my own sake."

"And for mine," she reminded me.

I felt a terrible sadness well within me. I suppressed it. "And for yours," I agreed.

We kissed. The pain continued to grow. I pulled away from her. I went to the corner of the room and began to wash myself. I noticed that my hands were shaking and that my breathing had become unusually deep. I had a wish, at that moment, to return to Hell, to summon up an army of all those poor damned souls and set them in rebellion against Lucifer, as Lucifer had set Himself against God. I felt that we were in the hands of foolish, insane beings, whose motives were more petty even than Man's. I wanted to be rid of all of them. It was unjust, I thought, that such creatures should have power over us. Even if they had created us, could they not, in turn, be destroyed?

But these ideas were pointless. I had neither the means, the knowledge nor the power to challenge them. I could only accept that my destiny was, in part at least, in their charge. I would have to agree to play out my role in Lucifer's terms, or play no role at all.

I drew on fresh linen. Sabrina sat with the curtain drawn back, watching me. I put on my breastplate, my greaves, my spurs. I buckled my sword and daggers about me. I picked up my helmet. I was ready, once again, for War.

"You say the horse will be ready?" I said.

"In the courtyard."

I stooped to pick up the pouch she had given me the previous day. I had regulated my breathing and my hands did not shake as much.

"I will stay here," she said.

I accepted this. I knew why she would not wish to accompany me to the courtyard.

"I intend to do my best in this matter," I said to her. "With you, I think that there is little chance of discovering any Grail, but I shall maintain my resolve if I know that you believe in me. Will you remember to trust me to return to you?"

"I will remember," she replied. "It is all that I will have to sustain me. Yes, Ulrich, I will trust you."

We were both desperate for certainty, and in that uncertain world we were attempting to make concrete that most amorphous and changeable of emotions, as people often will when they have no other sense of the future.

"Then we are pledged," I said. "And it is a more welcome bargain than any I have made in recent hours." I moved towards her, touched her naked shoulder with the tips of my fingers, kissed her lightly upon the lips.

"Farewell," I said.

"Farewell." She spoke softly. And then: "You must travel first towards Ammendorf, where you will seek out the Wildgrave."

"What can he tell me?"

She shook her head. "I know no more."

I left the room.

Outside her door I found that my legs were weak and that I could hardly make my way down the spiralling flights of stone steps to the main hall. I had never experienced such emotion before. I had hardly any means of coping with it.

In the main hall, upon the table, a breakfast had been prepared for me. I paused only to take a deep draught of wine, then continued to stride for the doors with long, faltering steps.

The courtyard was silent, save for the sound of my horse's breathing and the dripping of the drizzle upon the leafy trees. I sniffed the air. Apart from the warm smell of the horse there were no scents at all in it.

My horse stood near the central wall. He looked freshly groomed. There were large panniers on either side of his saddle. My pistols shone in their holsters. Every piece of harness had been polished, every piece of metal and leather was bright. There was a new cloth under the saddle. The horse turned his head to regard me with wide, impatient eyes. His bit clattered in his jaws.

With an effort, I mounted. The wine gave me enough strength and enough resolve to touch my heels to the steed's flanks. He moved smartly forward, glad to be on his way.

The portcullis was up. There were no signs of Sabrina's half-dead servants, no sign of our Master. The castle looked exactly as it had when I had first arrived.

It might have been an elaborate illusion. With that thought in mind, I did not look back: partly from fear that I would see Sabrina herself at a window, partly because I thought I might see nothing at all.

I rode out under the archway towards the path which wound down through ornamental gardens. The rain washed the statues and the bright, lifeless flowers; it obscured the outlines of the forest below. My horse began to gather speed. Soon we were cantering and I made no attempt to check him. Water poured from my helmet. As I rode I dragged my leather cloak from one of the panniers and wound it round me. The water washed from my face any trace of tears.

I rode down through the cold rain and into that deep, barren forest. It was only a little later that I looked back, briefly, to see the tall stones, the towers and the battle-ments, to confirm that they were, indeed, realities.

I did not look back again. The forest was dark and grey now and some part of me welcomed its embrace. We rode steadily until nightfall.

My journey to the outskirts of the forest took the better part of two days, and it was not until the morning of the third day that I awoke to birdsong and faint sunshine, to the smells of damp earth and oak and pine. The sense of joyful relief I felt upon hearing the whistling of finches and thrushes reminded me of the strangeness I was leaving behind me, and I wondered again at the reality of it all.

I never once believed that I had dreamed my experience, but it remained a very slight possibility that I had been victim to a sophisticated hallucination. Naturally, part of me desired that this be so. I could not, however, afford to indulge that hope.

I breakfasted lightly of the food provided and drew the maps from my case. I had determined not to consult them until Lucifer's wood was at my back. Ammendorf was not even a familiar name to me and it took me some while to discover it marked.

I as yet had no bearings, but at least I was again in the lands of mortal creatures, and sooner or later I would discover a village, or a charcoal burner, or a woodsman—someone to tell me where I was. Once I knew, I could head for Ammendorf, which appeared to be a relatively small town about fifty miles from Nürnberg.

My horse was eating the sweet-smelling grass with some relish. The grass we had left behind was nourishing enough, but presumably it had had no taste. He looked like a prisoner who had dined too long on bread and water and is suddenly offered a rich repast. I let him eat his fill, then saddled him and, mounted once again, continued on my way until I came,

very soon, upon a reasonably wide track through the forest.
This I began to follow.

By mid-morning I was riding across gentle hills towards a
rich valley. Mist lay upon the tops of the hills and through it
broke strong rays of sunshine which struck the deep greens of
fields and hedgerows and illuminated them. There was a faint
smell of wood smoke on the spring air and I was warmed, as
the rain lifted, by a southwesterly wind.

I made out old cottages and farmsteads, all apparently
untouched by the War. I saw cattle and sheep grazing. I
breathed in rich scents of the farmyard, of flowers and wet
grass, and my skin felt cleaner than it had felt in months. So
peaceful was the scene that I wondered if it might be another
illusion, that it was designed to snare me somehow, but
thankfully my rational, pragmatic mind refused such speculation. I had embarked upon an insane Quest, prompted by a
being who could, Himself, be insane; I had need to maintain
my sanity in small matters, at least.

As I approached the nearest cottage I smelled baking
and my mouth began to water, for I had eaten no hot food
since before my encounter with Lucifer. I stopped outside the
cottage door and cried a "halloo." At first I thought that, in
the manner of wary peasants, no one would answer me. I
took a step or two towards the time-darkened oak of the door
just as it opened. A small, plump woman of about forty-five
stood there. Seeing my warlike finery, she automatically
bobbed her head and said, in a thick accent which I did not
recognise: "Good morrow, Your Honour."

"Good morning to you, sister," I returned. "Is it possible
for an honest man to purchase some hot food from you?"

She laughed heartily at this. "Sir, if you were a thief and
prepared to pay, you would receive the same fare. We have
little coin, these days, and a pfennig or two would not go
amiss when the time comes to go to town and buy ribbon for
a new frock. My daughter is marrying two months from
now."

She ushered me into the dark warmth of the cottage. As
was typical of such places it was simple and neat, with rushes
on the flagstones and a few holy pictures upon the walls. I
noted from the pictures that these people were still loyal to
Rome.

She took my helmet and cloak and put them carefully

upon a chest in the far corner. She told me that she was about to bring a meat pie and an apple pie from her oven, if I could wait but quarter of an hour, and that she could offer me some good, strong beer of her own brewing, should I partake of such drink. I said that I would greatly welcome a sample of everything on her list and she retired to the kitchen to fetch the beer, chatting about the uncertainty of the weather and the chances of the various crops.

When she brought the beer I remarked that I was surprised the War had not touched them. Her little round face became serious and she nodded. "We believe that God hears our prayers." She shook her head. "But I suppose that we are luckier than most. There is only one road into the valley and it goes nowhere, after our village, save the forest. You must have travelled a very great distance, sir."

"I have indeed."

She frowned as she considered this. "You came through the Silent Marches?"

My ordinary caution made me lie. "I circled them," I said, "if you mean the lifeless forest."

The woman crossed herself. "Only Satan's followers can inhabit those marches."

I knew that she had tested me. For if I had admitted to having travelled through the Silent Marches she would have known that my soul was Lucifer's, and I doubt if I should have been able to have enjoyed her hospitality as much as I did. Both pies were soon forthcoming and they were both delicious.

As I ate I told her that I was an envoy for a prince and that I could not divulge his name. My mission was to attempt to bring peace to Germany, I said.

At this the good frau looked pessimistic. She picked up my empty plate. "I fear there will be no peace for the world until the Day of Judgement, Your Honour. We can merely pray that it comes soon."

I agreed with her wholeheartedly, for, after all, if my Quest were successful, Judgement Day must surely follow rapidly upon Lucifer's repentance.

"We live," said she, "in the century in which the world is bound to end."

"That is what many believe," I agreed.

"You suggest that you do not, sir."

"I might hope for that event," said I, "but I am not convinced that it will occur."

She cleared away the dishes. She refilled my stein. I was offered a pipe of tobacco from her husband's jar, but I told her that I did not take it. Her husband was at work in the fields, she told me, and would not be back until that evening. Her daughter was with her husband-to-be, helping with the spring planting.

All this wonderful ordinariness had begun to lull me and I thought that perhaps I might stay with these people for a while. But I knew if I did so I should not be fulfilling my pledge to Lucifer and might bring His vengeance not only upon myself but upon these people, also. It comforted me to know that there was one small corner of Germany where War and Plague were unfamiliar.

I finished my beer and asked directions for Nürnberg. The woman was vague, for she had never travelled very far from her village. But she gave me directions for Schweinfurt, which I decided to follow until I came to a larger settlement and more sophisticated people.

I left the woman with a piece of silver, which, had she known its origin, she would not have taken with such joy or such gratitude, and was soon upon my way.

The track wound through the valley, climbing gradually to the hills on the far side. I rode through widely spaced pines, over loamy, reddish soil, and looked back frequently at the cottages and farms with their heavy, peaceful smoke and their sense of dreamy security.

The track led me to a wider road and a signpost for Teufenberg, the nearest town. It was almost sunset when I embarked upon this road, and I hoped that I might come upon an inn or at least a farm where I could beg a bale of hay in a barn for the night, but I was unlucky. I slept again in my cloak, in a ditch by the side of the road, but was undisturbed.

I rose in the morning to warm sunshine and birdsong. Butterflies flew through the clumps of poppies and daisies at the edge of the track and the scents of those flowers were delicious to my nose. I regretted that I had not purchased a little more beer for my journey, but I had expected to be in Teufenberg by now. I promised myself that I would at least break my fast at the nearest inn, and when, by noon, I turned a bend and saw the carved gables of a substantial-looking hostelry, with outhouses, stables, and a little cluster of cottages at the back, I was glad of having made that promise.

The inn was called The Black Friar and it stood upon the banks of a broad but shallow river. A good-sized stone bridge spanned the river (although it seemed possible to ford it without wetting the thighs) and farther up on the far bank I saw a mill, its wheel working slowly as it ground corn. I guessed that both mill and inn were, as was quite common, owned by the same family.

I almost cantered into the courtyard, looking up at the wooden gallery, which went the entire circumference of the place, and crying out for the landlord as I dismounted.

A black-browed fellow, very heavily built and with red arms to match his nose, came through a downstairs door and took the bridle.

"I am Wilhelm Hippel and this is my tavern. You are welcome, Your Honour."

"It looks a well-kept place, landlord," I said, handing him my cloak as an ostler appeared to take my horse.

"We think so, Your Honour."

"And well-stocked, I hope."

I noticed a familiar peasant craftiness as he hesitated. "As best it can be in these times, sir."

I laughed at this. "Have no fear, landlord, I am not about to requisition your food and wine in the name of some warlike prince. I am on a mission of peace. I hope to be instrumental in putting an end to strife."

"Then you are doubly welcome, Your Honour."

I was taken into the main taproom and here enjoyed a mug of beer even better than that which I had had from the woman in the village. Venison and game were presented to me and I made my choice, feasting well and chatting with Herr Hippel about his trials and tribulations. These appeared extremely minor in comparison with those of men and women who had been directly touched by the War, but of course to him they were large enough.

There were robbers on this road, he warned me, and although they did not give him much trouble, some of his guests had been robbed and badly beaten (one even killed) during the previous autumn. The winter had not been so bad, but now he heard that the robbers were returning, "like swallows in spring," he said. I reassured him that I would journey warily. He said that he was expecting two or three more guests shortly and that it might be wise if we all travelled together to Teufenberg. I said that I would consider the idea, although privately I determined to continue alone, for I did not want the company of merchants or clerics on their slow, reliable horses.

In the shadows of the far corner, half-asleep with his tankard in his hand, I noted a surly red-headed youth dressed in a stained blue silk shirt with cuffs and collar of tattered lace; red silk breeches, baggy and loose after the Turkish fashion, tucked into high folded-over riding boots. He had on an unbuttoned leather waistcoat of heavy hide, of a sort which swordsmen often wear in preference to a breastplate. There was a long, curved sabre propped near him on his bench, and round his waist I detected a long knife and a pistol, both in black and silver, looking almost Oriental in design.

I had the youth for a Muscovite, since he was evidently no Turk. I raised a comradely tankard to him but he avoided my eye. The landlord whispered that he was well-behaved enough, but spoke poor German and seemed suspicious of even the friendliest action. He had been there since the day before and was apparently waiting for some soldier-priest who had agreed to meet him at the inn. The solider-priest, said the landlord, had some sort of Latin name which the youth had misheard or else could not pronounce properly. It was a little like Josephus Kreutzerling, he said. He seemed to hope that I might recognise it, but I shook my head. I had a wariness and dislike for those soldier-priests who, in my view, were capable of worse depredations, fouler cruelties, than almost anyone else I had ever encountered.

Having discovered that I could reach Teufenberg by nightfall, I decided to be on my way, and was just rising when the doors of the taproom opened and in came a tall, thin individual with hard grey eyes in a cadaverous face, a black wide-brimmed hat upon his head, collar and cuffs of plain linen, coat and breeches of black wool, black buckled shoes and gaiters which, as he sat down upon a stool, he proceeded to remove, revealing white stockings. He had a plain, straight blade at his side and he wore gauntlets, carrying one in his left hand. The only fancy thing he wore was a purple plume in his hat, and even this gave the impression that he was in mourning for someone.

He looked first at me and then at the landlord. Herr Hippel stood up.

"Can I be of service, Your Honour?"

"Some wine and a jug of water," said the newcomer. He turned his head and looked back at the young Muscovite who had grown more alert. "You are Gregory Sedenko."

"I am Grigory Petrovitch Sedenko," said the youth in his strange, rumbling accent, stressing vowels and consonants in a way which made me certain of his origin. He stood up. "Who knows me?"

"I am he who promised to meet you here."

I had, as I thought, recognised the face and manner of a soldier-priest. The man was typical of his kind; all human feeling had been turned into pride and cruelty in the name of his Crusade. "I am Johannes Klosterheim, Knight of Christ."

The young Muscovite crossed himself dutifully, but looked with boldness into the austere face of the fighting monk. "You have a commission for me, Brother Johannes, in Teufenberg."

"I have. I know the house. I have all the evidence. The case has been judged. It is left for you to execute it."

The boy frowned. "You are certain?"

"There is no question."

I wondered if I was listening to a witch-hunter. But if Klosterheim were an ordinary witch-finder, he would not be here at this time, talking to the youth. Witch-finders travelled with an entourage, with all the paraphernalia of their calling. If they did not travel, they stayed in one town or one area. Few of them were soldiers.

Gregory Sedenko reached for his scabbarded sabre and made to tuck it into his belt, but Klosterheim raised his naked hand and shook his head. "Not yet. There is time."

The landlord and myself listened in silence, for it seemed evident that Klosterheim had commissioned the boy to do murder, albeit murder in God's name. Both of us were uncomfortable in the presence of the pair. The landlord wished to leave. My instinct was to take the boy aside and warn him not to involve himself in whatever disgusting venture the soldier-priest must surely be initiating. But I had made a virtue of silence and inactivity in recent years. It did not do to speak one's mind in those days.

The boy sat down again. "I would rather have it done," he said, "as soon as possible."

"There are things I must tell you in private," said Klosterheim. "This is no ordinary work."

At this Sedenko laughed. "Ordinary enough in Kieff," he said. "It is how we spend our winters."

Klosterheim disapproved of his levity, even of his enthusiasm. "We must pray together first," he said.

"And pay?" said the youth.

"Prayer first, pay second," replied the soldier-priest. He looked at us as if to warn us not to interfere and preferably not to listen. The landlord went from the room, leaving only me as witness to what took place between the strange pair.

I decided to speak:

"I have not heard of the Knights of Christ, brother," said I. "Is that an order from these parts?"

"It is not an order, as such, at all," said Klosterheim. "It is a society."

"Forgive me. I am not entirely conversant with Church lore."

"Then you should make it your task to become conversant, sir," he said. His grey eyes were angry. "And you should consider your manners, also. You should think of making their improvement another goal."

"I'm much obliged for the advice, brother," I said. "I shall consider it."

"Best do so, sir."

Against my saner judgement I remained where I was, even though the older man wished me to leave. Eventually he rose and went to sit beside Sedenko, speaking in a voice too low for me to overhear. I continued to drink my beer, however, and to give them my attention. The youth was undisturbed, but the soldier-priest remained uncomfortable, which, out of sheer devilment, I wished him to be.

At last, with a curse ill-befitting a celibate man of God, he got up from the bench and drew the youth with him to the door. They went outside into the yard.

I had amused myself long enough. I drained my tankard, shouted for the landlord, paid him and asked that my horse be fetched for me.

In a little while I peered through the window to see that the ostler had returned with my steed. I donned my helmet, folded my cloak under my arm and opened the door.

Klosterheim and the Muscovite were deep in conversation on the far side of the yard. As I emerged, Klosterheim turned his back on me.

The sun was shining strong and hot as I mounted. I cried: "Farewell, brother. Farewell, Herr Sedenko." And I urged the beast out of the courtyard toward the open road.

The sun had gone down by the time I sighted, in the twilit mist, the spires and rooftops of Teufenberg. It was a pleasant enough little town with a population that was only reasonably suspicious of a man like myself, on a good horse and in armour, and I had hardly any difficulty finding a hostelry with room for me and my horse. Again, to relieve my host's perturbation, I told the story of being an envoy commissioned to try to bring peace to the warring factions and, naturally enough, was given a much-improved welcome.

In the morning I was directed onto the road for Schwein-furt and wished Godspeed in my mission by the landlord, his wife, his son-in-law and his three daughters. I had almost begun to believe that I was the hero I presented myself as being!

On the outskirts of the town I passed a house which had a crowd surrounding it. Men, women and children stood packed together, watching wide-eyed as a group of people in black began to emerge from the house. The women were wailing and the boys and girls were pale and stunned. They were carrying three corpses from the house.

I wondered if this had anything to do with the pair I had encountered on the previous day.

I asked one fat townsman what had happened.

"It's the Jews," he said. "All the men were struck down in the night by the Sword of God. It is His vengeance upon them for their crimes."

I was disgusted. Their fate was familiar enough, but I had not expected to witness such an event in the pleasant town of Teufenberg.

I did not wait to hear the catalogue of crimes, for it would be the same wretched list one heard from the Baltic to the Black Sea.

Grimly, I spurred my horse and was more than glad

when I reached the highway. The air seemed purer. I galloped a few miles until Teufenberg was completely out of sight, then I let my horse walk for a while.

In one sense I was grateful for what I had seen that morning in Teufenberg. I had been reminded of the realities of the world which lay ahead of me.

Chapter V

THE WEATHER GREW warmer and warmer as the miles between Teufenberg and Schweinfurt narrowed. It was almost like summer and I was tempted, against my ordinary caution, to divest myself of some of my armour. But I kept it on, pouring a dram of water into my shirt occasionally to cool me. The roads were fairly good, there having been little rain in recent days and few armies to churn them up, and I was lucky in that, every night, I found reasonably pleasant accommodation. Signs of the War began to increase, however. I passed the occasional gallows and more frequently came upon burnt-out ruins of farmsteads and churches.

I had reached a mountainous region, of pines and glittering limestone, one day and was emerging from a small gorge, when I saw before me a broad meadow in which, quite recently, some gory fight had taken place. There were bodies strewn everywhere, most of them stripped or at least partially shorn of their best clothing. Crows and ravens flapped and hopped, squabbling over the red, stinking flesh of the slain. There was absolutely no means of telling the loyalties of the combatants, and there was little point in trying to find out. It would probably emerge, as always, that their motives for fighting had been confused, to say the least.

Normally I should have skirted the battlefield, but my path took me directly through it and there were boulders on either side of the meadow. I was forced to let my horse pick his way between the corpses, while flies rose in clouds to attack me, presumably finding something more attractive about warm blood than cold.

I was halfway across the meadow, holding a cloth to my nostrils to try to block out the sickening smell of death, when I heard a noise from the rocks on my right and, looking up, saw a small boulder come tumbling down towards me. I detected a flash, as of metal, a hint of blue cloth, and immediately my old instincts came to my service.

The reins were wound around my pommel and both pistols were in my gloved hands. I cocked them carefully just as the men began to reveal themselves. They were all on foot, dressed in a motley of armour, carrying a variety of weaponry, from rusty axes and pikes, to glittering Toledo swords and daggers. The ruffians belonged to no particular army, that was certain. They were old-fashioned brigands, with sweating red faces, unshaven chins, and all manner of minor diseases written on their skins.

I levelled my pistols as they began to scramble down the hillside towards me.

"Stand back," I cried, "or I shall discharge!"

Their leader, almost a dwarf, wearing a stained black cloak and hat and a torn linen shirt, produced one of the largest pistols I had ever seen and grinned at me. Most of his teeth were missing. He squinted along the gun and said in a wheedling voice:

"Fire away, Your Honour. And we'll have the pleasure of doing the same."

I shot him in the chest. With a groan he flung up his arms and fell backwards, twitching for a second or two before he died. His pistol slithered towards his feet and none of his men were prepared to pick it up.

I reholstered the pistol I had used and drew my sword. "You'll not find me easy game, my friends," I said. "I would advise you that the cost of robbing me will prove far too dear."

One of the ruffians at the back raised a crossbow and loosed his bolt. The thing went just past my shoulder and I betrayed no sign that I had noticed it. My horse, well-trained, held his ground as well as did I.

"No more of that," said I, "or this other pistol will do its work. You have seen that I am a good shot."

I noted an arquebus lowered and a musket lifted from its aiming rod.

A creature with a squint and a Prussian accent said: "We are hungry, Your Worship. We have not eaten for days. We are honest soldiers, all of us, forced to live off the land when our officer deserted us."

I smiled. "I would hesitate to guess who had deserted whom. I have no food to spare. If you wish to eat, why don't you seek out an army and attach yourselves to it?"

Another began: "For the love of God . . ."

"I do not love God and neither does He love me," I said, with some certainty. "You cannot beg charity from a man you had hoped to murder."

They were creeping closer. I raised my pistol as a warning. They stopped, but then one of them, from the middle, brought up a pistol and fired it. The ball grazed the neck of my horse and he jumped, losing his composure for a moment. I fired back and missed my man, wounding another behind him.

Then they were upon me.

I had left it too late to run from them. They had quickly surrounded me, clutching at the horse's bridle, feinting at me with their pikes. I defended myself with my sword, loosening one foot from its stirrup to kick and shoving my pistol back into its holster so that I could tug a long poignard from its sheath at my belt. I took the lives of three and wounded several more, but they had lost their fear of me now and I knew that I must soon be borne under.

I received two small wounds, one in my thigh and one in my forearm, but they did not stop me from using either the leg or the arm. The brigands had begun to try to bring down the horse—a desperate action since he was probably the most valuable thing I owned—when I heard the sound of more hooves behind me and a wild, terrible yell cut through the general din. Some of the thieves detached themselves from me to deal with this new antagonist.

I recognised him at once. It was the young Muscovite from the inn. His sabre swirled this way and that as he rode low on his pony, slicing living flesh as a surgeon might dissect corpses. And he continued with his bloodcurdling yells until all the thieves were on the run. Then he flung back his head, dragged off his sheepskin cap and laughed, hurling insults after those few robbers left alive.

It was only then that I saw another rider some distance behind us. He was positioned at the mouth of the gorge, sitting almost motionless upon his chestnut cob and looking at both Grigory Sedenko and myself with pursed lips and a disapproving eye.

Sedenko wheeled his pony, still laughing. "That was good fighting," he said to me.

"I am grateful to you," I said.

He shrugged. "This journey was becoming boring. I was only too glad to relieve the boredom."

"You risked your life for a fool and an agnostic," said Klosterheim, pushing his wide-brimmed hat back from his face. "I am disappointed in you, Sedenko."

"He's a fellow soldier, which is more than you are, Klosterheim, for all your protestations."

I was pleased that the youth had grown impatient with the soldier-priest. But then I recalled the Jews at Teufenberg and I looked with a slightly wary eye upon the Muscovite, for I was almost convinced that he had slain the three Jews in their sleep.

Klosterheim's lips twisted in distaste. "You should have let him die," he told Sedenko. "You disobeyed me."

"And would again in similar circumstances," said the boy. "I am tired of your sermons and your quiet deaths, brother priest. If I'm to continue on to Schweinfurt, let this gentleman accompany us, for my sake if not for his."

Klosterheim shook his head. "This man is cursed. Can you not see it written on him?"

"I can only see a healthy soldier, like myself."

Klosterheim spurred his horse forward. His hatred of me seemed entirely reasonless. He rode on past me, through that meadow of fresh and not-so-fresh corpses.

"I'll travel alone," he said. "You have lost my friendship, Sedenko. And my gold."

"And good riddance to both," cried the red-haired youth. Then, turning to me: "Where do you journey, sir, and would you tolerate my company?"

I smiled. The boy had charm. "I go to Schweinfurt and beyond. I'll happily ride with such an excellent swordsman. What's your destination?"

"I have none in mind. Schweinfurt's as good as any." He

spat after the retreating Klosterheim. "That man is mad," he said.

I looked to my wounds. They were not serious. A little balm was smeared on each. Soon we were riding along together, side by side.

"How were you employed by Klosterheim?" I asked casually. "As a bodyguard?"

"Partly. But he knows that I have no love for Jews, Turks or any other form of infidel. Originally he wanted me to help him in the execution of some Jews in Teufenberg. He said he had evidence of their having sacrificed Christian babies. Well, everyone knows that Jews do that and they must be punished. I was quite prepared to help him."

I said nothing to this. The fierceness with which the southern Muscovite hated his Oriental, Mussulman neighbours was well-known. The boy seemed no worse than most in this.

"You killed those Jews?" I asked.

He scoffed. "Of course I did not. One was too old and the others were too young. But the main reason was that Klosterheim had deceived me. There was no evidence at all that they had done what he said."

"And yet they were killed."

"Naturally. I told Klosterheim to do his own work. In the end that is what he did, though reluctantly. Then he told me that there were more infidels to kill and that I would be well-paid for my trouble. Gradually I began to realise that it was murder, not fighting, he wanted me to perform. And whatever else I am, sir, I am not a murderer. I kill cleanly, in fair fighting. Or, at least, I make sure the odds are fair, in the matter of Jews and Turks. I have never struck one of them from behind."

He seemed proud of this last fact. I laughed tolerantly enough and told him that I had known a few decent Jews in my time and at least one noble Turk. He politely ignored this remark which, I am sure, he judged to be in extremely poor taste.

Sedenko's company had the effect of shortening the journey to Schweinfurt. Every so often, along the road, we saw ahead of us the purple plume and the black garb of Klosterheim, but he was travelling at speed now and was soon at least a day ahead of us. Sedenko's story was familiar enough:

He was a son of those hardy pioneers, the Kazaks, who had expanded Muscovite territory against the Tatars (thus his traditional hatred of Orientals) and had grown up in a village near the southern capital of Kieff. His people were famous riders and swordsmen and he had, according to his own boasts, excelled in every Kazak skill until he had become embroiled in a feud between rival clans over whether or not to rise against the Poles, and had killed a chief (or *hetman*). For this crime he had been banished, so had decided to strike westward and enlist in the army of some Balkan prince. For a while he had served with a Carpathian king in a war which, as far as I could tell, was no more than a quarrel between two gangs of robber-knights. Being of a fanatically religious bent, like most of his kind, he had heard of a "Holy War" in Germany and had decided that this was more to his taste. He had been disappointed to discover that he could find no particular sympathy with either side, for his religion recognised a Patriarch in Constantinople, not a Pope, yet in other respects was even more elaborate in its forms of worship than the Roman faith.

"I had thought I would be fighting infidels," he said in a disappointed voice, "Tatars, Jews or Turks. But this is a squabble between Christians and they do not appear to know the essentials of their arguments. They are all faithless fools, in my opinion. I decided I could fight for none of them. I enlisted as a personal bodyguard with a couple of noblemen, but they found me too wild, I think, for their taste, and I was close to starvation when I met Klosterheim."

"Where did you meet him first?"

"Where you saw us. I had had word through a third party—a monk in Allerheim—that this soldier-priest had employment for a defender of Christ's people. Well, I decided to see what it was, particularly since I had received a silver florin in advance. That was what paid my way to Teufenberg. Now we all know that a good Christian is worth twenty Jews, in any circumstance, and that twenty-to-one constitutes fair odds if one is attacking a village. I had expected a shtetl-full, at least. I had the impression that it was a veritable army threatening Teufenberg. But three! The only male Jews in the whole town! I felt insulted, sir, I can tell you. I have rarely tolerated such condescending behaviour as that which I tolerated in Klosterheim. Everyone is an infidel to him. He sought to convert me from the religion of my fathers to his own grey faith!"

I found his open naïveté, his unjustified and somewhat innocent prejudices, his enthusiasm, at once disarming and amusing. His prattle took little of my attention, but it served to keep my brain from morbidly dwelling on my own problems.

Schweinfurt was soon reached: a moderate-sized city which bore the usual traces of the War. Our presence was unremarked and I asked directions for the best road to Nürnberg. Sedenko and I put up at an inn on the outskirts of Schweinfurt and the following morning I prepared to say farewell to him, but he grinned at me and said: "If you've no objection, Captain von Bek, I'll stick with you for a while. I've nothing better to do and you have the air of someone who has embarked upon an adventure. You've said little of yourself or your mission, and I respect your silence. But I enjoy the comradeship of a fellow swordsman and, who knows, something might happen to me in your company which will lead to my finding decent employment with a company of professional soldiers."

"I'll not attempt to dissuade you now, Master Sedenko," said I, "for I'll admit that your company is as enjoyable as you claim mine to be. I head for Nürnberg, and from there go to a small town called Ammendorf."

"I have never heard of it."

"Neither had I. But I have instructions to go there and go there I must. It's possible that you would not wish to continue with me, once we reach Nürnberg, where there will be plenty of opportunities for you to find employment. And it is possible that, once I find Ammendorf, you will not be able to accompany me farther. You know that I have no wish to describe my true mission to you, but you are right in recognising its importance. You must agree, for your own sake as well as mine, to accept orders where they relate to my Quest."

"I am a soldier and accept a soldier's discipline, captain. Besides, this is your country and you know it a good deal better than I. I shall be proud to accompany you for as long as it suits you."

Sedenko pushed back his sheepskin cap on his head and grinned again. "I am a simple Kazak. All I need is a little food, a worthy master, my faith in God and a chance to ride and use this"—he drew his sabre and kissed the hilt—"and I am completely satisfied."

"I can promise you food, at least," I said. We mounted again together. I felt that I would come to miss Sedenko's companionship when the time came for our ways to part, but was selfish enough to allow him to stay with me until then.

A little later, as we took the highway to Nürnberg, he spoke more of Klosterheim. His distaste for his former employer was profound.

"He told me of the witches he's killed—some of them children. Christian folk, by the sound of them. I draw the line at children. What do you say, Captain von Bek?"

"I have a great deal of blood on my hands," I said. "Too much to let it grieve me immoderately, young Muscovite."

"But in War—the blood was spilled in War."

"Oh, indeed, in War. Or in the name of War. How many children do you think have died because of me, Sedenko?"

"You are a commander of men. There are always casualties which one regrets."

I sighed. "I regret nothing," I said. "But should I have regrets, I would regret that I ever left Bek. It is far too late for that now. I was not always a soldier, you see. You come from a race of warriors. Mine is a race of scholars and rural noblemen. We had no great tradition of warlike exploits." I shrugged. "There have been peasant children killed by my men, one way or another. And I was at Magdeburg."

"Ah," said Sedenko, "Magdeburg." He was silent for a while, almost, I thought, from a sense of respect. Nearly half an hour later he said to me: "It was an unholy shambles, Magdeburg, was it not?"

"Aye, it was that."

"Any true soldier would wish not to have been there."

"I'd agree," I told him.

It was the last we were to speak of Magdeburg.

Soon we began to detect the signs of large movements of armies upon the road and we took to travelling along tracks which, according to my maps (which were the most accurate I had ever used), roughly paralleled the main highway. Even then we occasionally encountered small parties and once or twice were challenged. As had become my habit I cried: "Envoy!" and we were permitted to pass without much in the way of questioning.

I determined that it would be unwise to go directly into Nürnberg. Rumour had it that a number of Saxony's greatest nobles were gathering there, perhaps to plan peace but more likely to consider fresh strategies and alliances. I had no wish to become involved in this and it would be harder, under sophisticated questioning, to maintain my deception. In those days one was the object of suspicion if one did not declare a loyalty or a master. It scarcely mattered what the cause might be, so long as one swore fealty to it.

About five miles beyond Nürnberg, in a glade where we had set up our camp, I asked Sedenko if he did not consider it time to part company. "They would welcome you in Nürnberg," I said. "And I can guarantee you that it would not be long before you saw an action."

He shook his head. "I can always go back," he said.

"There are lands ahead," I told him, "where you could not travel."

"Beyond Ammendorf, captain?"

"I'm not sure. I receive fresh orders there."

"Then let us determine what I do when you discover the nature of those orders."

I laughed. "You're as tenacious as a terrier, Grigory Petrovitch."

"We of the Kazak hosts are famous for our tenacity, captain. We are a free people and value our freedom."

"Yet you have picked me as a master?"

"One must serve something," he said simply, "or someone. Is that not so, captain?"

"Oh, I think I would agree," I said. But what would he think, I wondered, if he knew I served the cause of Satan?

Privately, I had another cause. I was maintained in my Quest by the thought that sooner or later I must be reunited with the Lady Sabrina. Witch or no, she was the first woman I had loved as I had always expected to be able to love. It was more than enough. If I dwelled too long on the implications of my Quest I would lose my ordinary judgement. Lucifer might speak of the fate of the world, of Heaven and Hell, but I preferred to think simply in terms of human love. I understood that imperfectly enough, but I understood it better than anything else.

The following morning we passed a long gallows-tree on which six bodies swung. The bodies were clothed in black habits and blood was encrusted on the limbs, showing that the

men had been tortured and broken before being hanged. At
the foot of one I saw a wooden crucifix. It was impossible to
determine to what order the monks had belonged. It scarcely
mattered, as I knew. What was certain was that they would
have been robbed of anything of value they had possessed. It
was no wonder that so many orders were these days renewing
their vows of poverty. There was no value in amassing wealth
when it could be taken from you on almost any excuse.

A mile or two farther along the road we came upon an
abbey. Parts of it were still burning and, for some reason, the
bodies of monks and nuns had been folded over the walls at
regular intervals, in the way a farmer might hang the corpses
of vermin to warn off others. I had seen many an example of
such dark humour in my years of War. I had been guilty of
similar acts myself. It was as if one wished to defy one's
conscience, to defy the very eye of God which, one sometimes felt, was looking down on all the horror and noting the
participants.

If Lucifer were to be believed, God had indeed looked
down upon me and judged me unfit for Heaven.

I was glad when, the next day, I consulted my map and
discovered that Ammendorf was only a few hours' ride away.

I had no notion of how I was to find the Wildgrave, the
Lord of the Hunt, but I would be relieved to have completed
the first stage of my Quest, come what may.

The road took us through a thick forest whose floor was
covered with mossy rocks and a tangle of vines which
threatened the footing of our horses. The smell of that
undergrowth, of the damp earth and the leaves, was so thick
that it seemed at times to cover my nostrils. The path rose
until we were riding a steep hill, still in the wood. Then we
had reached the crest but, because of the foliage, could see
little of what lay ahead of us. We rode down the other side.

Sedenko had become excited. He seemed to be gaining
more from my adventure than was I. He was evidently having
trouble in not asking me further questions and, since I could
in no way answer him, I encouraged his discretion.

When I judged Ammendorf to be little more than a mile
from us I reined in my horse and reminded my companion of
our earlier conversation. "You do know, Sedenko, that you
might not be able to follow me beyond Ammendorf?"

"Of course, captain." He offered me a frank stare. "It is
what you said before."

Satisfied with this, I continued to ride along the narrow trail which now twisted to follow the natural contours of the valley floor.

The trees began to thin and the valley to widen until at last we came to Ammendorf.

It lay beneath a huge, grey cliff streaked with moss and ivy. It was built all of dark, ancient stone which seemed to blend with the rock of the cliff itself.

No smoke lifted from Ammendorf's chimneys. No beasts stood in the walled yards, no children played in the streets; no townsfolk stood at Ammendorf's doors or windows.

Sedenko was the first to bring his horse to a halt. He leaned on his saddle-bow, staring in surprise at the strange, black town ahead of us.

"But it's dead," he said. "Nobody has lived here in a hundred years!"

Chapter VI

AMMENDORF AT CLOSE quarters gave off an odour of rot and decrepit age. Slates had fallen from roofs; thatch and wooden shingles were broken and tattered; only the heavy stones of the buildings were in one piece and they were covered in damp foliage and mildew.

The whole village had been abandoned suddenly, it seemed to me, and the green cast of the light through the gloom of the overhanging crag, the distinct and regular drip-drip of water, the soft yielding of the ground underfoot when we dismounted, all contributed to an impression of desolation.

Sedenko sniffed at the air and put his hand to the hilt of his sabre. "The place stinks of evil."

We peered upwards. I thought I detected more man-cut stone at the top of the crag, but a tangle of ivy and hawthorn obscured everything.

Could Lucifer, I wondered to myself, be losing His memory to send me to a place deserted for so long? There was none here to direct me to a Wildgrave doubtless long since dead.

Sedenko's look was questioning. Plainly he did not wish

to say what he was thinking: that I had been, at the very least,
badly misdirected.

The day was closing in. I said to Sedenko: "I must camp
here. But if you wish to travel on now I would suggest that
you do not hesitate."

The Muscovite grunted, fingering his face as he considered the prospect. Then he looked up at me and uttered a
small laugh. "This could be the adventure I have been
expecting," he said.

"But not one you would relish."

"It's in the nature of adventure, is it not, to risk that
possibility?"

I clapped him on the back. "You are a companion after
my own heart, Kazak. Would that you had been with me in
some of my former engagements."

"I have it in mind, captain, to be with you in some of
your future engagements."

The future for me was so mysterious, so numinous, that I
could not answer him. We began to explore the houses, one
by one. We found flagstones cracked and pushed apart by
plants. In some, small trees were growing. Everything was
damp. Pieces of furniture were rotting; fabric fell to shreds at
a touch.

"Even the rats have gone." Sedenko returned from a
cellar with a wine-jar. He broke the seal and sniffed. "Sour."

He dropped it into an empty fireplace.

"Well," he said, "which of these comfortable houses
shall we make our own?"

We decided in the end upon the building which had
evidently been the town's meeting place. This was larger and
airier than the others and we could light a fire in the big grate.

By dusk, with our horses billeted in one corner of the
room and the fire providing us with sufficient heat and some
light, we were ready to sleep.

Outside, in the deserted streets of Ammendorf, there
was little movement. A few birds hunted for insects and
occasionally we heard the bark of a fox. Soon Sedenko was
snoring, but it was harder for me to lose consciousness. I
continued to speculate on Lucifer's reasons for sending me to
this place. I thought about Sabrina and despaired of ever
seeing her again. I even considered retracing my steps
partway and seeking service with the Swedish King whose

army was just now marching at some speed through Germany. Then Magdeburg came back to me, as well as Lucifer's threats of what should happen if I betrayed Him, and I lapsed into despondency. Two or three hours must have passed in this useless state of mind before I nodded off, whereupon I was immediately aroused by what I was sure was the sound of hoofbeats.

I was on my feet almost with relief, picking up my scabbarded sword as I ran towards the window and looked out into the murk. A thin drizzle had begun to fall and clouds obscured moon and stars. I thought I saw the glow of an oddly coloured lantern moving between the buildings. The light began to grow brighter and brighter until it seemed to be flickering over half Ammendorf. And the hoofbeats grew louder, filling my ears with their din—yet still I could see no rider.

Sedenko was beside me now, his sabre ready in his fist. He rubbed at his face. "In the name of God, captain, what is it?"

I shook my head. "I've no idea, lad."

Even the meeting hall was shaking and our own mounts were stamping and whinnying, trying to break free of their halters.

"A storm," Sedenko said. "Some kind of storm, eh, captain?"

"It's like none I've ever witnessed," I told him. "But you could be right."

He was convinced that he was wrong. Every gesture, every movement of his eyes, betrayed his superstition.

"It is Satan's coming," he whispered.

I did not tell him why I thought that explanation unlikely.

All at once, from around a bend in the street, a horseman appeared. As he came into sight the hounds which surrounded his beast's feet, an undulation of savagery, began to bay. There were other riders behind him, but the leader was gigantic, dwarfing all. He wore a monstrous winged helmet framing a bearded face from which the eyes glowed with the same green-blue light which flooded the village. His great chest was encased in a mail shirt half-covered by the bearskin cloak which hung from his shoulders. In his left hand was a long hunting spear of a type not used in at least a hundred years. His legs were also mail-clad and the feet stuck into heavy stirrups. He lifted his head and laughed up at the sky, his voice joining in the note his hounds made until all seemed to be baying together, while his companions, shadows still behind him, began one by one to give forth the same dreadful noise.

"Mother of God," said Sedenko. "I'll fight any man fairly, but not this. Let's go, captain. They are warning us. They are driving us away."

I held my ground. "Drive us they might," I said, "and it would be a good sport for them, no doubt, for they would drive us like game, Sedenko. Those are hunters and I would say that their prey is Man."

"But they are not human!"

"Human once, I'd guess. But far from mortal now."

I saw white faces in the wake of the bearded horseman. The lips grinned and the eyes were bright (though not as bright as their leader's). But they were dead men, all of them. I had come to recognise the dead. And, too, I could recognise the damned.

"Sedenko," I said, "if you would leave me now, I would suggest you go at once."

"I'll fight with you, captain, whatever the nature of the enemy."

"These could be your enemies, Sedenko, but not mine. Go."

He refused. "If these are your friends, then I will stay. They would be powerful friends, eh?"

I had no further patience for the discussion, so I shrugged. I walked towards the door, strapping on my sword. The door creaked open.

The huntsmen were already gathering in Ammendorf's ruined square. I felt the heat of the hounds' breath on my face, the stink of their bodies. They flattened their ears as they began to lie down round the feet of their master's horse.

The chief huntsman stared at me from out of those terrifying eyes. White faces moved in the gloom. Horses pawed the weed-grown cobbles.

"You have come for me?" I said.

The lips parted. The giant spoke in a deep, sorrowing voice, far more melodious than I might have expected. "You are von Bek?"

"I am."

"You stand before the Wildgrave."

I bowed. "I am honoured."

"You are a living man?" he asked, almost puzzled. "An ordinary mortal?"

"Just so," I said.

He raised a bushy eyebrow and turned his head to look back at his white-faced followers, as if sharing a small joke with them. His reply was given in a tone that was almost amused:

"We have been dead these two hundred and fifty years or more. Dead as we once reckoned death, in common with most of mankind."

"But not truly dead." I spoke our High Tongue and this gave Sedenko some puzzlement. But it was the speech in which I had been addressed and I therefore deemed it politic to continue in it.

"Our Master will not let us die in that sense," said the Wildgrave of Ammendorf. He evidently saw me as a comrade in damnation. "Will you guest with me now, sir, at my castle yonder?" He pointed up the cliff.

"Thank you, great Wildgrave."

He turned his glowing eyes upon Sedenko. "And your servant? Shall you bring him?"

I said to Sedenko: "We are invited to dinner, lad. I would suggest you refuse the invitation."

Sedenko nodded.

"He will await me here until morning," I said.

The Wildgrave accepted this. "He will not be harmed. Will you be good enough to mount behind me, sir?"

He loosened his booted foot and offered me a stirrup. Deciding that it would be neither diplomatic nor expedient to hesitate, I walked up to his horse, accepted the stirrup and swung onto the huge beast's stinking back, taking a firm hold of the saddle.

Sedenko watched with wide eyes and dropped jaw, not understanding at all what was happening.

I smiled at him and saluted. "I'll return in the morning," I said. "In the meantime I can assure you that you will sleep safely."

The Wildgrave of Ammendorf grunted a command to his horse and the whole Hunt, hounds and all, turned out of the square. We began to race at appalling speed through the streets and onto an overgrown path which climbed through low-hanging foliage and outcrops of mossy rock to the top of the cliff, where it was now possible for me to see that my eyes had not earlier deceived me. I had thought that I had detected masonry from the village and here it was—a horrible old castle, part fallen into ruin, with a massive keep squatting black against the near-black of the sky.

We all dismounted at once and the Wildgrave, who stood more than a head taller than myself, put a cold arm about my shoulders and led me through an archway directly into the keep. Here, too, staircases and flagstones were cracked and broken. The hall was lit by a single guttering brand stuck into a rusting bracket above a long table. Over the fire a deer's carcass was turning. The white-faced huntsmen moved with agility towards the fire where they warmed themselves, paying no heed to two shaking servants, a boy and a girl, who were evidently neither part of this clan nor among the living-dead, but could have been as damned as the rest of us.

The Wildgrave's eyes seemed to cool as he placed himself at the head of the table and made me sit at his right. With his mailed hand he poured me brandy and bade me drink deep "against the weather" (which in fact was relatively mild). To him, perhaps, the world was permanently chill.

"I was warned of your coming," he told me. "There is a rumour, too, amongst the likes of us, that you are entrusted with a mission which could redeem us all."

I sighed. "I do not know, Lord Wildgrave. Our Master has greater faith in my capabilities than have I. I shall do my best, of course, for should I succeed, I, too, might be redeemed."

"Just so." The Wildgrave nodded. "But you must be aware that not all of us support you in your Quest."

I was surprised. "I cannot follow you," I said.

"Some fear that should our Master come to terms with God, they will be worse doomed than ever before, with no protector, with no further means of preserving their personalities against the Emptiness."

"Emptiness is not a term I am familiar with, Lord Wildgrave."

"Limbo, if you prefer. The Void, my good captain. That which refuses to tolerate even the faintest trace of identity."

"I understand you now. But surely, if Lucifer is successful, we shall all be saved."

The Wildgrave's smile was bitter. " What logic provides you with that hope, von Bek? If God is merciful, He provides us with little evidence."

I drank my brandy down.

"Some of us came to this pass," continued the Wildgrave, "through just such an understanding of God's nature. I am not amongst them, of course. But they believed God to be vengeful and unrelenting. And some, I would guess, will try to stop you in your mission."

"It is difficult and numinous enough as it is," I said as, with a clatter, the boy placed a plate of venison before me. The meat smelled good. "Your news is scarcely encouraging."

"But it is well-intentioned." The Wildgrave accepted his own plate. With the manners of a former time he courteously handed me a dish containing ground salt. I sprinkled a little on my meat and returned it to him.

He picked up his venison and began to munch. I noted that his breath steamed as it contacted the heat. I copied him. The food was good and was welcome to me.

"We have still to hunt tonight," said the Wildgrave, "for we continue to exist in our own world only so far as we can provide fresh souls for our Master. And we have caught nothing for almost a month."

I chose not to ask him to elaborate upon this, and he seemed grateful for my tact.

"I have been instructed to take you through into the Mittelmarch," he said. As he spoke, others of the Hunt brought their plates to table. They ate in silence, apparently without interest in our conversation. It seemed to me that they had an air of slight nervousness, perhaps because they resented this interruption to their nightly activities.

"I have not heard of the Mittelmarch," I told him frankly.

"But you know there are lands upon this Earth of ours which are forbidden to most mortals?"

"So I was told, aye."

"Those lands are known by some of us as The Middle Marches."

"Because they lie on the borderlands between Earth and Hell?"

He smiled and wiped his mouth on his mailed sleeve. "Not exactly. You could say they lie between Hope and Desolation. I do not understand much about them. But I am able to come and go between them. You and your companion shall be taken through tomorrow evening."

"My companion is not of our kind," I said. "He is a simple, innocent soldier. I shall tell him to return to a world he will better understand."

The Wildgrave nodded. "Only the damned are permitted to pass into Mittelmarch," he told me. "Though not all who dwell in Mittelmarch are damned."

"Who rules there?" I asked.

"Many." He shrugged his gigantic shoulders. "For Mittelmarch, like our own world, like Hell itself, has multitudinous aspects."

"And the land I go to tomorrow. It will be marked on my maps?"

"Of course. In Mittelmarch you will seek out a certain hermit who is known as Philander Groot. I had occasion to pass the time of day with him once."

"And what am I to ask of him? The location of the Grail?"

The Wildgrave put down his venison, almost laughing. "No. You will tell him your story."

"And what will he do?"

The Wildgrave spread a mailed hand. "Who knows? He has no loyalty to our Master and refuses to have any truck with me. I can only say that I have heard he might be curious to talk to you."

"He knows of me?"

"The news of your Quest is rumoured, as I said."

"But how could such news spread so quickly?"

"My friend"—the Wildgrave became almost avuncular as he put a hand upon my arm—"can you not understand that you have enemies in Hell as well as in Heaven? It is those you should fear worse than any earthly foe."

"Can you give me no further clue," I asked, "as to the identity of these enemies?"

"Naturally I cannot. As it is I have been kinder to you than is sensible for a creature in my position. I am feared in the region of Ammendorf, of course. But as with all our Master's servants, I have no real power. Your enemies could one day, therefore, be my friends."

I became distressed at this. "Have you no courage to take your own decisions?"

The Wildgrave's great face became sad for a moment. "Once I had courage of that sort," he said. "But had I had the courage to be self-determining in my own mortal life I would not now be a servant of Lucifer." He paused, looking out from eyes which, moment by moment, had begun to glow again. "And the same must be true of you, too, eh, von Bek?"

"I suppose so."

"At least you have a chance, however small, of reclaiming yourself, captain. And oh"—his voice became at once bleak and heartfelt—"how I envy you that."

"Yet if I am successful and God grants Lucifer His wish, we shall all be given the chance again," I said, innocently enough.

"And that is what so many of us fear," said the Wildgrave.

Chapter VII

SEDENKO, HE SAID, had slept well all night. When I returned at dawn he had been snoring, certainly, as if he was still a little boy in his mother's tent.

As he breakfasted he asked eagerly of my encounter with "the Devil."

"That was not the Devil, Sedenko. Merely a creature serving Him."

"So you did not sell your soul to him."

"No. He is helping me, that's all. I now know the next stage of my journey."

Sedenko was awed. "What great power must you possess to order such as the Wildgrave!"

I shrugged. "I have no power, save what you see. It is the same as yours—good wits and a quick sword."

"Then why should he help you?"

"We have certain interests in common."

Sedenko looked at me with some trepidation.

"And you must go back to Nürnberg," I said, "or wherever you think. You cannot go where I go tonight."

"Where is that?"

"A land unknown."

He became interested. "You travel by sea? To the New World? To Africa?"

"No."

"I would serve you well if you would permit me to go with you . . ."

"I know you would. But you are not permitted to follow where I travel now."

He continued to argue with me, but I rejected all his proposals until I was weary and begged him to leave, for I wished to sleep.

He refused. "I will guard you," he said.

I accepted his offer and eventually was able to sleep, waking in the later afternoon to smell Sedenko's cooking. He had found a pot, suspended it over the fire and was boiling some sort of stew.

"Rabbit," he told me.

"Sedenko," I said, "you must go. You *cannot* follow me. It is not physically possible."

He frowned. "I have a good horse, as you know. I am not prone to the seasickness, as far as I have been able to tell. I am healthy."

I again fell into silence. Only the damned could travel to Mittelmarch. Follow me as he would, he could not enter that Realm. I determined to waste no energy on the matter, contenting myself with advice to the young Kazak to go back to Nürnberg and find himself a good captain or, if he thought it a better idea, to leave the conflict altogether and begin to travel homeward, where he could direct his energies, if he wished, against his Polish overlords.

He became obstinate, almost surly. I shrugged. "The Wildgrave comes for me tonight," I said, "and I must ready myself for that journey. The stew is good. Thank you." I got up and began to see to my horse.

Sedenko sat cross-legged beside the fire, watching me. He hardly moved as I donned my battle-dress, strapping my steel breastplate tightly about my body, adjusting the set of my greaves. I thought it wise to enter the Realm of Mittelmarch with as much of the odds in my favour as possible.

Night fell. Sedenko continued to watch me, saying nothing. I refused even to look at him. I fed my horse. I oiled my leather. I polished my pistols and checked their locks. I cleaned my sword and my poignard. Then I gave close attention to my helmet. I whistled. Sedenko watched on.

By midnight I was beginning to grow a little nervous, but refused to show my state of mind to my silent companion. I looked through the windows at Ammendorf which, tonight, was lit faintly by the moon.

Even as I began to turn back I heard the echoing yell of a great horn. It sounded like the Last Judgement. It was a cold, desolate noise—a single, prolonged note. Then there came quiet again.

The building shook to hoofbeats. The green-blue glow flickered through the buildings outside. I heard the baying of the hounds.

I took my horse by his reins and led him through the hall and out down the steps into the square. I longed to say farewell to Sedenko but I knew I must discourage him at all costs from following me.

The Hunt came sweeping in. Red mouths gaped and tongues lolled. The Wildgrave's eyes seemed the single source of the hideous light. His men howled in unison with the dogs until all at once they were still as statues on frozen horses. Only the Wildgrave moved, his winged head turning towards me.

"You are ready, I see, mortal."

"I am ready, my lord."

"Then come. To the Mittelmarch."

I mounted my horse. The Wildgrave made a sign and the Hunt began to move again, with me riding beside him, my horse snorting and complaining in fear of the dogs. We did not ride back towards the castle, but out of Ammendorf and through a wood. The chill of the Wildgrave's monstrous body seemed to draw my own heat and I was shivering within half an hour. We rode beside a lake and I imagined that the lake shone with ice, an impossibility at that time of year. We rode until we saw the lights of a town ahead of us, and here the Wildgrave drew rein on the hill some miles above the town and wished me well in my Quest.

"But how shall I find Mittelmarch?" I was baffled.

"I have brought you to Mittelmarch," said the Wildgrave.

I noted that snow was falling on my sleeve.

"There was no transition," I said. "Or no sense of one, at any rate."

"Why should there be, for our sort? You merely follow certain trails."

"You could not have shown me the trail?"

"There is a way of looking," said the Wildgrave. "Do not fear. You are not trapped here."

"It snows late, in Mittelmarch," I said. I saw that the snow had settled. It was quite deep in some places. It weighted the trees. My breath was white.

The Wildgrave shook his head. "No later than in your own Realm, captain."

"Then I do not understand this," I told him.

"The seasons are reversed here, that is all. You will know when you have left Mittelmarch only by that sign."

His men glared anxiously at him. They wished to continue with their Hunt. For all the terror they must inspire, they were themselves more terrified than their victims—for they knew for certain what their fate must be should they fail Lucifer.

That cold, strangely friendly hand was placed again upon my arm. "Seek out Philander Groot. That is my best thought for you. And go wisely in this Realm as in your own, captain. I hope you find the Cure for the World's Pain."

He lifted his horn to his lips and blew that long, single note. Trees shook their snow from their branches. The dogs lifted their heads and bayed. In the forest behind me I thought that I heard beasts in flight.

The Wildgrave laughed: a sound even more hideous than his horn's cry.

"Farewell, von Bek. Discover for all of us, if you can, if there is such a thing as Freedom."

The ground trembled as the Hunt retreated, and then it was still, of a sudden, and I was alone. I drew my cloak about me and pushed my horse on towards the town below, guiding him carefully through the snow.

Overhead the sky fluttered and light appeared, first from a large yellow moon, then from the stars. There seemed something odd about the constellations, but I was no astrologer so could not tell what, if anything, was different. In the far distance were towering, jagged peaks. This land seemed somehow larger, more monumental, than the land I had left. It seemed wilder and was mysterious, yet it also contained in it an atmosphere if not of peace then at least of familiarity, and this sense in itself was comforting to me. It was almost as if I were back in Bek. As if I had gone into the past.

I knew that I must go warily in Mittelmarch and that I

could be in even greater danger here than in my own land. Nonetheless it was with lifting spirits that I continued on my way, and when I heard the sound of a rider behind me I became cautious, but was not unduly perturbed.

I turned my head, crying out a "halloo" to warn the rider that there was someone ahead of him.

No reply came back, so I drew my sword slowly and halted my horse before coming about to face whoever it might be.

The rider himself had slowed and now stopped. I could only dimly see him in the moonlight, stopped on the trail beside a great, snow-covered rock.

"Who are you, sir?" said I.

No reply again.

"I must warn you that I am armed," I said.

A movement of the figure, a slight stirring of the horse's feet, but no more. I began to approach at a walk. It was then that the rider decided to reveal himself.

He came out into the moonlight. He looked apologetic and defiant at the same time. He gestured with one gloved hand and he shrugged. "I am used to snow, master. Is that what you feared would distress me?"

"Oh, Sedenko," I said, without anything but sadness filling me.

"Master?"

"Oh, Sedenko, my friend." I rode forward and embraced him.

He had not expected anything but my anger and was surprised. But he returned the embrace with some vigour.

He did not know what I knew: that if he had been permitted to follow us into Mittelmarch it could mean only one thing. Poor Sedenko was already damned.

At that moment I railed against a God who could condemn such an innocent soul to Purgatory. What had Sedenko done that was not the result of his upbringing or his religion, which encouraged him to kill in the name of Christ? It came to me that perhaps God had become senile, that He had lost His memory and no longer remembered the purpose of placing Man on Earth. He had become petulant, He had become whimsical. He retained His power over us, but could no longer be appealed to. And where was His Son, who had been sent to redeem us? Was God's Plan not so much mysterious as impossible for us to accept: because it was a malevolent one? Were we all, no matter what we were or how we lived, automatically damned? Was Life without point? Did my Quest have any meaning? All these things were questions in my mind as I looked upon the Kazak youth and wondered what crime he could have committed that was evil enough to send him so young to Hell. Surely, I thought to myself, Lucifer is a more consistent and intelligent Master than the Lord Himself.

"Well, captain," said Sedenko with a grin. "Have I proved myself to you? Can I come another step of your journey with you?"

"Oh, by all means, Sedenko. You can, if it is only my decision, travel with me all the way to my ultimate destination."

Here was another soul whom I hoped Lucifer might spare in his gratitude were I successful.

Sedenko began to whistle some wild and rousing tune of his own people. He slipped sideways in his saddle and scooped up the fresh snow with his free hand, throwing it into the air and cheering. "This is more the kind of place for me, captain. I was born in the open snow, you know. I am a child of the winter!" His whistling turned into a song in his own language. He was like a happy boy. I did my best to smile at his antics, but my heart was heavy.

By morning we were in sight of a village which somewhat resembled the one we had left. A castle stood upon a crag, but this castle was in excellent repair. And the village was far from deserted. We saw smoke lifting and heard voices, sharp in the cold air. We rode down, through white trees, and plodded on our horses through the street until we came to the square where a market had already been set up.

I dismounted beside a stall which was selling slices of cooked meat and pickled fish and asked the red-faced woman in charge of it what the name of the town might be.

Her answer was one I had half-expected.

"Why, master," said she, "this is Ammendorf."

Sedenko had overheard me. "Ammendorf? Are there two, so close together?"

"There is only one Ammendorf," said the woman proudly. "There is nowhere else like it."

I looked beyond the town and the forest to the huge spikes of the mountains. I had not seen those mountains before. They seemed taller than the Alps. They might have stretched all the way to Heaven.

"Do you have a priest?" I asked her.

"Father Christoffel? You will find him at the church." She pointed to the other side of the village. "Up the little lane beyond the well."

Leading my horse, with a mystified Sedenko muttering behind us, I made for the lane. If anyone knew of the hermit Philander Groot it would surely be the priest. I found the lane. There were cart tracks in the snow, between tall hedges.

Sedenko continued to sing behind me. I think he was pleased with himself for being able to track me. I could hardly bear the sound of his voice, it was so sweet, so happy.

I turned a corner in the lane and there was the stone church with its spire and its graveyard. I tethered my horse to the fence which surrounded the graveyard and opened the wicket gate, bidding Sedenko to stay where he was and watch our mounts.

The doors of the church opened easily and I found myself in an unpretentious building, evidently Catholic but by no means reeking of incense and Mary-worship. The priest was at his altar, arranging the furniture there.

"Father Christoffel?"

He was fat and bore the scars of some earlier disease. His mouth was self-indulgent, like the mouth of a lazy, expensive whore, but his eyes were steady. Here was a man likely to commit sins of the flesh in abundance, but sins of the intellect would be few.

"I am Captain Ulrich von Bek," I said, doffing my helmet and pulling off my gloves. "I am upon a mission which is secret, but there are religious aspects to it."

He looked hard at me, cocking his little fat head to one side. "Yes?"

"I am looking for a man whom I heard to be dwelling in these parts."

"Hm?"

"A certain hermit. Perhaps you know him?"

"His name, captain?"

"Philander Groot."

"Groot? Yes?"

"I wish to speak to him. I hoped you would know of his whereabouts."

"Groot hides from himself and from God," said the priest. "And so he also hides from us."

"But you know his whereabouts?"

The priest lifted heavy brows. "You could say so. Why is a soldier looking for him?"

"I seek something."

"Something he possesses?"

"Probably not."

"Of military importance?"

"No, Father."

"You are interested in his philosophy?"

"I am not familiar with it. I have little curiosity where philosophy is concerned."

"Then what do you want from Groot?"

"I have a story for him, I think. I've been led to understand that he would wish to listen to me."

"Who told you of Groot?"

This was not a man to whom I wished to lie.

"The Wildgrave."

"Our Wildgrave," said the priest in some surprise. Then his face began to frown. "Oh, no. Of course. The other one."

"I suspect so," I replied.

"Do you serve Lucifer, too? Groot, for all his failings, is adamant. He will speak to none who do."

"I could be said to serve the world," I told the priest. "My Quest, some have suggested, is for the Grail."

The priest showed some surprise. His lips silently repeated my last two words. He peered into my face with those bright, intelligent eyes.

"You are sinless, then?"

I shook my head. "There are few sins unknown to me. I am a murderer, a thief, a despoiler of women."

"An ordinary soldier."

"Just so."

"So you have no hope of ever finding the Grail?"

"I have every hope."

The priest rubbed at the stubble on his jowls. He became thoughtful, glancing at me from time to time as he considered what had passed between us. Then he shook his head and turned his back on me, attending to the altar-furniture again.

I heard him murmur: "An ordinary soldier." He even seemed amused, though there was no mockery in him. Eventually he looked back at me.

"If you possessed the Grail, what would you hope from it?"

"A Cure," said I, "for the World's Pain."

"You care so much for the World?"

"I care for myself, Father."

He smiled at this. "Fear is a disease few of us know how to fight."

"It is also a drug," I said, "to which many are addicted."

"The World is in a sorry state, Sir Warrior."

"Aye."

"And any man who continues to hope that it can still be helped has my goodwill, my blessing even. Yet Philander Groot . . ."

"You think him evil?"

"There is no evil at all, I would say, in Philander Groot. That is why I am so angry with him. He refuses to accept God."

"He is an atheist?"

"Worse. He believes. But he refuses to accept his Creator."

I found this description sympathetic.

"And so," continued the priest, "he shall be refused Heaven and unjustly be swallowed up by Hell. I despair of him. He is a fool."

"But an honest fool, by the sound of him."

"There is none I know more honest, Captain von Bek, than Philander Groot. Many seek him, for he is said to have magical powers. He lives under the protection of a mountain kingdom which in its turn is also protected by powerful forces. To reach that kingdom you must journey to the far peaks and find the Hermit Pass, which leads into the valley where Groot dwells."

"The pass is named for him?"

"Not at all. It was always fashionable with hermits." There was a sardonic note to the priest's remark. "But Groot is no ordinary hermit. It is said that he spent his boyhood as the apprentice to a Speculator. Perhaps they are unknown in your part of the world. Speculators professionally spend their time watching for signs of the Coming of the Anti-Christ and Armageddon. The living can be good, particularly in troublesome times. But Groot, from what he has told me, became tired of the Future and for a while studied the Past. Now, he says, he cares only for an Eternal Present."

"Would that I could reject Past and Future," said I with some feeling.

"Oh, and then we should be able to reject Conscience and Consequence, eh?" said the priest. "But I have had this argument with my friend Groot and I will not bore you with it. Should you meet him, he will be able to present his position far more fluently than I."

I took the map-case from my pouch and drew forth several of the maps. "Is Hermit Pass marked here?" After much opening and closing I was able to withdraw the appropriate map (it showed both Ammendorfs) and display it to the priest. With a fat finger he indicated a road which led into the great mountains I had already seen. "Northwest," he said. "And may God, or whoever rules in Mittelmarch, go with you."

I left the church and rejoined Sedenko. "We will provision here," I told him, "and continue our journey in the afternoon."

"I saw what seems a good inn as we came through the town," he said.

"We'll dine there before we set off."

I had been at once cheered and disturbed by my encounter with Father Christoffel. I wanted to leave Ammendorf behind me as soon as possible and be upon my journey.

"Was your confession heard, captain?" innocently asked the young Kazak as I got into my saddle.

I shrugged.

Sedenko continued: "Perhaps I should also seek the priest's blessing. After all, it is some time . . ."

I became angry with him, knowing what I knew. I almost hated him at that moment for his ignorance of his own unfair fate. "That priest is next to an agnostic," I said. "He cannot unburden himself, let alone you or me. Come, Sedenko, we must be on our way." I paused, deciding that it was as well if I told him a little more of my story.

"I seek nothing less than the Holy Grail," I said.

"What's that, captain?"

Whistling, his breath clouding the sharp air, he fell in behind me.

I explained to him as much as I could. He listened to me with half an ear, as if I told a fabulous story which had not much to do with either of us. His very carelessness made me all the more gloomy.

Chapter VIII

As WE RODE out of Ammendorf my bitterness against a Deity who could consign such as Sedenko so easily to Hell continued to grow. There seemed no justice in the world at all, no possibility of creating justice, no being to whom one could appeal. Why should I be concerned about redemption in such a world? What would I escape, if I escaped Hell?

Sedenko had earlier attempted to interrupt my broodings, but for some while had said hardly a word, cheerfully accepting my silence and respecting my reluctance to answer his very ordinary questions. The day grew colder as night came nearer, yet I made no preparations for camp. I was tired. Ammendorf's good wine and food were sustaining me against weather and lack of sleep, and I told myself that Sedenko was young enough to lose another night's rest. Only the condition of the horses concerned me, but, they seemed fresh enough, for we did not push them hard. Movement was all that I desired. We passed through rocky hills and over snowy moorland, through woods and across streams, heading steadily towards the high peaks and Hermit Pass.

As night fell, I dismounted, leading my horse. Sedenko did not question me, but followed my example.

It had been some years since I had lost my Faith, save in my own capacity to survive a world at War, but evidently in the back of my mind there had always been some sense that through God one might find salvation. Now, as I journeyed in quest of the Holy Grail (or something identified as the Holy Grail), I not only questioned the possibility that salvation existed; I questioned whether God's salvation was worth the earning. Again I began to see the struggle between God and Lucifer as nothing more than a squabble between petty princelings over who should possess power in a tiny, unimportant territory. The fate of the tenants of that territory did not much seem to matter to them; and even the rewards of those tenants' loyalty seemed thin enough to me. For my own part, I believed that I deserved any fate, no matter how cruel, for I had used my intelligence in the service of my self-deceit. The same could not be said of Sedenko, who was merely a child of his times and his circumstances. I had received positive proof of the existence of God and the Devil and my Faith in them was weaker now than it had ever been.

My cloak would not keep out the bite of winter's night. I heard my teeth chattering in my skull. My heart seemed as if it were turning to ice. Even Sedenko was shivering, and he was used to far worse cold than this.

We were climbing higher into the foothills of the mountains. Their peaks were now tall enough to block off half the sky and the snow became deeper and deeper until it threatened to spill over into our boots. Towards dawn I began to realise that if we did not have heat and food soon we should probably perish, whereupon we should both go straight to Hell. The prospect reminded me of the reason I had accepted Lucifer's bargain.

Although it was difficult to see through the murk, I selected a place where an outcrop of rock had left the ground relatively clear of deep snow and told Sedenko to prepare a fire.

As he gathered wood, the dawn began to come up, red and cold. I watched him while he moved about in the nearby spinney below, bending and straightening, shaking snow from the sticks he found, and for some reason was reminded of the parable of Abraham and his son. Why should one serve a God who demanded such insane loyalty, who demanded that one deny the very humanity He was said to have created?

I watched as Sedenko prepared the fire for us and

selected food from our bag of provisions. He seemed cheerful merely to be in my company. He was excited, expecting great and interesting adventures. If he died on the morrow, he would probably look wonderingly at Hell itself and find it interesting.

And then it came to me that perhaps Lucifer had lied to me, that He had lied to all who served Him. Perhaps none of us were damned at all, but could somehow wrest our destinies free of His influence as He had attempted to wrest His own destiny free of God's. Why should we be controlled by such beings?

And the answer came to me, as it always did when I followed that logic: because they can destroy us at will.

I could almost sympathise with those the Wildgrave had warned me against; those who saw me as aiding in Lucifer's betrayal of His own creatures. They had seen Lucifer as representing if nothing else a defiance of an unjust God. A pact between God and Lucifer would find them without protection, sacrificed because Lucifer had found it expedient to change His mind.

But would God let Lucifer change His mind? Even Lucifer had no clue to that. And I, if I succeeded in discovering the Cure for the World's Pain, might not be finding a remedy at all. What if, when it was put to the lips of mankind, the Holy Grail was discovered to contain a deadly poison? Perhaps, after all, the only Cure for pain was the absolute oblivion of death, without Heaven or Hell.

My heavy sighs caused Sedenko to look up from where he was warming his hands against the fire. "What did the priest tell you, master? You have been distressed ever since you met him."

I shook my head. It had not been the priest, of course, who had disturbed me. And I could not explain to Sedenko that I knew him destined for Hell, that the God he claimed to serve had rejected him and had not even given him a sign of that rejection.

"Did he refuse you grace?" Sedenko continued.

"My state of mind has little to do with my encounter in the church," I said. "I received information from the priest. He has told me where I might look for a certain hermit, that is all."

"And you still do not know the purpose of your journey?"

"I know it, I think, as well as I ever shall. Make us our breakfast, young Kazak. And sing us one of those sonorous songs of yours, if you can."

I was asleep before he had begun to cook anything and it was noon before I woke up again. Simmering on the well-made fire was some soup. Sedenko himself had taken the opportunity to rest and was wrapped in his blankets a short distance from me. I ate the soup and cleaned the pan before waking him.

The mountains were taller than anything I had ever seen before. They were jagged and steep and the snow had frozen on them so that they glittered like crystal in the heavy winter sun. Everywhere was whiteness: the purity of Fimbulwinter, of the Death of the World. A few streams continued to run through the snow, which proved to me that it could not be as cold as it seemed. I had grown used to the warmth of spring, I suppose, and it was taking my body time to adjust. Sedenko seemed much easier with the elements than was I.

"A man can understand snow," he said. He told me that in his language there were a considerable number of words for different kinds of snow. "Snow can kill," he continued, as he packed our things back onto our horses, "but you also learn how to stop it from killing you. Or at least how to improve your chances. It is not so, captain, with men."

I smiled at this piece of philosophy. "True."

"Men will tell you what to do to avoid their killing you. You do it. They kill you anyway, eh?"

"Oh, very true, Sedenko." I consoled myself that this innocent would at least be good company in Hell, were we permitted to remain together. And I did not add that what he observed in Man, I observed the more sharply in God and His Fallen Angel. He would not have wanted to believe me. I did not wish to believe myself.

The smell of the snow was good in my nostrils now and I began to sense that peculiar elation which comes when you have lost all Hope of anything, save another hour or two of life. At one point, displaying considerable risk to my horse, I galloped for a short distance through the snow, sending it flying about me. Sedenko yelled and cheered and let his pony race, swinging his body from side to side of the beast with extraordinary agility, at one point leaping, apparently with a single movement, to stand on his saddle and balance there like an acrobat, arms outstretched.

He had boasted that the Kazak was the finest rider in the world and I must say that I could not dispute the fact, if his fellows rode as he rode. His ebullience infected me. I tried to push from my mind all thoughts of Good and Evil, of the War in Heaven, and did my best to sense again the pleasures of the scenery, while Sedenko gradually subsided, like a happy puppy, and eventually drew up beside me, panting and grinning.

That evening Sedenko again built a fire while I checked the map. We were high into the hills now and the mountains seemed to press in on us. There was the plain far behind us, but even this was obscured by the hills. Hermit Pass was not more than five miles to the northwest. We should be there, if we met no obstacles, by the middle of the next morning.

I wondered how this pass might be defended and what kind of danger, from what source, lay ahead of us. But I said nothing to Sedenko.

We reached the first range of mountains just before noon and the entrance to the pass was easily discovered. We had tied rags around our horses' feet. The rocky ground was patched with ice, so that it was better to walk our mounts whenever we could. The peaks of the mountains were invisible now. It seemed that we approached an infinitely tall wall of glittering crystal, white and pale blue, or grey where the rock was exposed. I continued to marvel at the height and shape of them; they were characteristic of nothing I had seen before.

The pass was a dark gash, seemingly in the side of a cliff. It was only as we drew nearer to it that we saw it lay between the mountains, turning sharply inwards so that it was not possible to see very far ahead. The snow was thinner here, but the ice thicker. We should have to move very carefully.

Without ado we stepped forward. The winter sun no longer fell on us and so the temperature dropped immediately, and we wrapped ourselves more thickly in our cloaks. The sound of our footfalls echoed in the canyon and we heard the rushing of water somewhere to one side of us, the drip of half-melted ice, the creaking and shifting noise of uncertain snow. Even as we moved some snow fell from overhanging rock and struck our heads and shoulders.

Sedenko looked upwards towards the crack of light far above us. "It's almost a cave," he said in some awe. "A monstrous huge tunnel, captain. Will it lead us into Hell?"

"I sincerely hope that it will not," I replied. I had a better idea of the implication of his words than did he.

We spoke quietly, as if we knew that too much noise could dislodge rock, ice and snow which would bury us within seconds. We turned the bend into deeper darkness. Every tiny noise from around us had significance, for it could herald a landslide. I realised that I was scarcely breathing and that I could hear my heartbeats in my ears.

Gradually the pass widened a little until the gap above admitted more light. The snow was deeper and wetter, but the ground was not so icy where the rays of the sun had fallen and we were able to relax into a more normal form of procedure. A few more bends and it had widened again until it was almost a narrow valley. Some bushes and small trees grew here and every so often I detected a patch of green. The noise of the ice and snow grew fainter and assumed less significance to us. After an hour or so into the pass, feeling somewhat more relaxed, we decided to rest and eat some of the bread and pickled herring we had purchased in Ammendorf.

It was as we cleared snow from a flat rock that I heard a scuffling sound and then what I was certain was a human gasp. I paused and listened, but heard nothing else like it. However, I removed my pistols from their holsters and placed them beside me on the rock as I ate.

Sedenko had not heard the sound, but he knew that something was alerting me and he watched my face, listening as he ate.

Another sound. Loose rock and snow fell towards us from our right. I put down my bread and picked up both pistols, levelling them in the general direction of the disturbance.

"Be warned!" I called. "And display yourself, so that we may parley."

A girl of about fifteen, thin-faced, freezing, wrapped in a miscellany of rags, shuffled from the other side of a rock. Her eyes were wide with fear, hunger and curiosity.

I did not lower my pistol. I had become wary of children in my profession. I levelled one of the barrels all the more firmly at her face.

"Are there more of you?"

She shook her head.

"Is your village near here?"

Again a shake of the head.

"Then what in the name of God and Saint Sophia are you doing here?" asked Sedenko of a sudden, slamming his sabre back into its scabbard and marching towards her. I felt he was incautious, but I did not warn him. He went up to her and looked at her face, taking it in his big hands. "You're quite pretty. What's your story, girl? Was your party waylaid by brigands? Are you the sole survivor? Are you lost?"

A sudden thought. He took a step backwards.

"Or are you a witch? A shape-changer?" He looked up at the far rocks. He looked behind him. He spoke over his shoulder to me. "What do you think, captain? Could she be tricking us?"

"Easily," I said. "But then I have assumed that since we saw her."

Another pace backwards. And another, until he was almost presenting his spine to my left-hand pistol. He was staring hard at her. He spoke very quietly to me now. "A witch, then?"

"A wretched girl, most likely, who has been abandoned in these mountains. No more and no less."

She pointed behind her. "My master . . ."

"There!" said Sedenko triumphantly. "A wizard she serves."

"Who is your master, girl?" said I.

"A holy man, excellency." She dipped a curtsey of sorts.

"A magus!" said Sedenko in an urgent whisper to me.

"One of the hermits who dwell in this pass, is he?" I asked.

"He is, Your Honour."

"She's no more than a hermit's companion," I told Sedenko. "You've seen such children before, surely?"

Sedenko rubbed at his lower lip with the joint of his thumb. He looked sideways at the girl. But he was almost convinced by my reasoning.

"And where's your master?" I asked her.

"Above, sir. And dying. We have had no food. He has been injured for many, many days. Since before the snow." She pointed.

Now I could see the shadow of a cave in the rock. There were several such caves here and there, which was no doubt why they were favoured by hermits. As well as providing the kind of living accommodation hermits seemed to find most satisfactory, they were also close to the pass and travellers could be prevailed upon to offer food, money or any other form of aid.

"How long have you been with your hermit?" I asked her. I decided to replace the pistols in their holsters. It was obvious to me that she was not lying. Sedenko, however, was not so certain now.

"Since I was a little girl, sir. He has looked after me from the time when my brother, my mother and my father were all killed. By the eagles, sir."

"Well, then," I said, "lead us to the dying hermit."

Sedenko had a thought: "Could this be your Groot, captain?"

"I think not. But he could know of Groot. Most of these hermits tend to be rivals, in my experience."

We clambered up the snowy rocks in the wake of the girl until the cave was reached. A dreadful stench came out of it, but again I was familiar with the kind of stink surrounding such holy creatures and braved it readily, with a hand over my mouth.

The girl pointed into a corner. Something stirred there. Sedenko remained outside, complaining. I made no attempt to force him to follow me.

A gaunt face raised itself a little and dark eyes stared into mine. If the smell and the sight were sickening, the worst was the smile I was offered by the hermit. It was radiant with insane piety. It offered itself as an example, it accused, it forgave all at once. I had seen such smiles before. More than once I had killed the ones who had presented them to me. I had once argued that a smile of that kind upon the lips was worth a second smile in the throat.

"Greetings, holy hermit," I said. "Your servant tells us that you are ailing."

"She exaggerates, sir. I have a wound or two, that is all. But what are my wounds compared to the wounds of our own dear Christ, whom we all wish to follow and to imitate? Those wounds take me closer to Heaven, in more than one sense."

"Ah, and they smell of Heaven already, do they not?" I replied. "I am Ulrich von Bek and I am upon a Quest for the Holy Grail."

I knew that this would have an effect. He fell back, almost resentfully. "The Grail? The Grail? Ah, sir, but the Grail would cure me!"

"And all others who are dying or lie sick," I said.
"However, I have not yet found it."

"Are you close to your Quest's end?" he asked.

"I do not know." I stepped closer. "I will get you
something to eat. Sedenko!" I called back to my companion.
"Food for this pair."

Sedenko with a certain reluctance scrambled back the
way we had come.

"I am honoured to be in the company of one so holy,"
said the hermit.

"But you are quite as holy as I," I said.

"No, sir, you are far holier than myself. It stands to
reason. How you must have suffered to have attained your
present state of grace!"

"Oh, no, Sir Hermit, I am sure that your sufferings
outstrip mine a hundredfold."

"I cannot believe that. But look!" He held up an arm.
There was movement in the arm which was not muscle or
bone. I peered hard at it.

"What must I see?" I asked.

"My friends, Sir Knight. The creatures I love more than I
love myself."

The main stink, I now realised, was coming from the arm
he displayed. And as my eyes grew accustomed to the gloom I
could see that his limb writhed with maggots. They were
feeding off him. He smiled at them, much as he had smiled at
me. He doubtless regarded them with more affection than he
felt for any human being. After all, these were actively aiding
him in his martyrdom.

I am a man used to disguising my disgust, but it took a
considerable effort of will not to turn away from that madman
there and then.

"Such pious suffering is outstanding," I said. I straightened and looked towards the cave-mouth, yearning for the
clean air and the snow.

"You are very kind, Sir Knight." With a sigh he fell back
into the general filth.

The thought of putting food into the mouth of this wretch
so that he might feed his maggots was obnoxious to me, but
the unwitting child deserved to eat. Sedenko reappeared and
I went towards him, taking the bread he gave me and handing
it to the girl. She immediately broke off the largest piece and
took it to her master. As she crumbled the bread and placed it

between his lips he chewed with a kind of eager control, the saliva running down his grimy chin and into his beard.

For a moment or two I stepped outside, barely able to quell my nausea.

Sedenko murmured: "That girl is wasted here. The old beast will be dead in a few more days at the most."

I agreed with him. "When he has finished eating I'll ask him what he knows of Groot, then we'll be on our way."

"There are holy men of his kind in many parts of my country," Sedenko said, "thinking that dirt and humiliation of the flesh bring them closer to God. But what can God want with them?"

"Perhaps He desires that we should all follow this hermit's example. Perhaps it satisfies God to see His Creations denying all the virtues they believe He has instilled?"

Sedenko muttered at me: "Heresy, captain. Or close enough." He did not like my tone, which I am sure contained more than a little mockery. I was in a darkly embittered mood.

I moved back into the cave. "Tell me, Sir Hermit, if you have heard of one of your kind. A certain Philander Groot."

"Of course I have heard of Groot. He dwells in the Valley of the Golden Cloud on the other side of these mountains. But he is not a holy man, though he may claim to be. Why, I have heard that he even denies God. He does not mortify his flesh. He is said to bathe very frequently, at least ten times in the year. His clothing . . ." The creature began to cough. "Well, suffice to say that he is not of our persuasion, though I am sure," added the hermit with some effort, "that he has his reasons for choosing his particular path and it is not for us to say who is wrong or who is right." Again that smile of exquisite and self-congratulatory piety.

"He has no maggots, I take it," said I.

"Not one," said the hermit. "So far as I know, Sir Knight. But I could be condemning him without cause. I have only heard of Philander Groot. There were once many other hermits living in these caves. I am the last. But they used to tell me of Groot."

"Thank you," I said with as much courtesy as I could muster. I looked from the hermit to the girl. "And what will become of your protégée when you finally attain Heaven, Sir Hermit?"

He smiled upon her. "She will be rewarded."

"You think she will survive this winter?"

The hermit frowned. "Probably not, of course, if I do not. She will rise up to Heaven with me, perhaps. She is, after all, yet a virgin."

"Her virginity will be sufficient passport?"

"That and the fact that she has served me so loyally all these years. I have taught her everything I know. When she came to me she was ignorant. But I have taught her of Sin and of Paradise. I have taught her of the Fall of Lucifer and how our parents were driven out of Eden. I have taught her of the Ten Commandments. I have told her of Christ's birth, suffering, death and resurrection and I have taught her of the Day of Judgement. For a woman, she has been blessed with more than is usual, you will agree."

"Indeed," I said, "she is a singularly fortunate young person. What else do you think she will inherit from you?"

"I have nothing," he said proudly, "but what you see."

"Shall you leave her your maggots?"

For the first time, now, he caught my irony. He frowned, lost for an answer.

I grew impatient with him. "Well, Sir Hermit, what's your answer?"

"You jest with me," he said. "I cannot believe . . ."

"I think it is time you received your reward," I told him, and I drew my sword. "It is not just that you should wait any longer."

The girl gasped. She ran forward, guessing my intention. I pushed her back with my free hand, shouting out for Sedenko's assistance. I advanced upon the hermit.

Sedenko appeared beside me, grinning. Plainly, he approved of my intention. He seized the girl in both arms and bore her from the cave as I raised my blade.

"Go with my friend, girl. There is no need for you to witness this."

"Kill me, too," she said.

"That would be unseemly," said I. "Should you die, too, it would be a veritable surfeit of sacrifice. I doubt if God Himself could contemplate so much at once. But if you wish to sacrifice something, do not make it your soul. I am sure that Sedenko here can think of some pleasurable alternative."

She had begun to sob as I turned my back on them and looked down on the holy man. He showed no fear.

He said: "You must do what you have to, brother. It is God's work."

"What?" I said. "Shall you and I take no responsibility at all for your murder?"

"It is God's work," he repeated.

I smiled. "Lucifer's my Master." I found his heart with my steel and began to push slowly. "And I suspect that He is yours, also."

The hermit died with only the smallest groan. I walked out of the cave. Sedenko was already carrying the girl down. He was grinning at her and saying something in his own language.

That night, while I tried to sleep, Sedenko took his pleasure with the girl. She became noisy at one point, but then grew quiet. In the morning she was gone.

"I think she will try to get to Ammendorf," he said.

I was not in a talkative mood.

For the next few days we travelled through the mountains while Sedenko sang all his songs several times over and I contemplated the mysteries of an existence I had come increasingly to consider arbitrary at best.

Chapter IX

I HAD FALLEN into the habit of deriving a kind of joy from the irony of my position, from the paradoxes and contrasts of my Quest. It led me to contemplate the most horrible crimes which could be committed by me in the name of the Grail Search. Was I strong enough, I wondered, to commit them? What kind of self-discipline was involved in forcing oneself, against one's own nature, towards vice? My inner debates became increasingly complex and unreal, but perhaps they served to take my mind off unwelcome actualities.

A hard week saw us through the heart of the mountains. We had experienced landslides, a couple of poorly organised attacks from local brigands, two or three near-falls on the higher passes and, of course, the ordinary vicissitudes of the climate. Sedenko's spirits had not declined a jot and my own gloom had begun to lift when we halted our horses on a high promontory and looked down into what we assumed must be our destination.

All we could see was glowing, golden mist, filling the wide basin of a valley, whose cliffs were snow-capped and whose sides were almost sheer.

"There's where Philander Groot dwells, captain," said Sedenko, leaning on his pommel, "but how do we reach it?"

"We must keep looking," I said, "until we find the way in. It must surely exist, if Groot has come and gone from there."

We began, by means of a narrow trail, to descend. There would be about four hours left until twilight, when we should of necessity camp. These mountains were too dangerous for night travelling.

The first intimation we had of the valley's guardians was a whistling in the air. When we looked back and up towards the clear blue of the sky we saw two of them, sharply outlined. Their intentions were clear. They meant to kill us.

I had never seen eagles so huge or so resplendent. Their bodies were pretty near as big as those of a small pony and their wings were, each one, about twice the length of their main bulk. They were predominantly white and gold and scarlet, with a certain amount of deep blue around the heads. The beaks shone like grey steel and were matched in appearance by their wide-stretched claws. As they came down on us, they shrieked their intention, celebrating their anticipated triumph.

Our horses began to rear and cry out. I pulled one pistol free, cocked it, aimed and fired. The ball struck the first eagle in the shoulder and it veered off silently, blood streaming from the wound. Sedenko's sabre cut at the second and caused it to stay its attack, fluttering over his head and making such a wind as to threaten to blow us down into the valley. My other pistol was produced and fired. This was a better shot, to the head. With a terrible wail the eagle tried to regain height, failed and fell heavily into the chasm. I watched its body pass through the mist and vanish. Its companion (perhaps its mate) sailed over the spot for some little while before its attention returned to us and, glaring and screaming, it resumed its attack. I had no time to reload. We had only our swords, now, for defence. The creature dived and snatched and, had not Sedenko ducked his head, the young Kazak would have been carried off for certain. As it was his sabre sliced several tail-feathers from the gigantic bird. These Sedenko grabbed from the air and brandished with a grin as a prize.

The bird came to me next. Those claws could easily impale me as readily as any pike. My horse was bucking and trying to flee and half my attention was on him, but I struck back with my sword and drew blood, though nothing worth the trouble.

The eagle was flying erratically, thanks to its wounded shoulder and lack of tail-feathers. Sedenko got in another blow which removed the better part of one claw and now the bird was weakening, though it had no thought of giving up its attack.

With every fresh dive it was driven off, having sustained another small wound or two.

And that was how we fought it. Slowly but surely we cut the great creature to pieces until all of its lower body and limbs, its neck and head, were a mass of blood and ruined feathers.

On the bird's final attack, Sedenko leapt onto his saddle and, standing on tiptoe, sliced so that a wing-joint was severed. The eagle fell to one side in the air, desperately trying to regain its balance, then smashed down into the snow which immediately became flecked with blood and feathers of white, gold and scarlet. It screamed in outrage at what we had done to it and neither of us had the stomach to watch it die or the courage to descend the slope and put it out of its misery. We looked at it in silence for a few minutes before sheathing our blades and riding on. Neither of us believed that we had won any kind of honourable victory.

Slowly the trail led down through the glowing, golden mist, until we could hardly see a couple of feet on any side. Again we dismounted and went with considerable caution, until night fell and we were forced to find a relatively flat stretch of ground where we might tether our horses and camp until morning.

Before he slept, Sedenko said: "Those birds were supernatural creatures, eh, captain?"

"I have never heard of natural creatures like them," I said. "I am certain of that, Sedenko."

"They were the servants of this magus we seek," he said. "Which means that we have offended him by killing his servants . . ."

"We do not know that they serve him or that he will be angry at our saving our own lives by killing them."

"I am afraid of this magus, captain," said Sedenko simply. "For it is well-known that the greatest sorcerer is the one who can command the spirits of the air. And what were those eagles but air-spirits?"

"They were large," I said, "and they were dangerous. But for all we know they saw us merely as prey. As food for their young. There can be few travellers in these parts, particularly during the winter months. And little large game, either, I would guess. Do not speculate, Sedenko, on things for which no evidence exists. You will waste your time. Particularly, I would guess, in Mittelmarch."

Sedenko took this to mean that he should be silent. He closed his lips, but it was obvious he had not ceased to consider the matter of the eagles.

We continued our journey in the morning and noted that the air grew gradually warmer, while the golden mist became thinner, until at last we emerged onto a broad mountain trail which wound down into a valley of astonishing beauty and which was completely without snow. Indeed, it might have been early summer in that valley. We saw crops growing in fields; we saw well-ordered villages and, to the east, a large-sized town built on two sides of a wide and pleasant river. It was almost impossible for either Sedenko or myself to realise that all around us lay stark crags and thick snow.

"We have gone from spring into winter in a single stride," said Sedenko wonderingly, "and now we are in summer. Are we sleeping, like the old man of the legend, through whole parts of the year, captain? Are we entranced without realising it? Or is this valley the product of sorcery?"

"If it be sorcery, it's of an exceedingly pleasing kind," I told my friend. I took off my cloak and rolled it up behind me.

"No wonder they guard this place with gigantic eagles." Sedenko peered down. He saw herds of sheep and cattle: a land of plenty. "This would be a place to settle, eh, captain? From here it would be possible to ride up into the snow when one wished, to sally out on raids . . ." He paused as he contemplated his own version of Paradise.

"What would we steal on the raids?" I asked him good-humouredly, "when all that we should need is here already?"

"Well"—he shrugged—"a man has to raid. Or do something."

I looked up. The golden mist stretched from end to end of the valley, giving it its name. I could not understand what caused this phenomenon, but I believed it to be natural. Somehow the cold, the snow, did not touch the valley. I had

known well-protected places in my time, which were harmed
less by the seasons than most, but I had never witnessed the
likes of this.

We rode down slowly and it took us well over an hour
before we had neared the bottom. Here, on the trail ahead of
us, we saw a great gate, impossible to pass, and before the
gate a mounted sentinel, standing foursquare on a giant
charger, dressed in all the warlike regalia of two or three
centuries since, with plate armour and crests and plumes and
polished iron and oiled leather, in colours predominantly
gold, white and scarlet, bearing a device of just such an eagle
as we had fought above.

From within the closed helm a voice called out:

"Stop, strangers!"

We drew rein. Sedenko had become cautious again and I
knew he was wondering if this being, too, were of supernatural origin.

"I am Ulrich von Bek," I said. "I am on the Grail Quest
and I seek a wise man who dwells in this valley."

The guardian seemed to laugh at this. "You are in need
of a wise man, stranger. For if you seek the Grail you are a
fool."

"You know of the Grail?" Sedenko was suddenly curious.

"Who does not? We know of many things in the Valley of
the Golden Cloud, for this is a land which is sought by those
who dream of Eden. We are used to legends here, stranger,
since we are ourselves a legend."

"A legend and you exist. So might the Grail exist," I
said.

"One does not prove the other." The guardian shifted a
little in his saddle. "You are the men who killed our eagle, are
you not?"

"We were attacked!" Sedenko became defensive. "We
protected our own lives . . ."

"It is not a crime to kill an eagle," said the guardian
evenly. "We of the Valley of the Golden Cloud do not impose
our own laws on strangers. We merely ask that strangers do
not bring their specific ideas of justice to us. But once you
have passed this gateway, you must agree to obey our laws
until you leave again."

"Naturally, we would agree," I said.

"Our laws are simple: Steal Nothing, whether it be an

abstract idea or another life. Examine Everything. Pay a Fair Price. And, remember, to lie is to steal another soul's freedom of action, or some fragment of it. Here a liar and a thief are the same thing."

"Your laws sound excellent," I said. "Indeed, they sound ideal."

"And simple," said Sedenko feelingly.

"They are simple," said the guardian, "but they sometimes require complex interpretation."

"And what are the penalties for breaking your laws?" asked Sedenko.

The guardian said: "We have only two punishments here: Expulsion and Death. To some, they are the same."

"We will remember all you have said," I told him. "We seek Philander Groot, the hermit. Do you know where we might find him?"

"I do not know. Only the Queen knows."

"She is the ruler of this land?" asked Sedenko.

"She is its embodiment," said the guardian. "She dwells in the city. Go there now."

He moved his horse aside and made a sign so that the iron portcullis might be lifted by unseen hands within the towers.

As we passed through, I thanked him for his courtesy, but such was my state of mind that I determined to look carefully about me. It had been many years since I had been able to believe in absolute justice, and some weeks since I had been able to believe that there existed in the world (or beyond it) justice of any kind.

The air was sweet as we followed a road of well-trodden yellow earth through fields of green wheat towards the distant city, whose towers and turrets were predominantly white, reflecting the gold of the mist above us.

"A noble creature, that guard," said Sedenko, in some admiration, looking about him.

"Or a self-righteous one," I said.

"One must at least believe in Perfection"—he had become serious—"or one cannot believe in the promise of Heaven."

"True," said I to that poor damned youth.

Chapter X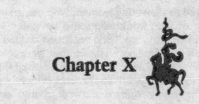

THE GUARDS AT the city gates were clad in the same antiquated regalia as the first guard we had encountered. They did not challenge us as we entered the wide streets to discover a well-ordered collection of houses and public buildings, a cheerful and dignified population and an active market. Since we had been ordered to present ourselves to the Queen of this land, we continued on our way until we reached the palace: a relatively low building of extreme beauty, with sweeping curves and pinnacles, bright stained glass and a general air of tranquillity.

Trumpets announced our coming as we passed under the archway into a wide courtyard decorated with all manner of shrubs and flowers. The unpretentiousness of the palace, its atmosphere, reminded me somehow of my boyhood in Bek. My father's manor had possessed just such a mood.

Ostlers came forward to take our horses and a woman in skirt and wimple of olden times emerged from the doorway to beckon us. She was an exceptionally lovely young female, with large blue eyes and an open, healthy face. She looked like the better type of nun.

"Greetings to you," she said. "The Queen expects you.

Would you wish to refresh yourselves, to bathe, perhaps, before you are presented?"

I looked at Sedenko. If I was half as filthy and as unshaven as he, I felt I would be happier for a bath and a chance to change my clothes.

Sedenko said: "We have been travelling through snow, lady. We hardly need to wash ourselves. See? Nature's done that for us."

I bowed to the young woman. "We are grateful to you," I said. "I, for one, would like some hot water."

"It will be provided." She beckoned and led the way into the palace's cool interior. The ceilings were low and decorated with murals, as were the walls. We passed through a kind of cloisters and here were apartments evidently prepared for guests. The young woman showed us into one of these. Heated water had already been poured into two large wooden tubs in the centre of the main room.

Sedenko sniffed the air, as if he saw sorcery in the steam.

I thanked the young woman, who smiled at me and said: "I will return in an hour to escort you to the Queen."

Refreshed, I was ready and dressed in my change of clothes when she came back. Sedenko had no change of clothes and had scarcely let the water touch his skin, but even he had deigned to shave his face, save for his moustache. He looked considerably more personable than when he had arrived.

Again we followed the young woman through a variety of corridors, cloisters and gardens, until we were led into a large-sized room with a high ceiling on which was painted a representation of the sun, the stars and the moon, what is sometimes called, I believe, a Solar Atlas.

There on a throne of green glass and carved mahogany sat a girl of perhaps fifteen years. Since she wore a crystal-and-diamond crown upon her dark red hair we naturally bowed and murmured what we hoped were the appropriate greetings.

The girl smiled sweetly. She had large brown eyes and red lips. "You are welcome to our land, strangers. I am Queen Xiombarg the Twenty-fifth and I am curious to know why you braved the eagles to visit us. You were not drawn here, as are some adventurers, by legends of gold and magic, I am sure."

Sedenko became alert. "Treasure?" he said, before he thought. Then he blushed. "Oh, no, madam."

"I am upon the Grail Search," I told the young Queen. "I seek a hermit by the name of Philander Groot and believe that Your Majesty knows where I could find him."

"I am trusted with that knowledge," she said. "But I am sworn never to reveal it. What help can Herr Groot provide?"

"I do not know. I was told to seek him out and tell him my story."

"Is your story an unusual one?"

"Many would believe it more than unusual, Your Majesty."

"And you will not tell it to me?"

"I have told it to no one. I will tell it to Philander Groot because he might be able to help me."

She nodded. "You'll trade him secret for secret, eh?"

"It seems so."

"He will be amused by that."

I inclined my head.

Sedenko burst out: "It's God's work he's on, Your Majesty. If he finds the Grail . . ."

I tried to interrupt him, but she raised her hand. "We are not to be persuaded or dissuaded, sir. Here we believe neither in Heaven nor in Hell. We worship no gods or devils. We believe only in moderation."

I could not disguise my scepticism and she was quick to notice.

She smiled. "We are satisfied with this state of things. Reason is not subsumed by sentiment here. The two are balanced."

"I have always found balance a nostalgic dream, Your Majesty. In reality it can be very dull."

She was not dismayed. "Oh, we amuse ourselves adequately, captain. We have music, painting, plays . . ."

"Surely such ideas of moderation require no true struggle. Thus they defeat human aspiration. What greatness have these arts of yours? How noble are they? What heights of feeling and intellect do they reach?"

"We live in the world," she replied quietly. "We do not ignore how it is. We send our young people out of the valley when they are eighteen. There they learn of human misery, of pain and of those who triumph over them. They bring their experience back. Here, in tranquillity, it is considered and forms the basis of our philosophy."

"You are fortunate," I said with some bitterness.

"We are."

"So justice requires good luck before it can exist?"

"Probably, captain."

"Yet you seek out experience. You tell your young people to search for danger. That is not the same as being subjected to it, willy-nilly."

"No, indeed. But it is better than not searching for it at all."

"It seems to me, madam, that you yet possess the complacency of the privileged. What if your land were to be attacked?"

"No army can reach us without our knowing of it."

"No army can march by land, perhaps. But what, for instance, if your enemies trained those eagles to come through the Golden Cloud carrying soldiers?"

"That is inconceivable," she said with a laugh.

"To those who live with danger and have no choice," I said, "nothing is inconceivable."

She shrugged. "Well, we are satisfied."

"And I am glad that you are, madam."

"You are a stimulating guest, captain. Will you stay at our Court for a few days?"

"I regret that I must find Philander Groot if I can, as soon as I can. My commission has some urgency to it."

"Very well. Take the West Road from the city. It will lead you to a wood. In the wood is a wide glade, with a dead oak in it. Philander Groot, if he pleases, will find you there."

"At what time?"

"He will choose the time. You will have to be patient. Now, captain, at least you will eat with us and tell us something of your adventures."

Sedenko and I accepted the invitation. The dinner was superb. We filled ourselves to capacity, spent the night in good beds and in the morning went by the West Road from the young Queen's town.

The wood was easily reached and the glade found without difficulty. We made a camp there and settled down to wait for Groot. The air was warm and lazy and the flowers softened our tempers with their beauty and their scents.

"This is a place to come home to when you are old," said Sedenko as he stretched himself on the ground and stared around at the great trees. "But I'd guess it's no place to be young in. No fighting, precious little hunting . . ."

"The lack of conflict could bore anyone under forty," I agreed. "I cannot quite get to the root of my irritation with this place. Perhaps there is a touch too much sanity here. If it is sanity, of course. My instincts tell me that this kind of life is in itself insane in some ways."

"Too profound for me, captain," said Sedenko. "They're rich. They're safe. They're happy. Isn't that what we all want for ourselves in the end?"

"A healthy animal," I said, "needs to exercise its body and its wits to the full."

"But not all the time, captain." Sedenko looked alarmed, as if I was about to expect some action from him.

I laughed. "Not all the time, young Kazak."

After three days of waiting in the glade neither of us was so willing to rest. We had explored every part of the surrounding country, its rivers, its meadows, its woods. We had picked flowers and plaited them. We had groomed our horses. We had swum. Sedenko had climbed every tree which could be climbed and I had studied, without much under-standing, the grimoires Sabrina had given me. I had also studied all the maps and had seen that Mittelmarch territories seemed to exist in gaps between lands where, in my own world, no gaps were.

By the time the fifth morning dawned I was ready to mount my horse and leave the Valley of the Golden Cloud. "I'll find my way to the Grail without Groot's help," I said.

And these words, almost magically, seemed to conjure up the dandy who sauntered into our camp, looking around him a little fastidiously but with the good humour of self-mockery. He was all festooned lace and velvet, gold and silver buckles and embroidery. He walked with the aid of a monstrous decorated pole and he stank of Hungary Water. His hat had a huge brim weighted down with white and silver feathers and his little beard and moustache were trimmed to the perfection demanded of the most foppish French courtier. His sword, of delicate workmanship, seemed of no use to him at all as he stared at me with a quizzical eye and then made one of those elaborate bows which I have never been able to imitate.

"Good morrow to thee, gentlemen," lisped the dandy. "I am enchanted to make your acquaintance."

"We're not here to pass the time of day with men dressed as women," said Sedenko, scowling. "We await the coming of a great sage, a hermit of the wisest disposition."

"Aha, forgive me. I will not keep you long, in that case. Pray, what are your names, sirs?"

"I am Ulrich von Bek, Captain of Infantry, and this is my companion Grigory Petrovitch Sedenko, swordsman. And yours, sir?"

"My name, sir, is Philander Groot."

"The hermit?" cried Sedenko in astonishment.

"I am a hermit, sir, yes."

"You don't look like a hermit." Sedenko put his hand on the hilt of his sabre and strode forward to inspect the apparition.

"Sir, I assure you that I am, indeed, a hermit." Groot became polite. He was distant.

"We heard you were a holy man," Sedenko continued.

"I cannot be held responsible for what others hear or say, sir." Groot drew himself up. He was somewhat shorter than Sedenko, who was no giant. "I am the same Philander Groot for whom you were looking. Take me or leave me, sir. This is all there is."

"We had not thought to find a dandy," said I, by way of apologising for Sedenko's frankness. "We imagined someone in homespun cloth. The usual sort of garb."

"It is not my way to fulfill the expectation of my fellow creatures. I am Groot. Groot is who I am."

"But why a dandy?" Sedenko sighed and turned away from us.

"There are many ways of keeping one's distance from the world," said Groot to me.

"And many others to keep the world at a distance from oneself," I added.

"You appreciate my drift, Sir Knight. Self-knowledge, however, is not self-salvation. You and I have a fair way to go in that direction, I think. You through action and I, coward that I am, through contemplation."

"I believe that I lack the courage for profound self-examination, Master Groot," said I.

He was amused. "Well, what a fine man we should be, if

we were combined into one! And how self-important, then, we could become!"

"I was told, Master Groot, that you might wish to hear my story and, that once you had heard it, you might wish to give me a clue or two to the solution of my problem."

"I am curious," admitted this gamecock philosopher, "and will be glad to pay for entertainment with information. You must rely on me, however, to set the price. Does that go against your wishes?"

"Not at all."

"Then, come, we shall take a walk together in the forest."

Sedenko looked back. "Careful, captain. It could be a trap."

"Grigory Petrovitch," I said, "if Master Groot had wished to ambush us, he could have done so at any time, surely."

Sedenko pushed his sheepskin cap high on his head and grumbled something before kicking violently at a clump of flowers.

Philander Groot linked his elegant arm in mine and we began to walk until we reached the stream. At its banks we paused.

"You must begin, sir," he said.

I told him where I was born and how I had come to be a warrior. I told him of Magdeburg and what followed. I told him of Sabrina. I told him of my meeting with Lucifer and of my journey to Hell. I told him of the bargain, of Lucifer's expectations. I told him what it was I sought—or rather what I thought it was.

We walked along the bank of the stream as I spoke and he nodded, murmured his understanding and very occasionally asked for clarification. He seemed delighted by what I had to say, and when I had finished he tugged at my arm and we stopped again. He removed his plumed hat and stroked at his carefully made curls. He fingered his little beard. He smiled and looked at the water. He brought his attention back to me.

"The Grail exists," he said. "And you are sensible to call it that because it frequently takes the form of a cup."

"You have seen it?" I asked.

"I believe I have seen it, on my travels, sir. When I travelled."

"So the legend of the Pure Knight deceives us?"

"It depends somewhat upon your definition of purity, I think," said Groot. "But suffice to say the thing is useless in the hands of one who would do evil with it. And as to the definition of evil, we can accept the crude, commonplace definition well enough here, I think. A certain amount of altruism exists in all of us and if properly maintained and mixed with appropriate self-interest, it can produce a happy man who gives offence neither to Heaven nor to Hell."

"I have heard that you refuse loyalty to either God or the Devil," I said.

"That's true. I doubt if I shall ever choose sides. My investigations and my philosophy do not lead me in their direction at all." He shrugged. "But who knows? I am yet a relatively young man . . ."

"You accept their existence, however?"

"Why, sir, you confirm it!"

"You believe that I have been the guest of Lucifer, that I am now His servant?"

"I must accept it, sir."

"And you will help me?"

"As much as I can. The Grail can be found, I believe, in a place known as the Forest at the Edge of Heaven. You will discover it, I am sure, marked on your charts. It lies on the farthest border of Mittelmarch. You must find it in the west."

"And are there any rituals I must follow?" I asked Philander Groot. "I seem to recall . . ."

"Ritual is the truth made into a child's game, at best. You will know what is for the best, I am sure."

"You can give me no more advice?"

"It would be against all I believe should I do so. No, Sir Knight, I have told you enough. The Grail exists. You will find it, almost certainly, where I said it can be found. What more could you need?"

I smiled in self-mockery. "Reassurance, I suppose."

"That must come from your own judgement, from your own testing of your conscience. It is the only kind of reassurance worth having, as I am sure you would agree."

"I agree, of course."

We were now walking back towards the glade. Groot mused. "I wonder if any object can cure the World of its Pain. It must be more than that. Would you say that your Master is desperate, captain?"

"His layers of defiance and rationalisation seem to fall away," I told the hermit, "to reveal little else but desperation. But can an angel fall so low in spirit?"

"There are entire monasteries, vast schools, debating such issues." Groot laughed. "I would not dare to speculate, Sir Knight. The Nature of Angels is not a branch of philosophy which captures my imagination much. Lucifer, I would say, cannot actually deceive an omniscient God, so therefore God must already know that the Grail is sought. If Lucifer has another purpose than the one He has told you, then God already knows it and continues, to some degree at least, to permit your Quest. This is the sort of talk which idle scholars prefer. But it is not for me."

"Nor for me," I said. "If I find the Grail and redeem my soul, that will be enough. I can only pray that Lucifer keeps His bargain."

"To whom do you pray?" asked Groot, with another smile. The question was rhetorical. He shook his hand to show that he was not serious.

"You seem an unusual subject of Queen Xiombarg," I said. "Or perhaps I misjudge her and this land."

"You probably misjudge the Queen and her country," he said, "but whether you do or you don't I can assure you that in all of Mittelmarch there is no more tranquil a valley, and tranquillity, at present, is what I seek above anything else, at this stage of my life."

"And do you understand the nature of Mittelmarch?" I asked him.

He shrugged. "I do not. All I know is that Mittelmarch could not survive without the rest of the world—but the rest of the world can survive without Mittelmarch. And that, I suspect, is what its denizens fear in you, if they fear anything at all."

"You are not, then, from Mittelmarch originally?"

"I am from Alsatia. Few who dwell here were born here. This valley and one or two other places are exceptions. Some exist here as shadows. Some exist as shadows in your world. It is very puzzling, captain. I am not brave enough to look at the problem with a steady eye. Not as yet. I have a feeling that if I did, I should die. Now, you will be wanting to be gone from the Valley of the Golden Cloud, eh? And on your way. I will escort you to the Western Gate. A trail will lead you through the mountains and onto a good road out of Mittelmarch."

"How shall I know which road it is?"

"There are not many roads in these parts, captain."

We had returned to the glade where a frowning Sedenko awaited us. "I believed you murdered or kidnapped, Captain von Bek."

I felt almost lighthearted. "Nonsense, Grigory Petrovitch! Master Groot has been of considerable help to me."

Sedenko sniffed at the strong odour of Hungary Water. "You trust him?"

"As much as I can trust myself."

Groot beckoned. "Pack your goods, gentlemen. I will walk with you to the Western Gate."

When we were ready to ride, the little dandy removed a lacy kerchief from his sleeve and mopped his brow beneath his hat. "The day grows warm," he said. With his tall cane held at a graceful angle, he began to stroll back to the road. "Come, my friends. You'll be out of here by nightfall if we hurry."

We walked our horses in Groot's wake as he moved rapidly along, more like a dancing master than anything else, humming to himself and commenting on the beauties of the fields and cottages we passed on our way, until at length we reached the far side of the valley and a gatehouse very similar to that by which we had entered. Here, Groot hailed the guard.

"Friends are leaving," he said. "Let them pass."

The guard, in the same livery as we had seen before, moved his horse aside and the portcullis was raised. At the gate Philander Groot paused, looking out at the trail, which wound up and up until it reached the golden mist. His expression was hard to read. I thought for a moment his eyes were those of a prisoner or an exile yearning to go home, but when he turned his face to me he had the same controlled, amused expression. "Here we are, captain. I will wish you good luck and good judgement on your Quest. It would be pleasing if we could meet again, in the fullness of time. I shall follow your adventure, as best I can, from here. And I shall follow it with interest."

"Why not come with us?" I said impulsively. "We should be encouraged by your company and I for one would be glad of your conversation."

"It is tempting, captain. I say that with all sincerity. But it is my decision to remain here for a while and so remain I shall. But know that I go with you in spirit."

A final elaborate bow, a wave, and Philander Groot was stepping backwards to let us ride through the gate. The portcullis closed behind us. A scented kerchief fluttered.

Soon we were engulfed again in golden mist and once more resorted to our cloaks as the weather grew colder.

By the time we were out of the mist, night had come and we camped upon the trail, there being no other suitable place. By morning we were able to look down at the far foothills of the mountains and know that very soon we should be on level ground again. We had not gone more than half an hour along our way before we heard the pounding of hooves and, looking back, observed some twenty armoured men coming up at a gallop.

Their leader was not armoured. I saw black and white. I saw a purple plume. I recognised Sedenko's former master and my sworn enemy, the warrior-priest Klosterheim.

We spurred our horses forward, hoping to outrun the armoured pack. There was something mysterious about them. Their armour glowed. Indeed, it seemed to burn, though only with black fire. Wisps of mist escaped the helms, and the mist was a terrible grey colour, as if the lungs which breathed it were in some way polluted.

"What can the Knight of Christ be doing with that company?" Sedenko gasped to me. "If ever creatures bore the stamp of Hell it is they. How can they be serving God's Purpose?"

I wanted to retort that if I served the Devil's then perhaps they could serve God's, but I bit back the comment and concentrated on doing my best to control my horse's descent of the trail. His hooves were slipping and twice he almost went over—once where a chasm loomed.

"We shall perish if we maintain this speed!" I said. "Yet Klosterheim means us harm for certain. And we cannot hope to defeat armoured knights."

We sought escape. There was none. We could go forward, or we could stand and wait for Klosterheim's devilish troop. As the trail widened I spied ahead that it entered a cleft in the rock, hardly space enough for one man to pass. It would be there, if anywhere, we could defend ourselves. I pointed, pulling at my reins. My horse reared. Sedenko saw my meaning and nodded. He dashed past me into the cleft, then turned his horse cautiously, inch by inch. I threw him one of my pistols and a pouch of shot and powder, backing my own horse round. With the cleft on both sides of us we could command our front without risk of attack from any other quarter.

Klosterheim scarcely realised what we had done as he raced forward. I aimed my pistol at him, drew back the hammer and then discharged. The shot went wide of him, but it served to halt him of a sudden. He shouted, glared, shortened his rein and held up a stilling hand to his pack. They stopped with unnatural discipline.

"Klosterheim," I called, "what do you want with us?"

"I want nothing from Sedenko, who can continue on his way without fear," said the thin-faced priest. "But it is your life I want, von Bek, and nothing less."

"Can I have given you so much offence?"

It was then that I realised we were still in Mittelmarch. I began to chuckle. "Oh, Klosterheim, what terrible things you have done in God's name! Were our Master still the creature He was, He would be more than pleased with you. You are as damned as the rest of us! And you are one of those who fears that my Quest shall bring an end to everything, that you will have no home, no master, no future, no identity. Is that why you fear me so, Klosterheim?"

Johannes Klosterheim almost growled in reply. His eyes darted from side to side of the trail. He looked upwards. He was seeking a means of outflanking us. There was none. "You reckon without my power," he said. "That has not been taken from me. Arioch!"

He cried the name of one of Lucifer's Dukes, perhaps his patron. He moved his hand as if he flung an invisible ball at the cliff. Something cracked high overhead. It might have been lightning. A disgusting smell came into my nostrils.

"Try the pistol, Sedenko," I murmured.

The gun boomed from behind me and I felt its flash. The ball went wide of Klosterheim, and I heard it strike a glowing black breastplate and then bounce against a rock.

"Arioch!"

Again the lightning and I glimpsed a huge piece of rock as it fell away from the outer wall of the crevice and dropped hundreds of feet into the chasm on the other side.

"You are a powerful magus, Klosterheim," said I. "And one wonders why you posed for so long as a holy priest."

"I am holy," said Klosterheim through his teeth. "My cause is the noblest there has ever been. I leagued myself with Lucifer to destroy God! I have been about the world showing, in the name of God, what horrors can exist. There was no cause nobler than Lucifer's—and now He seeks to capitulate, to abandon us, to let Hell and all it stands for be swept away. As Lucifer defied God, so it is my right to defy Lucifer. We are threatened with betrayal. He is my Master, von Bek, as well as yours. And I have served Him well!"

"But you do not serve Him now. He will be angered with you."

"What of it? He has no allies worth the name. His own Dukes are against Him. What will happen to them if God takes Him back?"

"Is Hell in rebellion?" I said in surprise.

"So it could be said. Lucifer loses authority by the hour. Your Master is weaker now, von Bek, than even the simpering Christ who first betrayed humanity! And I will not tolerate weakness! Arioch!"

Another crack of lightning. The burning black helms looked up as if in appreciation. Fragments of rock began to fall down on Sedenko and myself. "Ride fast, Sedenko," I cried. "Away from here. It is our only hope."

Sedenko hesitated. I insisted. "Ride! It is a command!"

From overhead the slabs of granite began to groan, and snow poured down the sides of the crevice until I thought I would be buried.

"Now you are alone, von Bek," said Klosterheim with relish. "I owe you much and would like to repay it slowly. But I'll be satisfied with taking your life and returning your failed soul to our Master."

"You deny that He is your Master," I reminded the warrior-priest. "And yet you know that He is. He will punish you, surely, Johannes Klosterheim. You cannot escape Him."

"Then why should Lord Arioch lend me twenty of his knights?" said Klosterheim with a sneer. "There is Civil War in Hell, Captain von Bek. You shall be a victim of that War, not I."

He cried out the name of his patron again. Again lightning cracked.

I did not wait, but turned my horse about and galloped along the crevice in Sedenko's wake, as rock tumbled down from above. I recalled something I had read in one of the grimoires and as I rode I leant into my saddlebag to find the book. I came out onto a clear part of the trail. The foothills were less than half an hour's ride ahead. There we should have more of a chance of escaping Klosterheim's hellish force.

I looked back.

The knights in their fiery black armour were riding their black horses over the rubble. I glimpsed a purple plume. I sensed that my own horse was weakening, that before long he must turn a leg and throw me. I reined him in and shortened his stride. He was panting. I could feel his heart thumping against my leg. I found the grimoire, took my reins in my teeth and sought the page I remembered. Here, in cramped letters, I discovered what I needed: *Words of Power Against the Servants of Duke Arioch.* Had Lucifer anticipated the treachery of His Dukes? The words themselves were meaningless to me but I brought my horse about, knowing I possessed no other weapon against the knights.

I cried out: *"Rehoim Farach Nyadah!"* in as loud a voice as I could muster.

I saw the knights begin to slow their pace, only to be urged on by a yelling Klosterheim.

"Rehoim Farach Nyadah! Gushnyet Maradai Karag!"

The knights drew up suddenly. Klosterheim emerged from the press, still galloping. He was glaring at me, his blade in his hand, and I dropped the grimoire back into the saddlebag as I drew my own sword, just in time to meet a fierce and accurate blow which, had it landed, would have removed my arm.

I thrust, was parried and blocked Klosterheim's retaliation. I saw that the knights were beginning to stir. They seemed confused.

Klosterheim was snarling like a beast as he fought. His very hatred might have been enough to destroy me. He struck and struck again. I defended myself. Then I heard hoofbeats behind me and Sedenko was riding up to my aid. A pistol exploded. Klosterheim's horse shouted and went down. The knights were beginning to move forward. Klosterheim struggled to his feet, his sword still in his hand. He ran at me, mindless with fury.

"Best leave now, captain," called Sedenko.

I took his advice. Even as we fled down the trail I saw Klosterheim stumbling towards Arioch's soldiers and pushing one of them from his steed so that he collapsed in a heap of blazing black metal.

We reached relatively flat ground at about the same time the sun came out and made the snow glitter. We heard Klosterheim and his men behind us. The sun grew warmer and warmer, threatening to melt the snow, by the time we dared to look back and see that they were almost upon us. I tried to recall the exact words I had used from the grimoire and I shouted them. But our pursuers did not this time stop.

Even as they gained on us the riders in black armour spread out in a widening semicircle to surround us.

The sun was uncomfortably hot. The road was dusty and so disturbed that it impaired my vision. I could see Sedenko ahead of me but I could only hear our enemies.

I was drenched in sweat as I caught up the young Muscovite and cried that we had no choice but to fight, though it was almost certain we were doomed. I fished for the grimoire and found the words of power again.

We set our horses back to back, peering through the dust and trying to see the riders as they closed in. *"Rehoim Farach Nyadah!"* I shouted with desperate authority.

The dust began to settle. Our pursuers were upon us. I saw Klosterheim's purple plume. I saw dark shapes advancing.

A long blade darted at me and I blocked it. I struck back, expecting to connect with plate armour. Instead my swordpoint entered flesh and I heard a grunt of pain.

I saw the face of my attacker. It was swarthy, unshaven, cross-eyed.

It had become the face of a common brigand.

Chapter XI

THE SUN WAS improbably hot. Out of the dust came a press of mounted ruffians clad in all manner of crude finery. Klosterheim still directed them. I almost lost my guard in my astonishment, wondering how the knights of Arioch had turned into these far less impressive creatures. But there were yet a good many more of them than could be easily dealt with. I coughed as the dust found my throat and nostrils. Sedenko and I were surrounded by what seemed a veritable forest of steel, and our horses and ourselves were cut with a myriad of minor wounds. Yet we had killed five or six within almost as many minutes and this caused the rest to proceed more warily. Behind them I could hear Klosterheim's voice, high with temper and eager bloodlust, urging them on.

I had a strong sense that my grimoires would be of no use here and that we had passed out of the Middle Marches and into our own world. Overhead the sun was strong and I glimpsed small trees and dry grass which reminded me of my journeys through Spain.

The rogues were pressing us hard. I saw Klosterheim's face now. He was relishing our defeat. We were being forced slowly off the road towards a precipice with a drop of some fifteen feet—quite enough to break our bones and those of our horses.

Sedenko shouted something to me but I did not catch it. The next moment he had vanished and I was fighting on my own. I could not believe he had abandoned me in order to save himself and yet it was the only sensible conclusion.

The snapguzzlers closed in tighter and I was moments from death when I heard Klosterheim's strangled tones from behind me. Suddenly my enemies had fallen away.

"Stop!"

Sedenko had Klosterheim by the throat. The witch-seeker's face writhed with anger and frustration.

"Stop, you oafs!"

The Kazak's steel was against Klosterheim's adam's-apple and had already drawn a thin line of blood. "Oh, Sedenko," he swore, "you might have been spared. But not now. Not if I can come back from Hell to destroy you."

I was laughing. I am not sure that I knew my reasons for mirth. "What? Is Duke Arioch not here to save you?" said I. "Why are his men all vanished?"

I kept my sword out as I rode up to Sedenko. Klosterheim's eyes had that mad, inturned look I had seen on more than a few denizens of Hell.

"Kill one of us," I said, "and we kill your master. If he dies, as you well know, you are doomed, every one. Go back up the road until you are out of sight."

The survivors became shifty, but another touch of the Kazak sabre had Klosterheim raving at them to obey. He knew what death meant for him. It was worse than anything he had threatened for me. He would hold onto life while there was the faintest chance. Pride and honour must be discarded, but anything was better than giving up his black soul to Him who owned it.

"Obey them!" called Klosterheim.

The survivors began to drag themselves away. I saw mountains behind them, but they were not the high peaks of the Mittelmarch. These were grassy and low.

Limping, leading their mounts, swearing at us, nursing wounds, the bewildered rogues retreated. We watched. When they were a good distance from us we saw that their breath began to steam and they showed signs of cold, shivering and stamping their feet, looking about them in some surprise. They had gone into the Mittelmarch. Then they vanished.

"Duke Arioch's warriors could not follow us," I suggest-ed. "And you had those men waiting if we succeeded in returning to this world. The damned can no more enter the Earth than the innocent can enter the Mittelmarch."

Klosterheim was shaking. "Are you going to kill me, von Bek?"

"I would be wise to kill you," I said. "And all my better judgement tells me to do so. But I am aware of what killing you means, and unless I am fighting you I cannot easily bring myself to kill you, Klosterheim."

He found my charity disgusting, it was plain, but he accepted it. He feared death more than anyone I had ever seen.

"Where are we now?" I asked him.

"Why should I tell you?"

"Because I could still summon enough anger, perhaps, to do what I know should really be done to cleanse the world of an obscenity."

"You are in Italy," he said. "On the road to Venice."

"So those mountains behind us would be the Venetian Alps?"

"What else?"

"We must go west," I said to Sedenko. "Towards Milan. Groot said that our goal lies in the west."

Klosterheim's pale features became tense as Sedenko wrenched the sword from his fingers and threw it away.

"Dismount," I said. "Your horses are fresher than ours."

We tied Klosterheim to a tree by the side of the road and transferred our saddles to his beast and another which had belonged to a dead ruffian. We kept our own horses and packed the remainder of our gear on them.

"We should not leave him alive," said Sedenko. "Shall I cut his throat, captain?"

I shook my head. "I have told you that I cannot easily consign any soul to the fate which inevitably awaits Kloster-heim."

"You are a fool not to kill me," said the solder-priest. "I am your greatest enemy. And I can conquer yet, von Bek. I have powerful allies in Hell."

"Not as powerful, surely, as mine," I said. Again I spoke in High German, which Sedenko could not understand.

Klosterheim replied in the same tongue. "Indeed they

could now be more powerful. Lucifer has lost Himself. Most of His Dukes do not want Reconciliation with Heaven."

"There is no certainty that it will come about, Johannes Klosterheim. Lucifer's plans are mysterious. God's Will is equally mysterious. How can any of us judge what is actually taking place?"

"Lucifer plans to betray His own," said Klosterheim. "That is all I know. It is all that is necessary to know."

"You have simplified yourself," I said. "But perhaps that is how one must be if one follows your vocation."

"We are betrayed by God and Lucifer both," said Klosterheim. "You should understand that, von Bek. We are abandoned. We have nothing we can trust—even damnation! We can only play a game and hope to win."

"But we do not know the rules."

"We must invent them. Join me, von Bek. Let Lucifer find His own Grail!"

We got up onto our horses.

"I have given my word," I said. "It is all I have. I hardly understand this talk of games, of loyalties, of betrayals. I have promised to find the Cure for the World's Pain if I can. And that is what I hope to achieve. It is your world, Klosterheim, which is a world of moves and countermoves. But such gamesmanship robs life of its savour and destroys the intellect. I'll have as little part of it as I can."

As we rode away Klosterheim shouted fiercely at me:

"*Be warned, war hound! All that is fantastic leagues against you!*"

It was a chilling threat. Even Sedenko, who did not understand the words, shuddered.

Chapter XII

WE RODE NOW across comparatively flat country which was broken by the low white buildings of farms and vineyards, yellow and light green under the heavy sun.

At the first good-sized town we came to I sought a doctor for our wounds. I had Satan's elixir, but preferred to keep it for more urgent purposes. By dint, however, of a little of Satan's silver we were able to get the doctor to tend to our horses as well. The man made a fuss but I argued that he had probably killed more men than horses in his career and that here was his opportunity to try to even up his score. He saw no humour in my jest, but he did his work skillfully enough.

We took the road to Milan, falling in with a mixed group of pilgrims, most of whom were returning to France and some to England. These men and women had visited the Holy City, bought all sorts of benefices, observed all the wonders, both ancient and modern, and seemed thoroughly satisfied that they had gained much from the hardships of travel. They had stories of maguses, of miracle-working priests, of visions and revelations. Many displayed the usual sorts of gimcrackery still sold as the bones of this or that saint, the feather of an angel, pieces of the True Cross and so on. At least three separate people I met had the real Holy Grail but considered themselves too sinful, still, either to perceive its actual beauty (these things were pewter got up to look like silver, mostly) or to be allowed to witness its magical properties. Naturally, I neither informed them of my Quest nor attempted to persuade them that the artefacts they had purchased were false.

When we got to that lovely city of Verona, we found the place in a bustle. Some Catholic knight, doubtless tired of the War in Germany and believing the Cause without much worth anyway, had aroused a group of zealous young men to join him in a Crusade. The object of the Crusade, it seemed, was to attack Constantinople and free it from the Turks. This idea appealed greatly to Sedenko, whose people lived to take the city they called "Tsargrad" out of Islam's chains. When he saw the leader of the Crusaders, however, a near-senile baron evidently eaten with syphilis, and the tiny force he had gathered, Sedenko decided to wait "until all the Kazak hosts can ride at once to Saint Sophia and destroy the crescent which profanes her altar."

Near Brescia we witnessed the trial and burning of a self-professed Anti-Christ: a gigantic man with wild black hair and a black beard, wearing a red robe and a crown of roses. He called upon the people to give up their false pride, their presumption that they were the children of Christ, and admit that as sinners they were followers of his. The Final War must come, he preached, and those who were with him would be triumphant. The Bible, he said, lied. It was plain that he believed every word he spoke and that his concern for others was sincere. He died at the stake, pleading with them to save themselves by following him. During his burning a thunderstorm began some miles away. The priests chose to see this as a sign of God's pleasure. The people, however, plainly expected the beginning of Armageddon and knelt to pray. In the main they prayed to Christ, though I believe I heard several praying to the charred bones of the Anti-Christ. And in Crema I was taken to meet another mad creature, some hermaphroditic monster, who claimed that it was an angel, fallen to Earth and, having lost its wings, unable to return to Heaven. The angel lived on what it could beg from the people of Crema. They were kind to it. Some of them half-believed it. However, I had met an Angel, albeit a Dark One, and I knew what they were like. But when this angel of Crema begged me, as a holy traveller and a Goodly Knight, to confirm that he had truly plummeted from Heaven, I told all those who would listen that, to the best of my limited knowledge, this was what an angel looked like and that it was quite possible that this one had lost its wings. I suggested it be given all possible comfort during its stay on Earth.

Five miles past Crema we saw an entire village destroyed by brigands clad in the hoods of the Holy Inquisition of Spain. They went off with the contents of the church, with all goods of value, with women and with children whom they plainly intended to sell as slaves. And those who survived believed, many of them, that they had been visited by Christ's servants and that what had been given up by them had been given up in support of Christ's Cause.

I met few good men on that road. I met many whose honour had turned to pride yet who were contemptuous of me for what they saw as my cynical pragmatism. Bit by bit I had told Sedenko most of my story, for I thought it fair to let him know whom he served. He had shrugged. After what he had witnessed of late, he said, he did not think it mattered a great deal. At least the Quest was holy, even if the men upon it were not.

Beyond Crema we passed again into the Mittelmarch. Save that the seasons were, of course, reversed, the landscape was not greatly different. We were in a kingdom, we discovered, which was the vestige of a Carthaginian Empire which had beaten Rome during Hannibal's famous campaign, conquered all of Europe and parts of Asia and had converted to the Jewish religion, so that the whole world had been ruled by Rabbinical Knights. It was a land so horrifying to Sedenko that he believed he was being punished for his sins and was already in Hell. We were treated hospitably and my engineering experience was called into play when the Chief Judge of this Carthaginian land pronounced a sentence of death upon a Titan. A gallows had to be built for him. In return for aid and some extra gold, I was able to design a suitable scaffold. The Titan was hanged and I received the gratitude of those people forever.

Shortly after this we entered a great, complicated city maintained by an infinite series of balances and relationships whose acute harmony was such that I could not then tolerate it. It was a place of divine abstractions and the citizens were scarcely aware of us at all. Sedenko was not as badly affected as was I, but we were both glad to leave and find ourselves soon in a familiar France near Saint-Etienne where, for some weeks, we were imprisoned as suspected murderers and heretics, released only through the intercession of a priest who had discovered several eyewitnesses. The priest was paid with the Carthaginian gold and we went on our way gladly. Both our own world and the world of the Mittelmarch seemed to have increased in peril, but we moved steadily westward through both, crossing the sea, at last, to England, where we did not fare particularly well.

In England we were regarded by almost everyone with deep suspicion. The nation was full of discontent and any stranger was considered either a Puritan traitor or a Catholic agitator, so we were pleased to leave that country and set sail for Ireland, where there were various small wars afoot. We found ourselves drawn into two such campaigns, once on the side of the Irish and once on the side of the English; Sedenko fell in love and killed the woman's husband when discovered. Thus we left Ireland in some haste and from there set foot, once more, in the Mittelmarch.

We had been on the Quest for almost a year and seemed no closer to the blue-green Forest at the Edge of Heaven, while I had seen much of the world but learned little, I thought, that I had not known already. I longed for my Lady Sabrina, whom I had in no way forgotten. My love for her was as strong as it had ever been.

Sometimes I believed I had caught sight of Klosterheim or that he had revealed his hand in several attacks on our persons, but I could not be sure. It did seem that his warning had been accurate. Fewer and fewer of the lands we visited would welcome us. We began to feel like criminals. The hospitality of even common folk declined. The struggle between Heaven and Hell, the struggle which was taking place in Hell alone, the wars which shook the lands of the Mittelmarch, were all reflected in the strife which tore Europe. There was no end to it. Death and Plague continued to spread. We wondered, should we continue our way west and come at last to the New World, if we should discover any better there. Young Sedenko had taken on a haggard look and seemed ten years older than when we had met. I, apparently, had not much changed in my appearance. I had become familiar with many of the spells in the grimoires and had on occasions used them. Of late, their use had become more frequent. And of late, also, they seemed to have become less effective. I wondered if Hell's Dukes were

massing and gaining strength over their Master. In which
case, I thought, my Quest and all my efforts were absolutely
without meaning.

It was raining in the Mittelmarch, one spring day, at
noon. Sedenko and I were drenched and our horses were
beginning to steam. We were crossing a wide plain of cracked
earth. At intervals on the plain we saw tall pyres burning,
sending black smoke low into the sky. The rain pattered on
our cloaks and made puddles in the mud. We had encountered and defeated four or five misshapen men who I
suspected were Klosterheim's, and I was following my compass which directed us to the way out of Mittelmarch. I was
beginning to know a deeper despair than any I had known
before, for I suspected my journey had no ending, that a
terrible trick had been played upon me.

The pyres were closer together. No mourners stood near
them, but upon each one was a heavily wrapped corpse. I
wondered if the occupants of those pyres had died of disease.
Then I saw a moving figure which was obscured by the smoke
and I pointed it out to Sedenko, but the Muscovite could see
nothing.

So long had it been since our last encounter with
Klosterheim that we had begun to think him gone directly
from our sphere, but now I was almost certain that the
shadow in the smoke was the witch-seeker himself. I drew up,
raising a cautionary hand to Sedenko, who followed my
example. The rain and the smoke continued to make it all but
impossible to see any distance.

Eventually we decided to ride on as the rain began to lift
and the sun emerged, dark red and huge in the eastern sky.

The smoke gave way to mist rising from the broken earth
and we left the pyres behind us, though the plain continued to
stretch for miles in all directions.

Sedenko saw the village first. He gestured. Distant metal
glittered in the heavy evening light. The houses seemed to be
rounded, topped by little spires. Coming closer, I saw that
they were in actuality leather tents mounted on wheels and
decorated with all manner of symbols. The glitter came from
their roof-spikes, of gold, bronze and silver inlay.

Sedenko drew in his breath. "Those yurts are a familiar
sight!" His hand went to the hilt of his sabre.

"What?" said I. "Are they Tatars?"

"By all the signs, aye."

"Then perhaps we should skirt that camp?" I suggested.

"And lose the chance of killing some of them!" he said, as if I were insane.

"There are likely to be rather more of them, friend Sedenko, than there are of us. I do not think my Master would be pleased if I diverted my time to the cause of genocide . . ."

Sedenko scowled and muttered. He was like a hound restrained from hunting its natural game.

"Besides," I added, "they are showing a keen interest in ourselves."

A score of horsemen were riding towards us. I spurred my steed into a trot, but Sedenko did not follow me. "I cannot run from a Tatar," he wailed.

I went about and got hold of his reins, dragging him and his horse after me. But the Tatars were moving with astonishing speed and within minutes we were surrounded, staring at their mounts, which were not creatures of flesh at all, but were fashioned from brass. They had dead, staring eyes and creaked a little as they moved. The Tatars, however, were evidently flesh and blood.

"Those horses are mechanical," I said. "I have never heard of such a wonder!"

One of the Asiatics pulled at his long moustache and stared at me for several moments before speaking. "Yours is the tongue of Philander Groot."

"It is German," I said. "What do you know of Groot?"

"Our friend." The Tatar chief looked suspiciously at the glaring Sedenko. "Why is your companion so angry?"

"Because you chased us, I suppose," I told him. "He is also a friend of Philander Groot. We saw him less than a year hence, in the Valley of the Golden Cloud."

"It was said that he would go there." The Tatar made a sign to his men. Pressing on either side of us, they began to steer us towards their village. "It was Groot who made our horses for us, when the Plague came, which destroyed all mares and lost us our herds."

"Is that what burns yonder?" I asked him, pointing back at the pyres.

He shook his head. "Those are not ours." He would say no more on the subject.

My opinion of Groot was even higher now that I had seen an example of his skill. I found it difficult to understand why the dandy had chosen to live the life of a hermit when he was capable of so much.

The mechanical horses clattered as we moved. Sedenko said to me: "They are not true Tatars, of course, but are creatures of the Mittelmarch, and so I suppose are not necessarily my natural blood-enemies."

"I think it would be politic, if nothing else, Sedenko," said I, "if you held to that line of reasoning. At least for the next little while."

He looked suspiciously at me, but then nodded, as if to say he would bide his time for my sake.

The village was full of dogs, goats, women and children and it stank. The Tatars brought their mechanical mounts to a halt and the creatures stopped, still as statues, where they stood. Fires and cooking pots, half-cured skins, wizened elders: all at odds with the sophistication of Groot's inventions.

We were led into one of the larger yurts and here the stench was more intense than anything we had experienced outside. I was almost driven out by it, but Sedenko took it for granted. I gathered that his own people had borrowed many Tatar customs and that, to a stranger, Kazaks would not be easily distinguishable from their ancient enemies.

"We are the Guardians of the Genie," said the Tatar chief as he bade us sit upon piles of exotic but unclean cushions. "You must eat with us, if you are Groot's friends. We shall kill a dog and a goat."

"Please," said I, "your hospitality is too much. A simple bowl of rice is all we need to eat."

"You must eat meat." The chief was firm. "We have few guests and would hear your news."

I was amused, wondering what he would make of our real story. I had learned in such circumstances to be a little vague, since oftentimes we had not even journeyed from any neighbouring kingdom, and thus could be unfamiliar with geography, customs and politics which might be the only experience of our hosts. We had become used to saying that we were upon a pilgrimage, in quest of a holy thing; that we were vowed not to mention it, nor the name of the Deity we worshipped. This way I, at least, was able to identify this fictitious god of mine with the gods of those we met. Sedenko, being still somewhat more pious than myself, preferred to say nothing.

As best I could, I described some of my adventures in the Mittelmarch and some of our experiences in our journey across Europe. There was quite enough for the Tatar chief to hear, and by the time we were setting to about the dog and the goat (both of which were stewed in the same pot, with a few vegetables) I think we had paid more than amply for our food and it was time for me to ask the chief:

"And what is this Genie which you guard?"

"A powerful creature," he said soberly, "which resides in a jar. It has been imprisoned there for eons. Philander Groot gave it to us. In return for the gift of horses, we guard the Genie."

"And what did you do before you became Guardians of the Genie?" I asked.

"We made war on other tribes. We conquered them and took away their horses, their livestock, their women."

"You no longer make war on them?"

The Tatar shook his head. "We cannot. Even by the time Philander Groot came to us we had destroyed everyone but ourselves."

"You wiped out every other tribe?"

"The Plague weakened them. We considered attacking Bakinax, but we are too few. Philander Groot said that with the power of the Genie we should not have to fear the Plague. And this seems to be so."

"And what is Bakinax?" asked Sedenko.

"The City of the Plague," said the Tatar chief. "It is where the Plague came from in the first place. It is created by a demon the citizens have with them. I have heard that they try to destroy the demon but that it feeds on the souls of men and beasts and that is why it sends the Plague to them. It sits in a sphere at the centre of Bakinax, eating its fill."

"Yet your souls are untouched."

"Quite. We have the Genie."

"Of course."

After we had eaten, the Tatar chief caused a brand to be lit and he took us to the outskirts of the camp where a little wooden scaffolding had been erected. From it, hanging by plaited horsehair, was a decorated jar of dark yellow glass. The Tatar held the brand close and I thought I saw something stirring within, but it might have been nothing more than reflected light.

"If the jar is broken," said the chief, "and the Genie is

released, it will grow to immense proportions and wreak a horrible destruction throughout Mittelmarch. The demon knows this and the folk of Bakinax know this and that is why we are left untroubled."

He took a woven blanket and with some reverence draped it over the scaffolding, hiding the jar from our sight. "We cover it at night," he said. "Now I will show you to our guest yurt. Do you require women?"

I shook my head. I had known no other woman since I had taken the Lady Sabrina's ring. Sedenko considered the offer a little longer than did I. But then he also decided not to accept. As he murmured to me: "To sleep with a Tatar woman would be tantamount to heresy amongst the Kazak people."

The yurt in which we were to sleep was relatively clean and had sweet straw upon the floor. We stretched out on mats and were soon asleep, although not before Sedenko had grumbled that he had lost considerable pride by missing the opportunity to kill a Tatar or two. "At very least I should have stolen something from them."

When I awoke at dawn Sedenko had already been out, to relieve himself, he said. "It's stopped raining, captain. One of the children said that it is only about a day's ride to Bakinax, due west. It lies directly on our way. What do you think? We're low on provisions."

"Are you anxious to visit a place known as the City of the Plague?"

"I am anxious to eat something other than dog or goat," he said feelingly.

I laughed at this. "Very well. We shall take the risk."

I arose and washed myself in the bowl of water provided us, breakfasted off the rice brought by a shy Tatar maiden and stepped out of the yurt. The camp was only just beginning to wake. I strode through it to the yurt of the chieftain. He greeted me civilly.

"Should you come upon our friend Philander Groot," he said, "tell him that we long to see him again, to do him honour for the honour he does us."

"It is unlikely," said I, "but I will remember your message."

We departed on good terms. Sedenko seemed overeager to reach Bakinax and I suggested, after about half an hour,

that he slow his pace. "Do the fleshpots become so attractive
to you, my friend?"

"I would feel more comfortable with a city wall between
myself and the Tatars," he admitted.

"They plainly mean us no harm."

"They might wish us harm now," he said. He looked
back in the direction of the camp. It was no longer visible.
Then he reached behind him into a saddlebag and withdrew
something which he displayed in his gloved hand.

It was the jar containing the Tatars' Genie.

"You are a fool, Sedenko," I said grimly. "That was a
treacherous action to perform upon those who treated us so
kindly. You must return it."

"Return it!" He was amazed. "It is a question of honour,
captain. No Kazak could leave a Tatar village without something they value!"

"Our friend Philander Groot gave that to them, and they
gave us their hospitality in the name of Groot. You must take
it back!" I drew rein and reached out for the jar.

Sedenko cursed me and pulled on his horse's head to
move out of range. "It is mine!"

I sprang from my horse and ran towards him. "Take it
back or let me!"

"No!"

I jumped for the jar. His horse reared. He tried to
control it and the jar slipped from his hand. I flew forward in
an effort to save the thing, but it had already fallen to the
hard earth. Sedenko was yelling something at me in his own
barbaric tongue. I stopped to pick the jar up, noticing that the
stopper had come loose, and then Sedenko had struck me
from behind with the flat of his sword and I momentarily lost
my senses, waking to see him clasping the jar to his chest as
he ran back for his horse.

"Sedenko! You have gone mad!"

He turned, glaring at me. "They were Tatars!" he cried,
as if reasoning with a fool. "They were Tatars, captain!"

"Take the jar back to them!" I clambered to my feet.

He stood his ground defiantly. Then he shouted wildly,
as I came up: "They can have their damned jar, but they shall
not have their Genie!" He dragged forth the stopper of the
jar.

I stopped in horror, expecting the creature to emerge.

Sedenko began to laugh. He tossed the jar at me. "It's empty! It was all a deception. Groot tricked them!"

This seemed to please him. "Let them have it, if you wish, captain." He laughed harder. "What a splendid joke. I knew Philander Groot was a fellow after my own heart."

Now, as I held the jar, I saw tiny, pale hands clutching at the rim. I looked down into it. There was a small, helpless, fading thing. As the air reached it, it was evidently dying. It was manlike in form, but naked and thin. A tiny, mewling noise escaped its wizened lips and I thought I detected a word or two. Then the miniature hands slipped from the rim and the creature fell to the bottom of the jar where it began to shiver.

There was nothing for it but to replace the stopper. I looked at Sedenko in disgust.

"Empty!" He guffawed. "Empty, captain. Oh, let me take it back to them. I threatened to ruin Groot's joke."

I forced the stopper down into the jar and held the thing out to Sedenko. "Empty," said I. "Take it back then, Kazak."

He dropped the jar into his saddlebag, mounted his horse and rode away at that breakneck pace he and his kind preferred.

I waited for some forty minutes, then I continued on westward, towards Bakinax, not much caring at that moment if Sedenko survived or not. I had consulted my maps. Bakinax lay not much more than a week's ride from the Forest at the Edge of Heaven.

My foreboding grew, however, as I came closer to the city.

Sedenko, grinning all over his face, soon caught me up.

"They had not noticed its disappearance," he said. "Is not Philander Groot a wily fellow, captain?"

"Oh, indeed," said I. It seemed to me that Groot had had his own reasons for deceiving the Tatars. By means of that Genie, alive or dead, they survived and the people of Bakinax dared not attack them. Groot had given the Tatars life and a reason, of sorts, for living. My admiration for the dandy, as well as my curiosity about him, continued to increase.

The vast plain was behind us at long last when we came to a land of dry grass and hillocks and thousands of tiny streams. It had begun to rain again.

I reflected that the Mittelmarch appeared to have become bleaker in the year of our journey. It was as if less could grow here, as if the soul of the Realm were being sucked from it. I told myself that all I witnessed was a difference of geography, but I was not in my bones content with that at all.

In the evening we saw a city ahead of us and knew that it must be Bakinax.

We rode through the streets in the moonlight. The place seemed very still. We stopped a man who, with a burning torch in each hand, went drunkenly homeward. He spoke a language we could not understand, but by means of signs we got directions from him and found for ourselves a lodging for the night: a small, ill-smelling inn.

In the morning, as we breakfasted from strange cheeses and mysterious meats, we were interrupted by the entrance of five or six men in identical surcoats, bearing halberds, with morion helmets decorated by feathers, their hands and feet both mailed. They made it plain that we were to go with them.

Sedenko was for fighting, but I saw no point. Our horses had been stabled while we slept and we had no knowledge of their exact whereabouts. Moreover, this whole country was alien to us. I had, as had become my habit, all Lucifer's gifts about my person and my sword was at my side, so that I did not feel entirely vulnerable as I rose, wiped my lips and bowed to the soldiers as an indication that we were ready to accompany them.

The streets of Bakinax, seen in daylight, were narrow and none too clean. Ragged children with thin, hungry faces stopped to look at us as we passed and old people, in rags for the most part, gaped. It was not an unusually despondent place, this city, compared to many I had seen in Europe, but neither did it seem a cheerful one. There was an atmosphere of gloom hanging over it and I thought it well-named the City of the Plague.

We were escorted through the main square where, upon a great wooden dais, stood a huge globe of dull, unpleasant metal, guarded by soldiers in the same uniform as those who now surrounded us. The square was otherwise empty of citizens.

"That must be the house of the devil the Tatar mentioned," whispered Sedenko to me. "Do you really think it lives on the souls of the people hereabouts, captain?"

"I do not know," said I, "but I would cheerfully feed it yours, Sedenko." I was not yet prepared to forgive him for his foolishness concerning the stolen jar. He, for his part, was absolutely unrepentant. He took my remark, as he had taken others, as a joke, craning his head to look again at the sphere as we were marched up stone steps and through the portal of what was evidently some important public building.

We were taken into a room lined on both sides with pews. Not one of the pews, however, was occupied. At the far end of the room was a lectern and behind the lectern, where a priest might stand, was a tall, thin man with a bright red wig, dressed in a gown of black and gold.

Said he in the Latin language: "Speak you Latin, men?"

"I speak a little," I told him. "Why have we been brought here so roughly, Your Honour? We are honest travellers."

"Not so honest. You seek to avoid the tolls. You have ridden through our sacred Burning Grounds and desecrated them. You have entered Bakinax by the East Gate and placed no gold in the plate. And those are only your main crimes. Do not offer me your hypocrisy, sir, as well as your offences! I am the Great Magistrate of Bakinax and it was I who ordered you arrested. Will you speak?"

"We cannot know your laws," I said, "for we are strangers here. If we had been aware that your Burning Grounds were sacred we should have ridden clear of them, I assure you. As for the gold which must be placed in the plate, we will willingly pay it now. None challenged us as we entered."

"Too late to pay in gold," said the Great Magistrate. He cleared his nose and glared at us. "You cannot claim that nobody told you of Bakinax as you journeyed here, for it is a famous place, this City of the Plague. Did no one mention our demon?"

"A demon was mentioned, aye." I shrugged. "But nothing was said of tolls, Your Honour."

"Why come here?"

"For fresh supplies."

"To the City of the Plague?" He sneered. "To this awful City of the Demon? No! You came to cause us distress!"

"But, sir, how can we two cause a whole city distress?" I asked. The man was mad. I believed, reluctantly, that probably all Bakinax was mad. I regretted my decision to come here and felt in agreement with the Great Magistrate when he suggested that only a fool would seek out Bakinax.

"By being what you are. By seeing what you see!" replied the Magistrate. "We shall not be mocked, travellers! We shall not be mocked."

"We do not mock," I told him. "We promise that we shall not ever mention Bakinax again. Only, good sir, let us continue on our way, for we have a holy mission to perform."

"Aye, indeed you have," said the old man with some relish. "You must pay for your stupidity and your contempt for us with your souls. You will be given to our demon. Two of us shall thus be saved for a little longer and you will receive fitting punishment for your crimes. Your souls will go to Hell."

At this I laughed. Sedenko had no idea what had passed between us. I told him roughly what had been said.

He was not as amused as I. Perhaps he did not really believe that his soul was already destined for Lucifer's Realm.

Chapter XIII

"You, sir," said the Great Magistrate, addressing me, "shall be the first to fight our demon. None has ever beaten him. Should you, however, manage to kill him, the door of the sphere shall be released and you will be free. If you have not emerged in an hour, your friend will be sent to join you."

"I am to be allowed to carry my sword?" said I.

"All you possess you may take with you," he told me.

"Then I am ready," I said.

The Great Magistrate spoke to his soldiers in their own tongue. One stood guard over Sedenko, while the rest escorted me from the Court and back into the square where the rain had again begun to fall.

We mounted steps onto the platform. The sphere had set in it a small round door which one of the guards approached. He was nervous. He put his palm against the handle and hesitated.

I saw a figure enter the square.

If anything, Klosterheim was even more gaunt than when last I saw him. He was grinning at me now. He was almost trembling with pleasurable anticipation. His black garments were stained and neglected; the purple feathers in his hat were matted and stringy and he had developed a peculiar, almost undetectable stoop. His eyes had that same inturned insanity. He removed his hat in a mock salute as the door groaned open and the soldiers pushed me forward.

"Was this your doing, Klosterheim?" I asked.

The witch-seeker shrugged. "I am a friend," he said, "to Bakinax."

"Is this demon your gift to the city?"

He ignored me, signing casually to the guards.

With a wave to him I bent and entered the foul-smelling darkness, salty and damp, of the sphere. Crouching there, I blinked, peered, but saw nothing. The round door clanked shut behind me. Gradually I began to see. The light came from a peculiar substance washing the floor of the sphere. It was white and it was viscous and it was obviously, too, the source of the smell. Something emerged from it at the farthest point from me. The fluid at the bottom of the sphere made sucking sounds. There was no colour here. All seemed grey, black and white. The thing which moved through the liquid was larger than I. It had scales. It had a great, sad, misshapen head which had fallen to one side and almost rested on its left shoulder. Its long teeth were broken and its lips were ragged, as if they had been chewed to destruction. From one large nostril came a little vapour. The monster squeaked at me, almost a question.

"Art thou the Demon of the Sphere?" I asked him.

The head lifted a fraction. Then, after some while, a voice came from the back of its throat.

"I am."

"Thou must know," said I, "that my soul is not for eating. It already belongs to our Master, Lucifer."

"Lucifer." The word was distorted. "Lucifer?"

"He owns it. I can offer you no sustenance, therefore, Sir Demon. I can only offer you death."

"Death?" It licked its torn lips with a ruined tongue. A smile seemed to appear on its features. "Lucifer? I wish to be free. I want to eat nothing more. Why do they feed me so much? All they have to do is release me from the pact and I will fly straight back to Hell."

"You do not want to be here?"

"I have never wanted to be here. I was tricked. Through my own greed I was tricked. I know your soul is not for me, mortal. I could smell it if it were mine. I cannot smell your soul."

"Yet you will still kill me, eh?"

The demon sat down in the fluid. He splashed at it with his taloned fingers. "Children and youths. This stuff is all that remains. There is not one soul in Bakinax—not one adult soul, that is—which is not already claimed. I will not kill you, mortal, unless you grow bored and want to fight. You are one of the few who has wished to talk. Most of them scream. The children, the youths and the maidens, I eat. It silences them. It entertains me. It feeds me for a little while. But I have more than enough. More than enough."

"But you will not release me from your lair?"

"How can I? I am trapped here myself. A pact. It seemed worthwhile all that time ago."

"Who was the magus who trapped you?"

"He was called Philander Groot. A cunning man. I roamed free before, across this whole kingdom. Now I am limited to Bakinax and this cage. Oh, I am so tired of the flavourless souls of the young." He took some of the fluid up on his finger and sucked. He sighed.

"But they fear you," I said. "It is why they keep you here. They believe you will escape if they do not placate you."

The demon said: "Is that not always the way with Men? What must I represent to them, I wonder?"

I leaned, as best I could, against the wall of the sphere. I was growing used to the smell. "Well, they will not release you and they will not release me unless I kill you. You have food. I have not. I must starve to death, it seems, or destroy you."

The demon looked up at me. "I have no desire to kill you, mortal. It would give offence to our Master, would it not? Your time is not yet arrived."

"I believe that," I said. "For I am upon a mission directly instructed by Lucifer."

"Then we have a dilemma," said the demon.

I thought for a moment. "I could attempt to exorcise you," I told him. "That would at least release you from the sphere. Where would you go?"

"Directly back to Hell."

"Where you would wish to be."

"I never want to leave Hell again," said the demon feelingly.

"I am no expert at exorcism."

"They have attempted to exorcise me, but those already pledged to Hell, whether they know it or not, cannot bid me leave."

"Therefore I cannot exorcise you either."

"It would seem so."

"We have reached impasse again," I said.

The demon lowered its head and sighed a deeper sigh than the first. "Aye."

"What if I killed you?" I said. "Where would your own soul go?"

"Oblivion. I would rather not die, Sir Knight."

"Yet I was told the door will open only after I have slain you."

"Since nobody has slain me, how are they to know that?"

"Perhaps Philander Groot told them."

I brooded on the problem for a while. "The door must be opened eventually, to admit my companion, who is to be your next victim. Why cannot we escape when his turn comes?"

"It might be possible for you to escape," said the demon. "But I am trapped by more than metal. There is the pact, you see, with the magus. Were I to break it, I would be destroyed instantly."

"Therefore only Philander Groot can release you."

"That is so."

"And Philander Groot has become a hermit, dwelling in a far kingdom."

"I have heard as much."

"Inevitably I am led to the logic," I said, "that my only means of escape is by killing you. And I know that my chances of doing so are virtually nothing."

"I am very strong," said the demon, by way of confirmation, "and also extremely fierce."

"I think that my only hope," I told him, "is to wait until the hour is up and, when my friend is sent to join us, attempt to leave by the door."

"It would seem so," agreed the demon. "But they would kill you anyway, would they not?"

"That is a strong likelihood."

The demon brooded for a moment. "I am trying to think of another solution, one which would benefit us both."

"Not to mention the remaining children and virgins of Bakinax," I said.

"Of course," said the demon. He became nostalgic. "Are there any Tatars left, do you know?"

"A few. They are protected against you by a Genie they have."

"The one in the jar?"

"That's the one."

"Aha." He frowned. "I was fond of Tatars."

It was beginning to seem to me that the supernatural creatures of this land were somewhat ineffectual beings. I wondered if not only the Mittelmarch but the whole of Hell was in decline. Or perhaps the powers had been marshalled to cope with the Civil War which Klosterheim had said was raging between Lucifer and His Dukes.

I thought I detected a movement overhead. I stretched out my hand to the demon. He placed his own scaly fingers in mine. "Would you oblige me," I asked him, "by allowing me to stand upon your shoulders so that when the door is opened I will be able to escape?"

"By all means," said the demon, "if you will agree one thing: should you escape and find Philander Groot again, tell him that I guarantee that if he will break the bond I will go home immediately and never venture into the regions of the Earth again."

"The likelihood," I said honestly, "of my seeing Groot is slender. However, I give my word that if I should meet him again, or be in a position to get a message to him, I will tell him what you have told me."

"Then I wish you Lucifer's luck," said the demon, bending so that I might climb upon his back. "And I hope that you kill that Great Magistrate who has caused me so much boredom."

The door was opening. I heard guards laughing. I heard Sedenko cursing.

His face appeared above me. I put my finger to my lips. His eyes widened in amazement. I whispered: "Draw your sword now. We are going to try to fight our way clear . . ."

"But—" began Sedenko.

"Do not question me," I said.

The Kazak shrugged and called back. "Wait, fellows, while I free my blade!"

The sabre was in his hand. I drew my own sword as the demon began to lift me higher towards the door. I took hold of the sill and jumped through, past Sedenko, lunging at the nearest guard and taking him in the heart. Two more fell to me before they realised what had happened. The remaining three set upon me and Sedenko and would have been finished easily, had I not been distracted by Sedenko's agitated gesturing. I turned to glance in the direction he pointed.

Klosterheim was there, mounted on a heavy black charger. At his back were twenty mounted suits of armour, glowing with eery black fire. Here were the demons-at-arms of Arioch, Duke of Hell.

For a moment I was tempted to scramble back into the sphere.

Klosterheim was laughing at me as he waited for the fight to end.

I killed one more guard and Sedenko sliced apart the other two.

Behind us, out of the open sphere, came the stench of rotting souls. Before us was the face of a triumphant Klosterheim and his impassive minions.

"We are certainly doomed," murmured Sedenko.

I had by now memorised the spell which held back these riders. I dismissed Sedenko's fears. I raised my hand:

"Rehoim Farach Nyadah!"

Klosterheim continued to laugh. Then he stopped and raised his own hand: *"Niever Oahr Shuk Arnjoija!"* His expression was challenging. "I have neutralised your spell, von Bek. Do you think I have wasted the past year in wondering how you stopped my men the last time?"

"So you have us," I said.

"I have you. I knew your destination. I knew you must come through this land, for you are seeking the Holy Grail in the Forest at the Edge of Heaven. You will never see that forest now, von Bek."

"How goes the War in Hell?" I said.

Klosterheim sat back in his saddle. "Well enough," he told me. "Lucifer is weakening. He retires. He will not fight. Our allies increase. You were a fool not to join me when I offered you the chance."

"I accepted a task," I said. "I knew that I had little hope of achieving it. But a bargain is a bargain. And Lucifer holds my soul, not you, Klosterheim."

A shadow fell suddenly across the whole town. I looked up and saw the strangest sight I had yet met in Hell or the Mittelmarch. A huge black cat was looking down on us. If he had moved one paw or flicked his tail, he could have destroyed the entire city. I thought at first that this was another of Klosterheim's allies, but it became plain that the witch-seeker was as surprised as were we.

"What have you conjured now, von Bek?" he said. He was disconcerted. Then he cursed at something he had seen behind us.

Sedenko turned first, yelling in astonishment. There was a great twittering: the kind of sound starlings make in the evening. I looked back.

A chariot, of bronze and silver, was drifting down through the sky towards us, drawn by thousands of small golden birds.

"Attack them!" cried Klosterheim. He drove his horse towards the platform, the black riders a mass of glowing metal in his wake.

As the chariot settled onto the platform, Klosterheim leapt his horse onto it and came riding directly at me. I parried his first blow. The armoured minions of Duke Arioch were dismounting, lumbering up the steps towards us. We were driven back rapidly.

I heard a voice from the chariot. It was a gentle, chiding, half-mocking voice. It said:

"Demon of the Sphere, I release thee from thy bondage on the condition thou hast made and on the further condition that you fight these enemies of your Master's, for they conspire against Lucifer."

In spite of the danger I turned my head. The little man in the chariot tugged at his beard and bowed to me. I caught the odour of Hungary Water. I saw lace and velvet. It was Philander Groot himself. "Will you join me, gentlemen?" he asked politely. "I think that Bakinax is about to become a battlefield and it will be no sight for sensitive men."

Sedenko needed no further invitation. He was running hell-bent-for-leather towards the chariot. I followed him.

From out of the sphere, blinking and snarling, came the demon. He screamed his exultation. His scales clashed and began to glow. He laughed in hideous joy. And I saw a snarling Klosterheim still riding at us, still determined to kill me, even as we climbed into Groot's chariot.

Now the Demon of the Sphere and the Knights of Duke Arioch were joined in battle. It seemed to me an unequal match, but the demon was accounting well for himself.

Klosterheim's horse reared beneath us as we rose into the air, pulled by the little birds. His teeth were bared. He cried out almost as a child might cry out when it has been deprived of some favourite food.

The last I saw of the witch-seeker, he had leapt his horse from the platform and was riding away from the terrifying carnage taking place on the platform. I saw two armoured knights flung so far that they crashed into the Court. Bricks and stone collapsed. A horrible fire began to flicker wherever Duke Arioch's knights fell.

Then, beneath the tranquil stare of that great black cat, we passed beyond Bakinax and over the red plain.

"I planned none of this," said Philander Groot, as if he apologised to us. "But I knew that the state of balance which I had achieved could not last. I am glad to see that you are well, gentlemen."

I was speechless. The dandy raised an eyebrow. "You are doubtless wondering why I am here. Well, I spent some time contemplating your story, Captain von Bek, and contemplating my old decision to remove myself from the affairs of Men, Gods and Demons. Then I considered the nature of your Quest and, you must forgive me this, I decided that I would like a part in it. It seemed momentous."

"I had no idea that you were so great a magus," I told him.

"You are very kind. I have had the sense, of late, that important events are taking place everywhere. Vain creature that I am, and growing a little bored, I must admit, with the Valley of the Golden Cloud and its decent moderation, I thought I might once again see if I could make use of my old powers, though I regard them, as I am sure do you, as childish and vulgar."

"I regard them as Heaven-sent," I told him.

He was amused. "Well, they are not that, Captain von Bek. They are not that."

The dandy was silent for a little while as we continued on our journey through the upper air. Then he spoke more seriously than was his wont. "At present," he said, "no soldier of the Dukes of Hell can pass into the ordinary Realm of Earth. But should Lucifer be defeated, there will be a wild carelessness come upon Creation and it will be the end of the world, indeed. There will be no single Anti-Christ, though Klosterheim could be said to represent them all. There will be open warfare, in every region, between Heaven and Hell. It will be Armageddon, gentlemen, as has been predicted. Mankind will perish. And I believe, no matter what the Christian Bible predicts, that the outcome will be uncertain."

"But Lucifer does not wish to make war on God," I said.

"The decision could be Lucifer's no longer. Nor God's. Perhaps both have lost their authority."

"And the Grail?" said I. "What part can the Grail play in all this?"

"Perhaps none at all," said Groot. "Perhaps it is no more than a diversion."

Chapter XIV

PHILANDER GROOT'S CHARIOT came to earth eventually on a quiet hillside overlooking a valley which reminded me very much of my own lost Bek.

In the valley a village was burning and I could see black smoke rising from farmsteads and mills. Dark figures with brands marched across the landscape, setting fire to anything which would ignite. It was familiar enough to me. I had ordered such destruction many times myself.

"Are we still in the Mittelmarch?" I asked the dandy. "Or have we returned to our own Realm?"

"It is the Mittelmarch," he said, "but it could as easily be the ordinary Earth, you know. There is very little now which is not destroyed or threatened."

"And all this," I said, "because Lucifer sent me upon a Quest for the Grail!"

"Not quite." Groot motioned with his hand and the chariot ascended again into the air. He said as an aside: "That will be the last we shall see of that, I fear. Mostly such things are leased by the Powers of Darkness, even if not used in their work. Did you know that, Captain von Bek?"

"I did not."

"Now that I am no longer of the Grey Lords, as those of

us who are neutral are named by Hell, I do not expect to conjure things so easily." He paused, smoothing back his little moustache. "You are an unusual man, captain, but your Quest has not brought all this about. Lucifer's decision to attempt peace with His Creator is what has exacerbated a crisis which has been in the making since at least the Birth of Christ. The lines have become confused, you see. The pagan faiths are all but destroyed. Buddha, Christ and Mahomet have seen to that. To many the death of paganism heralded the coming decay of the world (and I will not elaborate, for it is a sophisticated theme, though it does not sound it). We have given up responsibility, either to God or to Lucifer. I am not sure that God demands that of us, nor am I sure that He wishes it. Nothing is certain in the universe, captain."

"Nothing will be gained if I discover the Cure for the World's Pain?"

"I do not know. Perhaps the Grail is no more than a bartering tool in a game so mysterious that not even the two main participants understand its rules. But there again, I could be utterly wrong. Know this, however: Klosterheim is now more powerful than you begin to realise. Do not think, because his pride made him bring the same twenty knights who lost you before, that he can command only twenty. He is now one of the main generals of rebellious Hell. Your Quest, you will recall, is the ostensible cause of that rebellion. They will stop you if they can, Captain von Bek. Or they will take the Grail from you if you find it."

"But with you to help, magus," said Sedenko, "we stand a better chance."

Groot smiled at him. "Do not underestimate Klosterheim, gentlemen. And do not overestimate me. What little I know has been worked for. It has been wrested away from others, the power itself. They can claim much back, whenever they wish. My conjuring tricks with genies and demons are small things. They are pathetic in the eyes of Hell. Now I have not much left. But I will travel with you, if I may, for my curiosity is great and I would know what befalls you. We are a day or two farther on in the journey towards the Forest at the Edge of Heaven, and I fancy we shall see little of Klosterheim for a while. He must have lost some valuable knights in that brawl at Bakinax. But when he comes again into our ken he will come with far more power than he has ever possessed in the past."

"Everything that is fantastic leagues against me," I said, repeating Klosterheim's warning.

"Aye. Everything that is fantastic is threatened. Some believe all these marvels you have witnessed to be productions of the World's Pain. Without that Pain, some say, they would not be necessary. They would not exist."

"You suggest that mankind's needs create them?"

"Man is a rationalising beast, if not a rational one," said Philander Groot. "Come, there are horses waiting for us in yonder spinney."

We followed him down the hill a little way, and sure enough the horses were there. As we mounted, Groot chatted urbanely, telling anecdotes of people he had known and places he had visited, for all the world as if we went on a merry holiday. We rode along the crown of the hills, avoiding the soldiers in the valley below, and continued through the night until we were well past it. Only then did we think of resting. We came to a crossroads in the moonlight. Philander Groot considered the signs. "There," he said at last. He pointed to the post which said: *To Wolfshaben, 3 miles.*

"Do you know Wolfshaben, captain? Herr Sedenko?"

We both told him that we did not.

"An excellent town. If you take pleasure in women you will want to visit the harlotry they have there. I will entertain myself at the harlotry, where the beds are anyway more comfortable."

"I'll gladly join you," said Sedenko with some eagerness.

"If I can have a good bed and no harlot," said I, "I'll cheerfully keep you company."

My friends were entertained royally at Wolfshaben's wonderful harlotry (which is quite famous, I gather, amongst the travellers in the Mittelmarch) and I slept like a dead man until morning.

The spring morning was fresh as we rode away from Wolfshaben, and there was dew on the light-green grass and a touch of rain upon the leaves of the trees so that everything smelled sweet.

Philander Groot, riding ahead of myself and Sedenko, sniffed at the air, for all the world like one of Versailles's courtiers on a frolic, and cried: "A beautiful day, gentlemen. Is it not wonderful to be living?"

The road descended to another valley, as green as the last, and this was deserted of soldiery, apparently completely

untouched by War of any kind. But as we took a turn we came
upon a great procession of men, women and children, on
horseback, in carts, with bundles on their backs and a look of
terror about their eyes. They were from all walks of life.
Philander Groot hailed them merrily, as if unaware of what
they signified. "What's this? Pilgrims seeking Rome?"

A man in half-armour, which had been hastily strapped
about his person, rode up urgently. "We are fleeing an army,
sir. You would be warned not to go any farther in this
direction."

"I'm grateful for the warning, sir. Whose army is it?"

"We do not know," said a wretched woman with a cut
across her brow. "They came upon us suddenly. They killed
everything. They stole everything. They did not speak a
word."

"Nothing justified. No threats. No chivalry," said the
man in half-armour.

"I think, sir," said Groot, glancing at us for confirmation, which we readily gave, "that we will travel with you for a
while."

"You would be wise, sir."

And so it was in the company of more than a thousand
people that we took another road than the one we had
originally hoped to follow, though we did not go back the way
we had come. We were with them for almost two days. For
the most part they were educated men and women: priests
and nuns, astronomers, mathematicians, surgeons, lords and
ladies, scholars, actors. And not one of them could understand why they had been attacked or who had attacked them,
though there were many theories, some of them exceedingly
farfetched. We could only conclude that these were mortal
soldiers serving the Dukes of Hell, but even that was by no
means certain, particularly since a few of the clerics had come
to the familiar conclusion that their community had committed some dreadful sin against God and that God had sent the
soldiers to punish them.

We departed from this concourse eventually and found
upon our maps a fresh road to take us westward. But armies
were galloping everywhere. We hid frequently, being too
faint-hearted to offer battle to anyone who might be a minion
of a Duke of Hell.

Yet now all the world seemed to be afire. Whole forests

burst into flame; whole towns burnt as fiercely as ever
Magdeburg had burnt.

"Ah," said Philander Groot, "it could be the End, after
all, my friends."

"And good riddance to it," I said. "It is a poor world, a
bad world, a decadent world. It expects love without sacrifice.
It expects immediate gratification of its desires, as a child
might, as a beast might. And if it does not receive gratification it becomes pettish and destroys in a tantrum. What's the
use of seeking a Cure for its Pain, Philander Groot? What's
the use of attempting, by any means, to divert it from its
well-earned doom?"

"Because we are alive, I suppose, Captain von Bek.
Because we have no choice but to hope to make it better,
through our own designs." Philander Groot seemed amused
by me.

"The world is the world," said Sedenko. "We cannot
change it. That is for God to do."

"Perhaps He thinks it is for us to do," said Groot quietly.
But he did not press this point. "Oh, look ahead! Look
ahead! Is that not beautiful, gentlemen?"

It was a tall structure which reached to the sky, all curves
and angles of crystal. A great building of glass and quartz
such as I had never seen before.

"It's gigantic," said Sedenko. "Look inside. There are
trees growing there. It is like a jungle."

Philander Groot put fingers to lips and drew his brows
together. Then his face cleared. "Why, it is the famous aviary
of Count Otto of Gerantz-Holffein. Shall we go through it,
gentlemen? You will see that the road passes directly into the
aviary and out the other side. I did not realise it was so close.
I have heard of it, but never seen it before. Count Otto is
dead now. His obsession was with exotic birds. He had the
aviary built by a friend of mine many, many years ago. That is
why it is full of trees, you see. Trees for the birds. And it still
stands! It was a miracle of architecture. Or are you nervous?
Should we skirt the place?"

"We'll go through," said Sedenko.

"I should like to see it," I agreed. I felt that I would be
glad of any relaxation, however temporary.

"Count Otto was so proud of his aviary and his collection
of birds that he insisted on all travellers visiting it," said

Philander Groot, "which is why he had the road going through it." He seemed genuinely delighted.

As we came closer I saw that the entrance to the vast aviary was overgrown and neglected; it seemed to have been abandoned for years. I listened for birdsong. I heard a noise, a kind of chattering and murmuring, like the inner musings of a disconsolate giant.

"Count Otto had at least one example of every known bird," said Philander Groot as he led the way into the miniature jungle. Branches tangled over our heads, but the road was fairly clear. "When he died his nephew would have nothing to do with the aviary. That is why it is now as it is."

There was a strong odour of mould and ancient undergrowth and far ahead of us, through soft, diffused, greenish sunlight, I saw the glitter, I thought, of bright feathers.

"It's a large enough bird," said Sedenko. He glanced about him. "A perfect place for Klosterheim to set an ambush . . ."

"He's behind us," I reminded the Muscovite.

"He has hellish aid," said Philander Groot. "He is now one of Arioch's chief generals. He is not constrained by the considerations of mortals; not at present. But no one place is any more dangerous to us than another, given the powers Klosterheim commands."

"Is that why you seem so insouciant, Philander Groot?" I asked the dandy-magus.

He turned to me with a smile and was about to speak when it came crashing out of the foliage.

It was at least four times the size of a horse and limping on three of its legs. The other, the right foreleg, was lifted above the ground and had plainly been wounded a long while. Its scales were what I had seen and mistaken for feathers: primarily glowing reds and yellows. Its gaping jaws were full of silvery teeth, and its heavy tail thrashed behind it like the tail of an angry cat.

It came at us with incredible speed. Groot went one way, Sedenko the other, and I had drawn my sword and was left facing the lame dragon.

I had no experience of dragon-fighting. Until now I had not believed that such creatures existed. This one did not breathe fire, but its breath stank mightily. And it meant us harm. There was no doubt of that.

My horse was shrieking with terror and trying to escape, but I knew that I could not flee and live. I struck at the beast's snout with the point of my sword and drew blood. It roared and snapped, but it slowed its progress. I struck again. It half-reared on its hind legs, unable to strike with its single front leg without toppling forward. I rode past it, leaping over the thrashing tail and forcing it to turn, its passage hampered by the heavy tree-trunks. Silver teeth snapped at my sleeve and caught some flesh. I cried out, but I was not seriously hurt. I glimpsed Philander Groot and Sedenko riding up behind the dragon, striking at it with their own swords.

I was being forced farther and farther back into the undergrowth until I came to a great wall of glass and was trapped. Again the dragon's head darted down and the teeth narrowly missed me, fastening on the neck of my horse which screamed. I fell backwards out of the saddle as the horse was lifted clear of the ground. I landed heavily, amongst branches, and began to get to my feet at once.

The horse was dead, hanging twitching in the dragon's jaws. It sniffed at the air for a moment before dropping the beast, which crashed down a few yards from me. The dragon plainly had me for its prey and would be satisfied with nothing else. I had only my sword for protection. I tried to crawl into the cover of a large tree-trunk, but I knew there was nowhere I could find safety in that ruined aviary.

Glass cracked as the dragon's tail struck it. From the roof came a strange chiming and then, as if awakened, a flock of varicoloured birds went flapping upwards, twittering and crying. Then they began to descend upon the corpse of the horse. They ignored the fight and the dragon ignored them. They began to feed.

The long snout sniffed at the air again and found my scent. Hobbling, the dragon continued in pursuit of me, while behind it Philander Groot and Grigory Petrovitch Sedenko yelled and struck, to no effect. My strength was fast going. Shards of crystal began to fall all around me, one of them almost impaling me.

Again the teeth found me and I felt my left arm raked. It was as if the dragon had shredded the whole limb in a single movement. I became faint, but continued to flee.

Philander Groot was calling to me, but I could not distinguish the words. I struck again at the dragon's mouth, driving my sword up into its palate. It grunted and lifted its head, taking my sword with it, then spitting it out. I was totally without defence now.

I fell. I began to drag myself along the ground, hoping to find some temporary sanctuary. A claw found my right leg and pain sang up to my spine and suffused my whole body. Yet I continued to move, grasping low branches to pull myself along.

Then my hand fell upon something smooth and cool. Through fading eyes I looked and saw that it was one of the shards from the broken roof. It was like a long icicle. I saw that it tapered to a sharp point. With one hand I attempted to lift it, using my good leg as a lever, until it was braced on the ground between two roots, the thin, jagged edge jutting towards the dragon.

The beast reared again and tottered forward on its hind legs. Saliva ran from the jaws. The silver teeth snapped. I rolled behind the huge shard of crystal even as the dragon dropped down upon me.

The point caught it in the chest, just below the throat, and went straight through. The dragon roared and bellowed, glaring down at me as if it recognised me as the source of its pain.

Black blood burst from the body as the dragon struck with its good leg at the shard, and every blow had the effect of forcing the wound wider so that more blood came. I was covered from head to foot with the horrible liquid, but I fancy I was grinning, too.

Philander Groot and Sedenko had dismounted. They came running towards me, ducking under the branches. Groot had another spear of crystal in his arms. He drove this with all the strength of his tiny body into the side of the dragon.

The beast groaned and turned towards this new source of pain. A terrible coughing began to sound in its throat.

Then it had heeled over against one of the walls, already cracked, and smashed through. For a moment it seemed that it would try to rise as it lay amongst leaves, bits of broken tree, the fallen fragments of glass and crystal. It snorted and blew blood through its nostrils for several feet. The birds were rising from the body of my horse. They had picked its bones completely clean. Again the awful, almost pathetic coughing began to sound from the dying dragon.

One last, long sigh and it had expired.

The bright birds began to settle on the scales until the dragon was completely buried under a wave of bustling feathers and bloody beaks.

Philander Groot and Grigory Sedenko came to my aid. Their faces were full of concern. I turned my head and looked at my arm. It was torn to the bone. My leg had fared scarcely any better.

I gestured towards the skeleton of my horse. My saddle-bags were untouched. "The little bottle." I gasped as the pain began to manifest itself.

Sedenko knew the bottle I meant. He ran to the saddle-bags and found it. It was dented and buckled, but still in one piece. It took him some while to tear the cork free and put it to my lips. I drank sparingly. The pain gave way to something akin to a kind of cold ecstasy and then there was oblivion. I dreamt that I was a youth again in Bek and that this adventure had, itself, been nothing more than a nightmare.

When I awoke, my friends had cleaned my body and changed my clothes. I wondered, for a moment, if, like Siegfried, I would be made immune by dragon's blood. My left arm was a mass of scars, but I could move it and there was only a soreness and a stiffness to it. Similarly, my leg had healed.

Philander Groot was smiling at me, tugging at his little beard. He appeared as composed as ever. His dress was perfect, as was his poise. "Now you are a true Knight of Chivalry, Captain von Bek," he said. "You have slain a dragon in pursuit of the Holy Grail!"

From his sash he withdrew his scabbarded sword. He offered the beautifully wrought hilt to me. "Here," he said, "you cannot be a knight without a blade."

I did not hesitate in accepting his gift. I am still unsure why he made the gesture or why I so readily responded to it.

"I am grateful to you," I said.

I was sitting upright in a corner of the great aviary. Through the foliage I could see the shattered wall and the bones of the dragon beyond it. There was no longer any sign of those birds. It was as if they awoke only when they smelled death.

I climbed to my feet.

"You have been insensible for a full day," Philander Groot told me as I strapped his sword to my belt.

"Precious hours," said I, "lost to Klosterheim."

"Perhaps," said the magus.

Sedenko came forward, leading the two remaining horses. "I have ridden ahead," he said. "There is a great plain beyond us. And beyond that is a blue-green forest which reaches to the sky. I think that we have found the edge of the world, captain."

Chapter XV

"It is just like my homeland," said Grigory Petrovitch Sedenko with considerable joy, "just like the steppes of Ukrainia."

Beyond this rolling grassland the world seemed to curve upwards so that it was possible to see the hazy blue-green of a great, tranquil forest.

We were crossing a small stone bridge which appeared to have been built for a town no longer in existence. "Count Otto loved to live here, by all accounts," said Philander Groot. "It is said that he built his castle within sight of Heaven and that when he died not only did he rise up to Heaven, but that the castle was taken with him. Certainly there is no sign of it in these parts."

"Well," I said, "it should be only a little while now before I am at the end of my Quest."

"The Grail really lies yonder?" said Sedenko.

"I shall know soon." I hesitated. "I shall know if all these adventurings, all these ordeals, have been meaningless or not. Man struggles in the belief that he can, by dint of perseverance, affect his own destiny. And all those efforts, I think, lead to nothing but ruin."

"You remain a fatalist, then," said Philander Groot quietly.

"I know that Man is mortal," I said. "That famine and disease are not his to control. I sought to become a man of action in response to what I experienced. And all I brought to the world was further Pain."

"But now you could be in reach of its Cure." Philander Groot's tones were kindly. "It might be possible to free Man from his captivity, his dependency on either God or Lucifer. We could see the dawning of a New Age. An Age of Reason."

"But what if Man's Reason is as imperfect as the rest of him?" I said. "Why should we praise his poor logic, his penchant for creating laws which only further complicate his lot?"

"Ah, well," said Philander Groot. "It is all we have, perhaps. And we must learn, must we not, through trial and error."

"At the expense of our natural humanity?"

"Sometimes, perhaps." Philander Groot shrugged. "You must take my horse now, Sir Knight. I shall follow on foot as best I can."

"You have no further magic to aid you in your journey?" I asked.

"It is all used up, as I said. The Dukes of Hell are recalling every scrap of power they have leased to the likes of me. Let them have the fantastic and the sensational. I had rejected it once and now reject it again. Though I do not believe I have the choice, as I once had. However, since when I had the choice I made the same decision, I have no great sense of loss. And my need for it disappeared many years ago."

Sedenko cried out suddenly: "Look! Look back!"

We turned our heads.

Beyond the bridge, beyond the hills, a great, dark cloud had gathered and was moving.

"It is Klosterheim and the Forces of Hell," said Philander Groot simply. "You must make haste now, Captain von Bek. They pursue only you."

"So many?" I said.

He smiled quietly. "Are you not flattered?"

"They will kill you, Philander Groot," said Sedenko. "I insist that you ride pillion with me."

"I love life," said the magus. "I will accept your offer, Muscovite."

And so we continued our journey, with Philander Groot clinging to Sedenko's back. We travelled far more slowly than our urgent hearts demanded, with the black cloud looming larger, it seemed, with every step. And soon we felt the ground trembling beneath us, as though an earthquake had begun, yet we ignored it as the far horizon became filled with blue-green haze.

Soon it seemed that half the world was dark and half was light. Behind us were the Forces of Hell and Klosterheim; ahead lay Heaven, which we could not enter. We were in a kind of timeless Limbo, the last three mortals caught between adversaries in a mysterious and meaningless War which threatened to destroy all the Realms of Earth.

We were still several miles from the forest when we heard shouts in our rear and saw about a dozen riders bearing down on us. Outriders from Klosterheim's main army.

These were fearfully hideous looking warriors with distorted, disease-racked faces—some with half the flesh missing from their bones. All of them grinned the familiar grins of the decomposing dead.

Out came our swords and we were at once in battle, our effectiveness impaired by the fact that Groot not only was a passenger but was now unarmed. Neither were our spirits improved by the awful giggling noises which escaped the lips of our attackers whenever our swords struck them.

Round and round us they galloped, making it impossible for us to progress, while I racked my memory for a spell to hamper them. Groot it was who succeeded, with:

"Brothers! Why do you not pursue von Bek? He will destroy you if he succeeds. See—there he is now, almost at the forest!"

As they turned lustreless eyes in the direction he pointed, he murmured to me: "I find that the dead are in the main a dull-witted breed."

The riders ceased their giggling and began to confer amongst themselves, whereupon we were again spurring our horses towards the blue-green haze. Behind us we could see an army stretching the length of the horizon and above them the blackness which now crept towards the sun. Soon it would be blotted from view.

A coldness came from the east now, like a wind yet with

no power. It was more reminiscent, I thought, of a vacuum which threatened to suck us in. We shivered as we laboured on, the Hell-creatures once more in pursuit.

"Duke Arioch spreads his wings," said Groot of the black cloud. "He has put his entire army at Klosterheim's disposal."

Dead flesh stank in our nostrils; dead hands reached out for us. And more came up behind the first riders: running things, half-ape, half-man, in knotted leather with spears and hardwood clubs, their teeth like tusks. And behind them came thin-faced, long-bodied warriors with waving grey hair, in green-and-white livery and no armour. These carried great two-handed blades and guided their thick-bodied mounts with their thighs. And to one side of them were demons, all horns and warts, on demon-horses, and there were women with filed teeth, and women with the snouts of pigs, and apparitions whose flesh ran liquid on their bodies, and there were lizards bearing monkey-riders, and ostriches carrying lepers in arms, and hooded things which cawed at us—and still we galloped, barely in front of them, while Sedenko set up a wailing and a crying out to God, the Tsar and Saint Sophia for their aid and Groot was pale, exhausted, no longer able to maintain his poise.

The gabbling, squeaking and giggling din filled our ears. It alone might have driven us mad, just as the smell brought us close to fainting. Our horses were tiring. I saw Sedenko stumble once and almost dislodge the magus. It seemed to me that Philander Groot was as frightened as I was, that he had spent all his resources. Yet now he had no option but to run with us in the faint hope that the forest might offer at least some temporary sanctuary.

We were not far enough ahead of our pursuers. Little by little they caught up with us again and began to surround us.

"O God, have mercy on me. I repent! I repent!" shouted Sedenko, even as he slashed with his sword at a demon and took off its head. "I confess that I am a sinner and a rogue!" Another head went clear of a body. Blood spattered the Kazak's face. He was weeping, pale with fear, scarcely conscious, I guessed, that he prayed even as he killed. "Mother of God, take me to thy bosom!"

The stinking press grew tighter and tighter. Yet not a single sword had cut at us. Not one blow had landed on us. I

realised that Klosterheim had ordered that we be taken alive.
His nature was such that he would be gratified only if he could
supervise our deaths.

"The grimoire!" cried Sedenko to me. "There must be
something in the grimoire!"

I drew out first one and then another. I called out words
of power. I chanted the spell which had previously commanded Duke Arioch's forces. But nothing affected those Hell-
creatures now. It spoke much for Arioch's growing strength
and for Lucifer's waning authority. I flung the grimoires at
laughing, hideous faces. I flung my maps at Klosterheim even
as his horse parted the ranks and he rode slowly, stiff-backed,
towards us, a little smile upon his thin lips, a slight swagger to
his shoulders. He reached out a hand and caught the map-
case, emptying it onto the ground. He shrugged. "Now you
are mine, von Bek," he said.

It was then that Philander Groot quietly dismounted and
placed himself between me and my old enemy.

"Klosterheim," he said in a quiet, small voice which
nonetheless carried enormous weight, "thou art the personifi-
cation of intellectual poverty."

Klosterheim sneered. "Yet here I am, Philander Groot,
in the ascendant, while all you can hope for is a merciful
death. Perhaps you would argue that there is no justice. I
would argue that the strong make their own justice, through
action and through the gathering of power to themselves."

"You have been granted power, Johannes Klosterheim,
because Duke Arioch finds it worth his while to grant it. But
when you have no further use, Johannes Klosterheim, you
will be discarded."

"I command all this!" Klosterheim swept his hand to
indicate the endless ranks of the damned. "Lucifer Himself
trembles. See! We have reached the borders of Heaven itself.
When we have done with you, we shall march upon the Holy
City, if we so decide. We lay siege to the feeble, decadent old
God residing there. We lay siege to His idiot Son. Duke
Arioch uses me, it is true, but he uses me as Lucifer uses von
Bek. For my courage. For my mortal courage!"

"In von Bek it is courage," said Philander Groot. "In
you, Johannes Klosterheim, it is madness."

"Madness? To seek power and to hold it? No!"

"Despair leads to many forms of thought," said the

magus, "and many kinds of action. Despair drives some to
greater sanity, towards an analysis of the world as it is and
what it might be. Others it drives to deep and dangerous
insanity, towards an imposition of their own desires upon
reality. I sympathise with your despair, Johannes Klosterheim, because it has no solace, in the end. Your despair is the
worst there is to know. And yet men often look upon the likes
of you and envy you, as you doubtless envy Duke Arioch, as
Duke Arioch doubtless envies his master Lucifer, whom he
would betray, and perhaps as Lucifer envied God. And what
does God envy, I wonder? Perhaps he envies the simple
mortal who is content with his lot and envies nobody."

"I'll not listen to this drivel," said Klosterheim. "You
become boring, Philander Groot. I shall kill you all the
sooner if you bore me!"

Philander Groot had straightened his back. He seemed
far more relaxed now. He struck one of his old poses and
tweaked for a moment at his moustache. "Fa! This is crude,
even for you, Johannes Klosterheim. If you demand entertainment in others, you should at least be prepared to offer
some yourself!"

All around us the Forces of Hell were snuffling and
snorting, growling and drooling. They were so hungry for our
deaths.

"Is this—" Groot continued, waving a fastidious hand at
the demons and the misshapen living-dead, "is this all you can
offer? Mere sensation? Terror is the easiest of all human
passions to arouse. Did you know?"

Klosterheim was not cowed by the magus. He shrugged.
"But you will admit that terror is most effective in winning
one's goals. By far the most economical of emotions, eh,
philosopher?"

"I suppose that we are temperamentally opposed," said
Philander Groot, for all the world as if he played host to a
guest at dinner, "and that we shall never quite understand the
other's motives or ambitions."

He reached up into the air and appeared to pull on
something, an invisible cord. Then in his hand there was a
ball of blazing gold. The gold flared brighter and brighter
until his whole body seemed to burn with it. His calm,
somewhat bored face continued to look out at us as the
hordes of Hell fell back, muttering and dismayed. He moved

one of his hands and a swath of fire spread across the nearest group of demons. Instantly they began to burn, howling and stamping and beating at their bodies. Another movement and several score more monsters were afire.

Klosterheim staggered backwards, shielding his face from the heat. "What? You have tricked me. Kill him!"

Philander Groot spoke to me in a conversational tone. "I shall be dead within moments, I think. I would advise both of you to flee while you can."

"Come with us!" I said.

"No. I am content."

I looked westward and there was the blue-green haze, my goal.

"Here!" I threw him the flask containing the last of Lucifer's elixir. He took it with a nod of gratitude and put the rim to his lips.

"Sedenko!" I shouted to my companion. Then I lashed at my horse and was away.

"Oh, you must kill them now!" I heard Klosterheim shout.

We broke out onto the grass again. I looked back. Everything was shadow save for the golden fire which seared through the ranks of the damned. Sedenko was white. He was clutching at his back, even as he rode. He seemed to be weeping.

I saw Philander Groot move. I saw fire spring between us and the Hell-horde. The stink of that army gave way to purer air and there was softness ahead of us.

As we reached the forest and entered the first clumps of trees, Sedenko fell forward on his horse's neck. His breathing was ragged. Small sounds came from his lips.

I saw that he had a gash in his back which stretched from his shoulders to his hip. He continued to weep. "They have killed me. Oh, by all that is holy, they have killed me, captain."

The golden fire was out now. The black army was on the move again. Then it stopped.

I knew that it would not come into the Forest at the Edge of Heaven, but that it would be waiting for me should I ever emerge again.

I jumped from my weary horse and went to tend to Sedenko. I supported his body as it slid from its saddle. Blood flowed over my arms and my chest. He looked up at me and his face was now innocent and pleading. "Am I truly damned, captain? Am I bound for Hell?"

I could not reply.

When he was dead I raised myself to my feet and I looked about me. Everything was still. A loneliness had come upon my soul.

There was darkness everywhere now but in the forest. And even here there were wisps of grey, as if evil crept in.

I lifted my head to the sky and I shook my fist. "Oh, I reject you. I reject your Heaven and I reject your Hell. Do as you wish with me, but know that your desires are petty and your ambitions have no meaning!"

I addressed no one. I addressed the universe. I addressed a void.

Chapter XVI

A SILENCE HAD fallen over the world.

The plain now seemed filled from end to end by Kloster-heim's army, a frozen, waiting gathering. The forest itself was like the forest I had first entered when I discovered Lucifer's castle. No animals, no birds, nothing moving; only the sweet scent of the flowers and the grass.

I gathered leaves and wild tulips and covered Sedenko's body with them. I did not have the strength to bury him. I left his horse to guard him and mounted my own beast, striking due west into the depths of the blue-green forest. My mind and my body both were consumed by a curious numbness. Perhaps they were incapable of accepting any more terror or grief.

I knew, too, that I had changed as much since I had left Lucifer's castle as I had since I had left Bek on the road to Magdeburg. The changes were subtle. There had been no strong sense of revelation. My bitterness was of a different order. I blamed nobody, not even God, for the woes of the world. Neither did I blame myself too hard for past crimes. However, I was determined to follow a path that was entirely my own. Should I ever return to the world I had left, I would

not serve Protestant or Catholic. I would use my soldier's
skills to protect myself and mine, if need be, but I would not
volunteer to go a-warring. I mourned for Sedenko and for
Philander Groot and I told myself that should I have the
chance to avenge their deaths, I would probably take it,
though I felt no special anger, now, towards the wretched
Johannes Klosterheim, who daily increased his own terror as
he increased his power.

The ground began to rise upwards, almost following the
curve I thought I had detected from a distance. And now,
away from the influence of Klosterheim's forces, I heard a
wren's voice, then the sound of blackbirds and magpies.
Small animals moved in the undergrowth. All was natural
again.

I rode for many hours before I realised that night did not
fall in this forest. The sky was cloudless and still and the sun
was benign. And eventually I heard the sound of children
laughing as I breasted a rise and looked down into a little
glade, with a thatched cottage and a few outbuildings, a cow
and a plough-horse. Three little boys were playing in the yard
and at the door stood a grey-haired woman with a straight
back and clear, youthful skin. Even from that distance I saw
her eyes. They were as blue-green as the forest and they were
steady. She smiled and gestured.

I rode down slowly, savouring this scene of peace.

"I must warn you," said I, "that a great army out of Hell
besieges your forest."

"I know," said the woman. "What are you called, man?"

"I am called Ulrich von Bek and I am upon a Quest. I
seek the Holy Grail so that the World's Pain might be cured
and Lucifer taken back into the Kingdom of Heaven."

"Ah," said she, "at last you are here, Ulrich von Bek. I
have it for you."

I dismounted. I was astonished. "You have what, lady?"

"I have what you would call the Grail. It is a cup. It is
what you seek, I think."

"Lady, I cannot believe you. I think that up to now I
never did truly believe that I would find the Grail, and never
so easily as to be offered it by one such as you."

"Oh, the Grail is a simple thing. And it has a simple
function, really, Ulrich von Bek."

My legs were weak. I felt faint. I had not realised how
exhausted I had become.

The woman signed to one of the boys to take my horse. She put her arm about my waist. She was extremely strong.

She led me into the cool peace of her parlour and sat me down upon a bench. She brought me milk. She gave me bread with honey on it. She took off my helmet and she stroked my head and murmured soothingly to me so that I wept.

I wept for an hour. And when I had finished I looked up at the lady and I said: "All that I love is threatened or is lost forever."

"So it must seem," she said.

"My friends are dead. My true love is in Satan's thrall, as am I. And I cannot trust my Master to keep His bond."

"Lucifer cannot be trusted," she agreed.

"He offered to return my soul," I told her.

"Aye. It is the only thing He can offer, Ulrich von Bek, which has any value to a mortal. He can offer power and knowledge, but they are worthless if the price is one's soul. Many have come to me, at the Forest at the Edge of Heaven. Many soldiers and many philosophers."

"Seeking the Grail?"

"Aye."

"And you have shown it to them?"

"To some, yes, I have shown it."

"And they have taken it forth into the world?"

"One or two have taken it forth, aye."

"So it is all a trick. There is no special power to the Grail."

"I did not tell you that, Ulrich von Bek." She was almost chiding. She poured me more milk from a pitcher. She spread honey on the good bread. "But most of them expected magic. Most expected at very least some heavenly music. Most were so pure, Ulrich von Bek, and so innocent, that they could not bear the truth."

"What? The Grail, surely, is not a deception of Satan's. If so, the implications of what I have been doing . . ."

She laughed. "You expect worse, for your experience has led you to expect worse. Oh, I have seen great-hearted men and women kneeling in worship of the cup. I have seen them pray for days, awaiting its message, some sign. I have seen them ride from here in disappointment, claiming that they have been offered a false Grail. I have even been threatened with death, by that same Klosterheim who now commands Hell's armies."

"Klosterheim has been here? When?"

"Many years since. I treated him no differently. But he expected too much. So he got nothing. And he went away. He stabbed me here"—she indicated her left breast—"with his sword."

"And yet he did not kill you, plainly."

"Of course not. He was not strong enough."

"He has strength with him now."

"That he has! But he has refused to learn," she said, "and it is a great shame. He had character, Johannes Klosterheim, and I liked him, for all that he was naïve. He refused to learn what Lucifer refused to learn. Yet I believe you have learned it, Ulrich von Bek."

"All I have learned, lady, is to accept the world's attributes as they are. I have learned, I suppose, an acceptance of my own self, an acceptance of Man's ability to create not sensations and marvels but cities and farms which order the world, which bring us justice and sanity."

"Aha," she said. "Is that all you have learned, then, young man? Is that all?"

"I think so," I said. "The marvellous is of necessity a lie, a distortion. At best it is a metaphor which leads to the truth. I think that I know what causes the World's Pain, lady. Or at least I think I know what contributes to that Pain."

"And what would that be, Ulrich von Bek?"

"By telling a single lie to oneself or to another, by denying a single fact of the world as it has been created, one adds to the World's Pain. And pain, lady, creates pain. And one must not seek to become saint or sinner, God or Devil. One must seek to become human and to love the fact of one's humanity."

I became embarrassed. "That is all I have learned, lady."

"It is all that Heaven demands," she said.

I looked out through her window. "Is there such a place as Heaven?"

"I think so," she said. "Come, we shall walk together, Ulrich von Bek."

I was much refreshed. She took my hand and led me from the cottage and through the forest behind it until we stood upon a precipice, whence issued the blue-green haze. I felt a sudden soaring of the mind and senses, such as I had never before experienced. I felt a joy and a peace, previously unknown. I wanted to plunge from that place and into the cool haze, to give myself up to whatever it was I felt. But the woman tugged at my hand and I had to turn my back on Heaven.

Even now I cannot be sure if I experienced a hint of what Heaven might be. It seemed a kind of clarity, a kind of understanding. Can Hell and Heaven be merely the difference between ignorance and knowledge?

I turned my back on Heaven.

I turned my back on Heaven and walked with the lady to her cottage. The children had disappeared and only the cow and the horse were there, placid.

I sat at the table and she poured me milk from her pitcher.

"Where is this?" I asked her. "Where does Heaven lie?"

"That must be obvious to you by now." She went to the wooden dresser behind her and she opened a drawer. From the drawer she took a small clay pot and she placed it on the table before me.

"Here. Take this back to your Master. Tell Him you have found the Grail. And tell Him that it was fashioned by the hands of an ordinary woman."

"This?" I could not touch it. "This is the Holy Grail?"

"This is a production of that which you believe inhabits the Grail," she said. "And it is holy, I think. And it was made by me. And all it brings is Harmony. It makes those who are in its presence whole. Yet, ironically, it can be handled only by one who is already whole."

"I, whose soul is in Lucifer's charge, can be called whole, lady?"

"You are a man," she said. "A mortal. And you are not innocent. Neither are you destroyed. Yes, von Bek, you are whole enough."

I reached fingers towards the little clay pot. "My Master will not believe in this."

She shrugged. "Your Master is a fool," she said. "Your Master is a fool."

"Well," I said, "I will take it to Him. And I will tell Him what you have told me. That I bring the Cure for the World's Pain."

"You bring Him Harmony," she said. "That is the Cure. And the Cure is within every one of us."

"Has this cup no other power, lady?"

"The Power of Harmony is power enough," said she quietly.

"But difficult to demonstrate," said I in some amusement.

She smiled. Then she shrugged and would say no more on the subject.

"Well," I told her, "I thank you for your hospitality, lady. And for this gift of the Holy Grail. Must I believe in it?"

"Believe what you like. The cup is what the cup is," she said. "And it is yours to take."

I picked up the cup at last. It was warm in my hand. I felt a little of what I had experienced as she and I looked into the abyss beyond her house. "I thank you for your gift," I said.

"It is no gift," she told me. "It is truly earned, Ulrich von Bek. Be sure of that."

"I have a scroll," I said, "which I must open if I am to return to my Master."

"You cannot open it here," she said. "And even if you did open it, you could not return to Hell from here, nor any part which Hell commands. It is the rule."

"Ah, but madam, I have come so far! Am I to be cheated now?"

"You are not cheated," she said kindly, "but it is the rule. Use your scroll once you are out of the forest again. It will serve you then."

"Klosterheim and Duke Arioch's horde await me there."

"That is true," she said. "I know."

"So I am to be doomed just as it seems I achieve my goal?"

"If you think so."

"You must tell me!" I was close to weeping. "Oh, madam, you must tell me!"

"Take the Grail," she said. "And take your scroll. They will both serve you well. Show Klosterheim the Grail and remember that he has seen it before."

"He will mock me."

"Of course Klosterheim will mock you if he has any chance at all. Of course he will, Ulrich von Bek. He is all armour, that Klosterheim."

"And then he will kill me," I said.

"Then you must have courage."

She rose from the table and I knew she meant me to leave.

One of the little boys was holding my horse for me as I went out into the yard. Another sat on the pump, watching me. The third was unconcerned. He was studying the chickens.

I sat down upon my horse and set my feet in my stirrups. I felt the clay pot in my purse, together with Lucifer's scroll.

"There will be no legend told of you," said the grey-haired woman, "yet you are my favourite amongst all those who have come to me."

"Mother," I said, "will you tell me your name?"

"Oh," she said, "I am just an ordinary woman who made a clay pot and who dwells in a cottage in the Forest at the Edge of Heaven."

"But a name?"

"Call me what you will," she said. She smiled and her smile was warm. She put a hand upon mine. "Call me Lilith, for some do."

Then she had struck my horse upon his flank and I was riding east again. Back to where Klosterheim and all his horrid army awaited me.

Chapter XVII

I KNEW THAT it was a foolish hope, yet I deliberately went to where I had left Sedenko's body. I recalled a legend concerning one of the properties of the Grail, that it could bring the dead back to life. I held out the little clay pot over the corpse of my poor damned friend, but his eyes did not flicker and his wounds did not magically heal, though his face seemed more at peace than when I had covered him with flowers and leaves.

This dream, I thought, has no meaning. This clay pot is nothing more than a clay pot. I have learned nothing and I have gained nothing. Yet I rode on, out of the blue-green Forest at the Edge of Heaven, and I stood alone against all the ranks of rebellious Hell, reaching for my parchment even as Klosterheim rode out from the infinite black cloud and came slowly towards me.

"I give you the opportunity to join in this adventure," he said. He was frowning. He pursed his lips. "You and I have great courage, von Bek, and together we could storm Heaven and take it. Think what would be ours!"

"You are mad, Johannes Klosterheim," I said. "Philander Groot has already told you that. He was right. How can Heaven's gifts be taken by storm?"

"The way I take Hell's, fool!"

"I have found the Grail," I said, "and would ask you to let me pass, for I am on my way to my Master. I have been successful in my Quest."

"You have been deceived. You are not the first to be so deceived."

"I know that you have looked upon the Grail and have rejected it," I said, "but I have not rejected it, Klosterheim. Do not ask me why, for I could not tell you, though I am sure you have many reasons as to why you would not accept it."

"I would not accept it," he said, "because it was a trick. There were no miracles. Either God deceived us or He had no power. It was then that I decided to serve Lucifer. And now I serve myself against even Lucifer."

"You serve nothing," I said, "save the Cause of Dissension."

"My Cause has far more meaning! Von Bek, I offer you all that you desire."

"You offer me more than ever Lucifer offered," I said. "Do you believe that His power is already yours?"

"It shall be!"

He signalled and the black weight of Hell came moving in on me. I smelled the stink. I heard the gibbering and the other noises. I saw the hideous, malformed faces. Rank upon rank upon rank of them. "This is what rules now," said Klosterheim. "Death and terror are the means by which all power is maintained. I make my justice for myself. A just world is a world in which Johannes Klosterheim has everything he desires!"

I took the little clay pot from my purse. "Is this what you rejected?"

The ground began to tremble again. It seemed the whole Earth swayed. From the ranks of Hell came a monstrous ululation.

Klosterheim looked hard at it. "Aye. It's the same. And you've been deceived by the same trick, von Bek, as I told you."

"Then look upon it," I said. "Let all your forces look upon it. Look upon it!"

I hardly know why I spoke thus. I held the Grail up high. No shining came out of it. No music came out of it. No great event took place. It remained what it was: a small clay pot.

Yet, here and there in the ranks of Hell, pairs of eyes

became transfixed. They looked. And a certain sort of peace came upon the faces of those who looked.

"It is a Cure," I cried, following my instincts, "a Cure for your Pain. It is a Cure for your Despair. It is a Cure."

The poor damned wretches who had known nothing but fear throughout their existence, who had faced no future but one of terror or oblivion, began to crane to see the clay pot. Weapons were lowered. The gruntings and the gigglings ceased.

Klosterheim was stunned. He made no protest as I moved towards his army.

"It is a Cure," I said again. "Look upon it. Look upon it."

They were falling to their knees. They were dismounting from their beasts. Even the most grotesque of them was transfixed by that clay pot. And still no special radiance came out of it. Still no miracle occurred, save the miracle of their salvation.

And thus it was, with Klosterheim coming beside me, that I rode through the ranks of Hell and was unharmed. Klosterheim was the only one who was not affected by the Grail. His face writhed with a terrible torment. He was fascinated by what happened, but did not wish to believe it. He coughed. He began to groan. "No," he said.

We passed together through his entire army. And that army lay upon the ground. It lay upon the ground and it seemed to be sleeping, though it might also have been dead; I did not know.

And Klosterheim and I were now the only two who were conscious, just then.

Klosterheim was shaking. He moved his head from side to side and he bit at his lip and he glared at me and the little clay pot. And he could not speak. And he had tears in his tormented eyes.

"No," said Klosterheim.

"It is true," I told him. "You might have had the Grail. But you rejected it. You rejected your own salvation as well as the salvation of your fellow men. You might have had this Grail, Johannes Klosterheim."

And he put fingers to his wretched lips. And now tears ran down his gaunt, pale cheeks. And he said again: "No."

He said: "No."

"It is true, Klosterheim. Yes, it is true."

"It cannot be." This last was a terrified shout. He stretched gloved hands towards the Grail, as if he still believed he might be saved.

Then he fell forward from his horse. His soul had been taken out of him. Duke Arioch had claimed him.

I dismounted. Klosterheim was quite dead.

Duke Arioch's forces either continued to sleep on or were beginning to rise and disperse. Those who had awakened wandered off, perfectly at peace with themselves. Not only was the Forest at the Edge of Heaven no longer threatened, but Lucifer would be victorious in Hell.

I wondered at the significance of my Quest and of the cup itself. Somehow it had served both God and the Devil. And then I remembered the woman's words. She had spoken of Harmony.

From out of my purse I took the scroll and opened it. I read the words that had been written there, and even as I read them I found myself in the library of the castle where I had last seen my Master, Lucifer.

The library was empty, save for its books and its furniture. Morning light came in through the great windows. Outside, the trees were moving in a breeze. Birds perched in them. Birds sang in them.

I realised that this place was no longer within the domain of Hell.

Chapter XVIII

I WONDERED NOW if Lucifer had been defeated and if, in His defeat, He had taken Sabrina's soul with Him and would continue to claim mine.

For some time I stood by the window, looking out on that ordinary and comforting beauty. I placed the little clay pot upon the table at which Lucifer had been sitting. Then I left the library and I went into the cool hall and climbed the staircase to Sabrina's room. I did not expect her to be there.

I opened the door.

She was lying in her bed. Her expression was so full of peace that momentarily I believed her to be dead. Her face was as lovely as ever and her wonderful hair flooded the pillows. She was breathing softly as I stooped to kiss her brow. Her eyes opened. She looked at me without surprise. She smiled and she opened her arms to me. I bent to embrace her.

"You have brought the Grail with you," she said.

"You know?" I sat beside her. I stroked her shoulder.

"Of course I know." She kissed me. "We are free."

"I thought I had lost everything," I said. "Everyone."

"No," she said. "You have gained much and you have

gained it for all. Lucifer is grateful. You achieved your goal and in so doing you defeated His worst enemy."

"And He is no longer our Master."

"No longer." She looked at me with intelligent eyes. "He has gone back to Hell. He claims no part of Earth for His Realm."

"We shall never see Him again?"

"We shall see Him. In the library. At noon." She rose from the sheets and sought her gown. I handed it to her. It was white, like a wedding dress.

"And God?" I asked. "Does He still parley with God?"

"I do not know." She glanced out the window. "It is almost noon. Lucifer asked us to come together."

We embraced again, more passionately now. Then we left the room and walked down the staircase to the library.

Once more, as she had done a year before, Sabrina opened the huge doors of the library. And once more Lucifer sat at the table. But He was not reading. He was holding the clay cup in His hands. He turned beautiful eyes upon us. Some of the terror, I thought, had gone out of Him, some of the defiance.

"Good morrow to thee, Captain von Bek," He said.

"Good morrow, Prince Lucifer." I bowed.

"You would wish to know," He said, "that your friends do not reside in Hell. I have released their souls as I have released yours."

"Then Hell still exists," I said.

He laughed His old, melodious laugh. "Indeed it does. The antidote for the World's Pain cannot abolish Hell, any more than it can bring immediate surcease to all that ails Man."

He replaced the cup gently upon the table and He got to His feet. His naked skin glowed like silver fire and His fiery copper eyes still contained that element of melancholy I had seen before. "I had sought to have no more to do with your Earth," He told us. Gracefully He moved towards us and looked down on us. There seemed to be love in His eyes, too, or at least a kind of affection. I still did not know if He lied. I still do not know. He reached out His marvellous hands and touched us. I shivered, sensing that strange ecstasy which, to many, could be a compelling drug. I gasped. He withdrew his hands. "I have spoken with God," said Lucifer.

"And He has refused you, Your Majesty?" Sabrina spoke softly.

His sweet, vibrant voice was almost as low as hers when He replied. "I do not think it is a refusal. But I hoped for more." The Prince of Darkness sighed and then He smiled. It was a bitter and it was a very sad smile.

"I am not accepted into Heaven," Lucifer continued. "Instead, Heaven has put the world into my sole charge. I am commissioned to redeem it, in the fullness of time. If I help mankind to accept its own humanity, then I, Lucifer, shall be all that I was before I was cast down from Heaven."

"Then you are now the Lord of this Earth, Your Majesty?" I said. "God no longer rules here?"

"I do not rule, as such. I am charged to bring Reason and Humanity into the world and thus discover a Cure for the World's Pain. I am charged to understand the nature of this cup. When I understand its nature and when all mankind understands its nature, we shall both be redeemed!"

Lucifer raised His head and He laughed. The sound was musical and full of irony as well as humour.

"How things turn, von Bek! How things turn!"

"So you are still our Master," said Sabrina. She was frowning. She had come to be afraid again.

"Not so!" Lucifer turned, almost in rage. "You are your own masters. Your destiny is yours. Your lives are your own. Do you not see that this means an end to the miraculous? You are at the beginning of a new age for Man, an age of investigation and analysis."

"The Age of Lucifer," I said, echoing some of His own irony.

He saw the joke in it. He smiled.

"Man, whether he be Christian or pagan, must learn to rule himself, to understand himself, to take responsibility for himself. There can be no Armageddon now. If Man is destroyed, he shall have destroyed himself."

"So we are to live without aid," said Sabrina. Her face was clearing.

"And without hindrance," said Lucifer. "It will be your fellows, your children and their children who will find the Cure for the World's Pain."

"Or perish in the attempt," said I.

"It is a fair risk," said Lucifer. "And you must remember, von Bek, that it is in my interest that you succeed. I have wisdom and knowledge at your disposal. I always had that gift for Man. And now that I may give it freely I choose not to do so. Each fragment of wisdom shall be earned. And it shall be hard-earned, captain."

This time Lucifer bowed to us. His glowing body seemed to flare with brighter fire and the library was suddenly empty.

He had taken the clay cup with Him.

I reached out for Sabrina's hand.

"Are you still afraid?" I asked her.

"No," she said, "I am thankful. The world has been threatened too long by the extraordinary, the supernatural and the monstrous. I shall be happy enough to smell the pines and hear the song of the thrush. And to be with you, Captain von Bek."

"The world is still threatened," I said to her, "but perhaps not by Lucifer." I held her hand tightly.

"Now we can go home to Bek," I said.

Sabrina and I were married in the old chapel in Bek. My father died soon after we returned and he was pleased that I was there, to maintain the estates as he would have wished. He said that I had "grown up" and he loved Sabrina, I think, as much as did I. She bore us two girls and a boy, all of whom lived and all of whom are now well. We continued with our studies and came to entertain many great men, who were impressed with Sabrina's grasp of Natural Philosophy in particular, though I think they sometimes found my own speculations a trifle obscure.

I was not to meet Lucifer again and perhaps I never shall.

I continue to remain unclear, sometimes, as to whether my soul is my own. It is still possible that Lucifer lied to us, that God did not hear Him, that God did not speak to Him. Has Lucifer claimed the whole Earth as His domain in defiance of God? Or did God ever exist at all?

These are not thoughts I express to anyone, of course, save now, when I believe myself to be dying. The world is unsafe for a man who utters such heresies. I see little evidence that Reason is triumphant or that it ever shall be triumphant. But if I have Faith, it is in the faint hope that mankind will save itself, that Lucifer did not, after all, lie.

I have entered into Hell and know that I should not like to spend Eternity there. And I believe that I have been permitted a taste of Heaven.

We came to be happy in Bek. We sought Harmony, but not at the expense of muscular thought and passionate argument, and I believe that we achieved it in a small measure. Harmony is hard-won, it seems.

The War eventually subsided and did not touch us much. And as for the War which had threatened the supernatural Realms, we heard no more of it. The Plague never visited Bek. Without deliberately pursuing commerce we became well-to-do. Musicians and poets sought our patronage and returned it with the productions of their talents, so that we were consistently and most marvellously entertained.

In the year 1648, through no particular effort of goodwill and chiefly on account of their weariness and growing poverty, both of money and of men, the adversaries in our War agreed a peace. For several years afterwards we were to receive men and women at our estates who had known nothing but War, who had been born into War and who had lived by War all their lives. We did not turn them away from Bek. Many of them continue to live amongst us, and because they have known so much of War, they are anxious to maintain a positive Peace.

In 1678 my wife Sabrina died of natural causes and was buried in our family crypt, mourned by all. As for myself, I am alone at present. Our children are abroad; our son teaches Medicine and Natural Philosophy at the University of Prague, where he is greatly honoured; my elder daughter is in London as an ambassadress (there, I gather, her salon is famous and she enjoys the friendship of the Queen), and my younger daughter is married to a successful physician in Lübeck.

To my subjective eye, the Pain of the World is a degree less terrible than it was some thirty years ago, when our Germany was left in ruins. If Lucifer did not lie to me, I pray to Him with all my heart and soul that He can lead mankind to Reason and Humanity and towards that Harmony which might, with great efforts, one day be ours.

I pray, in short, that God exists, that Lucifer brings about His own Redemption and that mankind therefore shall in time be free of them both forever: for until Man makes his own justice according to his own experience, he will never know what true peace can be.

With this, my testament, I consign my soul to Eternity, offering it neither to God nor to Lucifer but to Humanity, to use or to discard as it will. And I urgently beg any man or woman who reads this and who believes it to continue that which my wife and myself began:

Do you the Devil's work.

And I suspect that you will see Heaven sooner than ever shall your Master.

Signed by my own hand in
this Year of Our Lord
Sixteen Hundred and Eighty:
BEK

About the Author

Michael Moorcock was born in London, England, in 1939. By the time he was eighteen he had started a career editing magazines while also playing and singing in various bands and pamphleteering for a political party. Beginning in 1964 he became the editor of *New Worlds Magazine,* which he ran under a radical editorial policy which created a great stir both in the world of science fiction and among the reading public (at various times attempts were made to censor the magazine and to hamper its distribution). The magazine is still published irregularly and remains a strong influence for experimentation and variety.

Concurrently with his editorial work, Moorcock has pursued an extremely productive career as a writer of science fiction and heroic fantasy. Among his more famous continuing characters are Jerry Cornelius and Elric of Melnibone. He won a Nebula Award in 1967 for his novella *Behold the Man;* has twice won the Derleth Award for fantasy (for *The Sword and the Stallion* and *The Hollow Lands);* received the Guardian Fiction Prize in 1977 for *The Condition of Muzak* and the John W. Campbell Memorial Award for *Gloriana.* He has also released one record album of his own and has appeared on albums with the group Hawkwind.

Moorcock has been married twice and has three children. He "leads a quiet life keeping three households" and currently resides in Ingleton, Lancashire, where he is working on an ambitious four-volume novel *Some Reminiscences of Mrs. Cornelius Between the Wars,* the first volume of which, *Byzantium Endures,* has already appeared.